THE BALLAD
OF THE
Realm Trotters

La Daryn Lockett

LOCATIVE
PRESS

The Ballad of the Realm-Trotters / La Daryn Lockett – Second edition.

ISBN 979-8-9878671-0-5

Printed in the U.S.A.

Second edition. 2024

Copyedit byAlexandra Ott

Cover design by

Glori Alexander

Dedication

For my friends, Tanner Paget and Armando Lopez
whose friendship and shared love of fantasy helped

inspire me to write this story.

Acknowledgments

If you had told me that it would take nearly ten years for me to produce a debut book from start to finish, I probably would not have started. Now that we're here, I am glad that I saw it to the end. I was twenty years old and in college when I pursued this seriously while studying for a bachelor's degree. Naturally, I had a lot of change and growth in that time that showed through those early drafts, which made the story better. There were a lot of inspirations that went into writing this story, and it simply wouldn't exist without the people who helped me craft this world and the characters we brought to life in it. These main characters would be very different without the misfit quirk and charm my friends (Tyler Porter, Tanner Paget, Vyvy Pham, and Leah Jumper) provided. Thank you all for all the encouragement and enthusiasm.

I owe thanks to all the people I've met and welcomed into my life in the last five to seven years who fed my creativity. In my experience, the older I get, the more I feel discouraged from expressing that side of myself. I want to thank my friends and acquaintances who shared their wisdom with me. I must also acknowledge the strangers I met while reading and writing in the coffee shops and bookstores who sat and talked with me. I've become a firm believer that sharing thoughts and ideas and listening to others' stories will always better a person. I'm grateful for those opportunities.

I'd like to thank you for reading.

THE BALLAD
OF THE
Realm Trotters

Prologue

FAR INTO THE DESERT, where the sand dunes rolled like ocean waves, was an oasis that no man or beast could reach on foot without dying of thirst or the heat from the burning sun. This island in a sea of sand was home to a kingdom, and in that kingdom was a white and gold palace belonging to a king among kings. This was where a sorceress was held prisoner for days. She did not eat nor drink, and when she thought she would finally pass, her captors took her from their dungeon and into the glaring firelight of a golden throne room. She was escorted by a pair of the Throne's Guard. The throne itself was an eight-foot solid gold pyramid with a pair of winged white bulls lying on either side.

This king of the oasis and the entire province was Theod-Rah, a king of mankind. He sat regally at the top in his golden seat. The Throne's Guards made the sorceress kneel at the steps and took a step back. From the shadows, the sorceress noticed an older man coming to her side. He was dressed in a fine white robe with a golden silk cape and a sash that came across his surprisingly gaunt waist. He wore the symbol of his cabal on his robe, a golden-winged sun that represented the Order of Fire — a sanctioned group of sorcerers that helped Theod-Rah's family keep their seat of power. A sweltering heat came from the Fire Lord's direction as he spoke. "Presenting his lordship, the master of gold and king of kings, Theod-Rah." His worn voice bounced off the walls.

The king stood. He was young. Younger than the sorceress by twenty years or more. He was shorter than his bronze statues depicted him, but they captured his physique perfectly. He wore a short beard and accented his long locks of hair with gold cuffs. From where the sorceress knelt, the chandelier hanging above them looked like a fiery crown upon the king's head. "My informants tell me you're a seer for hire. Where are you from?" he asked.

"I do not know, my king. I was born almost half a century ago to my mother who had no home and did not know my father."

"When did you first learn you had a connection to the Primordial Power?"

The sorceress hesitated and her lips were parched from thirst. "My mother said I was three years old when she discovered what I could do. We were hiding from marauders in a river when I had fallen from my basket into the water. She said she saw me at the bottom of the river lying so peacefully that she thought I had drowned. Instead, I was sleeping as if I were still cradled peacefully."

"I was told you were not easy to capture. That you are more skilled with the powers of water than any man is with a sword."

The sorceress said nothing.

"That my warlocks had to keep you busy for days so that they could starve you of your source of power. You must wonder why you've been brought to me."

"Yes, my king. Are you going to kill me?" the sorceress said stoically.

"Not if you comply with what I ask of you. My informants told me you shared a vision. That you claimed to see a magickally burning feather in the possession of three creatures."

She nodded. "Yes, I saw it, but my visions are of the future. Three hands holding its golden flames."

"The Phoenix Flame," the weathered man whispered. He was no longer beside her but standing over a brazier with his arms stretched out in the flames. His exposed arms didn't burn. Like her with water, he was using his second sight through the primordial power of fire. His eyes were rolled back into his head, and he muttered softly. The sorceress felt an intruding presence within her like her essence was making room for another. "She tells the truth," he said. "I see the flame, but the ones who carry it, I cannot see clearly." The man's eyes came back, and he withdrew his arms from the brazier.

11

"Three thieves are responsible for its disappearance," the king retorted.

"No," said the sorceress. "The vision is of the future. The three are the ones who will find the flaming feather abandoned in a dark place."

"Where is it now?" the king demanded.

"I know not where it is now, only where it will be."

The king stared at her, displeased. "Tell me more like your life depends on it."

"I can only do that if I have water. It is the source of my power." The two locked eyes for a moment. Both waited for the other to speak.

The weathered man marched to the front of the throne. "My king, I don't advise —"

"Silence," the king interrupted with a raised hand. He sighed and returned to the gold chair. He took his time getting comfortable and then nodded. "Very well. Fetch her water." The sorceress relaxed her shoulders and looked to either side of herself. A young servant emerged from behind a curtain with a large ceremonial bowl filled with fresh water. The servant placed the bowl before her, and the weathered man stood between her and the throne. As thirsty as she was, the sorceress restrained herself from drinking from the bowl. She dipped three fingers in its water, creating three overlapping ripples, which fed her primordial magick, a power that had connected her with her surroundings in a way that her other senses could not.

One of the white-winged bulls mooed at her as she felt thousands of hearts beating in the city outside the king's palace. She felt the uneasiness the guards were experiencing watching her enter the second sight as her eyes rolled back.

"I see a woman of light," she said. "She glows in the night with hair shining silver as bright as the moon. She is running from a place I do not know, a place with great magick, and she finds herself among us here in the province of Pryden alongside a monster. It's a powerful behemoth like an upright lizard with stag horns." People throughout the room gasped. "The third is a white-skinned man. An adventurer of the sea far from here, by the looks of it. These are the three who will find the flaming feather in the dark." The sorceress's eyes rolled back into place as the second sight left her.

"When will they find it?" the king asked.

"I do not know, my king. I cannot make the Primordial Power give more than it is willing me to see."

The king looked at the weathered man. "She tells the truth," he assured him. "Sorcery is powerful but fickle when engaging with time and space, my king."

"I need to know who stole from me, and none of you sorcerers with all your power can tell me that?"

"I suspect a power-hungry wizard, my king," said the weathered man in a soothing voice. "The spymasters are still at large tracking the arcane residue left behind at the scene."

"It has been two months, Firelord Zitane, and we are no closer to finding the thief or thieves."

"No, but we know who is fated to claim it next," the weathered Firelord said with his finger in the air. "We just need to bring them to you with allegiance to your crown."

"How could that be achieved?"

"This water hag said they are destined to arrive in Pryden. Which means the flame is still here, my king. We find the three, and we reclaim what is rightfully yours."

"How will you find them, Firelord?" the king asked.

"I will meet with my cabal tonight and have answers soon if it pleases my king."

"Very well."

"What will you have me do with the sorceress?" he said, standing over her.

"The knowledge worth your life was the location of the Phoenix Flame or who took it from me. You know both too little and too much."

"No, please! I will try again," she begged, dry lips quivering.

"If only you could have seen *your* future," the weathered Firelord whispered over her. The hair on her neck stood on end as balls of fire flew from two braziers on opposite sides of the throne room and into the fire

14

lord's hands. He reached for the sorceress, who splashed her hands into the bowl and magickally lifted the water from it like reaching tentacles and doused his burning hands. A hissing sound and steam came over them, but before the sorceress could make her next move, she was engulfed by streams of fire coming from every source in the throne room. All the braziers, the chandelier, and the iron torches held by Throne's Guards all came together to make a tentacled fire beast that consumed the single woman in a controlled inferno, leaving behind her charred corpse. Firelord Zitane rubbed his aching wrists. His hands were still red-hot from the magick. He cracked his neck before turning his attention back to the king. "My apologies, my king. I was hoping not to make a spectacle."

"I'm impressed as always, Lord Zitane."

"I will ignite the signals and leave for the cabal by morning."

"Very good. Bring your nephews with you."

"My king?"

"You may be a Firelord, Zitane, but outside these city walls I do not trust one sorcerer is enough to fend off an insurrectionist attack."

"You give them too much recognition, my king."

"And you don't give them enough, Zitane. Do as I say and bring your young sorcerers with you."

"Yes, my king." Firelord Zitane started to leave the throne room but paused at the entrance. "We are closer to recovering the Phoenix Flame, but it still may take some time."

The king sat comfortably in his gold chair, smelling the singed flesh in the air, and stroked the rings on his fingers. "Luckily I'm a patient man."

PART ONE

The Emerald Rainforest

Chapter One
RIKER

THE HARBOR BELLS PULLED Barron Von Riker from his daydream. He was on a ferry preparing to dock in the Narabari territory, a seafaring place of trade on the Gulf Coast in the South Seas. The surrounding fog pulled back like a curtain as his boat passed twenty-foot moss-covered boulders and a small island shipyard. "Look, Mama! Mermaids!" cried a child behind him. She was pointing at an aggregation of manatees grazing at the seagrass in the shallows.

"Dipendra, darling, keep your voice down," the child's mother said, smoothing the girl's hair with her hands. Riker wagered he looked the most out of place on the boat. He was tanned from years out at sea, but unlike the folk of this region, he was fair-skinned and not all human. Waiting for the ferry to moor the docks ahead, Riker noticed the same little girl staring at him. Her mother, realizing what was going on, playfully covered her eyes. "It's not polite to stare, dear!"

"No, it's quite alright," Riker insisted. He knelt to her level and swung his lute from his back to his front. The girl's eyes widened with amusement. The instrument was white with brown motifs and brass pegs and strings. She plucked one of the strings, and the hum made her giggle. She looked back up at him and upon seeing him closer, she gave a confused look.

"What are you?" she asked him, smiling.

"My mother was an elf. What gave it away?" he asked before her mother could chastise her.

"You're really pretty for a boy," she told him. Riker reached into his shirt pocket and took out a coin. It was an eroded piece of metal with a vague portrait on the face.

"Here. It's good luck," he said, handing it to her. The girl looked to her mother, who gave an approving nod. The girl took the coin and thanked him before she and her mother walked away. He had two coins left from his last job out at sea. For two weeks he had entertained the merchant ship's crew and learned to play their shanties while they worked and drank themselves silly. He did this for seven years, moving from boat to island and from island to a new boat. He enjoyed the ocean life, but in truth, he used the work to escape life waiting for him on the great continent at the center of the world. Only out in the open water could the days pass without mattering to him. It was like life on the continent froze in time, waiting for him to return. Seven years came and went, and by then Riker couldn't ignore the truth. The people he left behind were still there, living their lives without explaining why he left them so suddenly. He was on this ferry to finally come home and make amends.

As the boat moored, Riker noticed the silhouetted city behind the orange, glowing fire coming from the lighthouse. There was a great green banner hanging below the basin of fire off the ledge. It featured a saffron-red anchor that circled under three river dolphins, symbolizing the province's three major rivers of trade. On the beach, an odd-looking fellow approached him. "Welcome to Narabari!" he said with a big smile. Riker recognized him as an ebu-gogo, a race of dark-skinned smaller folk in these parts that stood shorter than a man by half the average. They were hairy all over the body, but those who lived close to humans wore clothing akin to the local humans but never wore shoes because of their agile lifestyle in the trees. They had unsettlingly large yellow eyes and exaggerated facial features.

The one that greeted Riker was among a line of humans offering an escort to the city, which was a long distance up a forestry hill. Riker spent a coin to hire the ebu-gogo and climbed into his cart pulled by a single bovine. With them were two more, a female and a youngling. Like the first, they were short and pudgy with wide faces and big noses, dark skin with large yellow eyes, and long, wild black hair. "What brings you inland, friend?" the driver asked Riker. Riker found that the trio made up a family.

"I'm going home to Southaven."

The wife sat next to the driver and looked back at Riker, smiling wide. She was finely dressed in a blouse and skirt. "Southaven! Do you live in the Land of Elves? We've heard of that place, haven't we, love?"

The driver scoffed. "Not much. Only that elves come and go from those woods."

"I've heard the same," Riker confirmed, "but I'm not from there. I lived in a town not far from there called Bloowood."

"What's Southaven like?" the wife asked, fully turned around and facing him. Her large expressive eyes fixed on him.

"It rains a lot, or it did. I haven't been home in some years."

"Why did you leave?" the son asked. He sat next to Riker, hugging a barrel of what smelled like pickled fish.

"Leave him be, son. He has been traveling all day. I'm sure he would rather not entertain us, little people," the driver said sternly. "We will be up the hill very soon, sir." Riker leaned back and took in the scenery. The cart was escaping the seaside fog as they ascended into the emerald-green forest. He listened to the howler monkeys and colorful bird calls as he pondered about home and how different it must be since he had left a few years ago. Looking at the tropical trees, he wondered if his home still smelled like pine when it rained. If it snows the same during winter. Most of all, he wondered about the person he missed the most and whether her family still lived there.

"You don't seem nervous, stranger," said the son.

"Why would I be nervous?"

"Most folk don't trust our kind."

"Hush, Tirto!" his mother scolded.

"Most people don't trust what they do not understand," Riker replied. "I am curious, however. Why is a family of ebu-gogos traveling this close to a human city? Your people are forest dwellers, no?"

"Most are," said the driver. "But there are those like ourselves who prefer a more civilized way of life, and the Narabari folk are more tolerant of us than some other human groups. Though they sometimes forget we are now like them."

"I see," Riker continued, not knowing what to say next.

At the top of the hill, Riker said his thanks and farewells to the family and entered the city. He was welcomed by a guard, who assessed him suspiciously. "What are you?" he asked.

"I am an entertainer," Riker replied, pulling on the strap of his lute and giving the man a slight bow. The guard looked to his companion, who stood in front of the gate. The companion shrugged and pushed the gate open. It had the design of a pair of fighting peacocks painted on it.

"Stay out of trouble, 'entertainer.'" Inside was a bustling street that smelled of spices and manure. Riker made way for the large hooved beasts that pulled carts full of bamboo, sugarcane, and grain while monkeys came here and there in front of his path taking things from unsuspecting traders. This was a place that demanded one's attention. Every other person he passed offered him something to buy, but with one coin left, Riker refused them. He was there to find his next ride across the gulf. He started searching for a tavern in hopes of finding a captain. The smell of fruits and smoke led him to a hookah lounge.

Inside, he approached a man enjoying a pipe on the balcony. On his right arm was a tiger tattoo. "What do you want?" the burly man asked.

"Straight to the point, I see. I'm looking for passage across the gulf," said Riker. "Can you help me?"

The man gazed at his face for a moment before taking a long drag from his pipe. "An elf, eh?"

"Half-elf actually."

"Of course, no such thing as a whole male elf these days. To answer your question, no, I will not help you."

"You have something against elves, Stranger? I can pay you and earn my keep."

The man took another drag of smoke. "Not about you or your coin. I'm on the job and don't have time to detour across the gulf."

24

Riker smirked dismissively. "What is your occupation, sailorman?"

"Why?"

"I can smell the blood coming from under your shirt and the medicine in the herb of your pipe. I'd say you deal in a lot more than fish." The man turned his whole body towards Riker and rested his hand on the hilt of the dagger strapped to his hip. Riker kept his smirk while flashing the flute he kept on a chain wrapped around his neck. He made sure the man could see the runes inscribed on it.

"Magick… You're bluffing."

"Want to find out if I am?" The man took his hand off the dagger and resumed his position against the balcony. "Not as dumb as you let on. Now I recall asking you a question."

"I poach animals of the monstrous kind."

"What's your game?" "Dragons. If you must know," the man said, lighting his pipe again.

"There are no dragons," Riker replied. He was sure of this. Everyone the world over knew dragons and wyverns had died out centuries ago. The man said nothing but opened his shirt to reveal lacerations across the charred skin on his shoulder in the shape of a large bite mark.

"The wyrm's mouth was still molten hot when it bit me trying to get on my boat."

"You brought a sea wyrm to port?"

"Look around you," the man said coarsely. "This city is where the money is for selling to the sort who want a live sea snake for gods-know-what. For food? A potion? I care not and neither should you, so why don't you go annoy someone else and leave me be?" Riker stepped away from the man and turned to go back into the lounge. "Wait," the man called. "Visit the Salty Sea Serpent down the way. It's a tavern where the adventuring types go looking for work."

Riker nodded to him. "Thank you." He later found the Salty Sea Serpent. It was a charming green and brown corner building on the edge of the better side of Narabari City. As he approached the front door, he stopped noticing the music coming from the other side of the building. He thought about what the man had said about keeping to himself and scoffed at the advice. He let go of the door handle and followed the music through an alley, where on the other side was another entrance, and beside it was a band of ebu-gogos playing wooden instruments.

A crowd was forming around them, and Riker followed suit. Throughout the performance, a pointy-haired ebu-gogo child no taller than Riker's shin walked around collecting coins in his triangular cap. Riker knew he was near when he heard the bells around the child's ankles approach. Though he had been reserving his last coin for his voyage across the gulf, Riker felt an urge to support his fellow musicians. When he reached to drop the coin in the cap, he sensed a lingering stare from the stranger beside him. He saw that the pale green eyes on him belonged to a young woman with skin as white as cream and platinum hair that came out of the hood on her head and down to her waist. Narabari City was the last place he'd thought he would find another elf.

Chapter Two

LLORVA

EARLIER THAT DAY, the cloaked Llorva was studying materials in the lounge of the inn beside the Salty Sea Serpent. She tried her best to ignore the noise from the patrons next door while reading the inn's library of atlases. "If I take the Peddlersroad north, I could arrive in about a year," she concluded, tapping on a page with her finger. She noticed how unkempt her nails were. She sighed and slumped in a chair. Traveling was getting harder without anything left to trade. That was her last night at the inn, and she'd spent the last of her shinies buying food from the innkeeper. The sound of music outside the window distracted her from her woe.

She saw that a crowd was forming in front of the Salty Sea Serpent tavern. Normally she avoided crowds during her journey but decided then to take a break from her isolation for a bit of entertainment. With the hood of her cloak up, she stepped out on the street and shouldered her way to the front of the crowd so that she could see the musicians. They were small, dark folk, fat, and with large yellow eyes. Llorva wanted to retreat, but their music kept her feet planted. It wasn't remarkable by her standards, but

29

the music was different in a way that piqued her curiosity like listening for the ending of a story.

One of them, smaller than the rest, approached her holding a dingy hat full of coins. At first, she assumed he was offering the hat to her. *An odd custom,* she thought, but noticed the humans around her started dropping coins into the hat. Even if she wanted to give the little creatures her money (and she did not), she had nothing left to give. He remained in front of her, waiting, and she froze, unsure of what to do. She was startled when someone came behind her and tossed a coin into the hat. It satisfied the beggar, and he walked away from her. Llorva turned around and took note of the stranger.

He was unlike the humans on this side of the world. He was around her height, with short auburn hair that he tied back. His complexion had once been fair-skinned, but exposure to the sun had tanned him. Even more unusual was that he possessed alfr features. He was halfr, an elf sired by a human male. He was the first of near kin she had seen in two months and hundreds of miles away from home. By the looks of him, she deduced that he was a musician and no stranger to interactions with humans.

Perhaps there was a community of others like him, a band of nomadic, alfar deserters she could travel with to help her reach the north safely.

He had disappeared in the crowd once they started dispersing after the last song. She looked for him, wondering what she would say.

How many halfr are there?

Are there whole-blood deserters with him?

She was distracted from her pondering questions when she heard a child's scream, and before she could look over her shoulder to see where it came from, she was pushed aside by a human carrying the small creature with the dingy hat from before.

Offended, she adjusted her clothes but then noticed the halfr chasing after the human. She wanted to walk away, but with nowhere to go the next day, she felt she needed to find out if this halfr could help her on her journey north. She strode after them. It was a chase that took her deeper and deeper into the city. Before she knew it, she was running into the slum where the old and sick were lying in the street and the ocean was out of view. She stopped herself before turning a corner into an alley. She could hear the men argue inside. "I shouldn't be here," she said to herself.

Having come this far, she took a breath and entered the alley. "Who is she?" the human said in a thick Haran accent.

The halfr looked over his shoulder with a knowing smile. "Ah! Good, my backup has arrived. Now, I suggest you put the boy down before this gets ugly."

Llorva approached cautiously. Ready to turn and run.

"You don't know what you're doing! You are interfering with a bounty," the human explained, holding the little thing. She had seen the young creature's kind before coming to this part of the world. She would see them watching her with their large yellow eyes from the trees on the road. What was more startling was finding some in the city among the native humans. The little one squirmed in the human's hands.

The halfr straightened his posture, putting his hands on his hips. "A bounty, you say. On a child? You expect us to believe that."

"He's lying!" cried the little one in a similar accent. "He's going to kill me!"

The human shook his captive violently. "This ebu-gogo and his family are thieves moonlighting as street performers. The city has a sizable reward for each of them, and you're going to tell me where you're all hiding," he said to the child. Llorva saw then how young the creature was compared to the others she had seen of its kind. He was frightened like a helpless pup, and she noticed he'd peed himself. Despite this, she considered the reward for his family's capture and how a fraction of it could buy her a few more weeks to survive her journey to the north of the continent.

"How much is the bounty?" Llorva finally said.

The halfr turned to face her. "What are you doing?" "How much is the bounty?" she repeated.

"Two hundred and fifty union coins per family member," the human replied deviously.

"Can I speak with you for a moment?" the halfr interrupted, standing between Llorva and the bounty-hunting human who seemed unsure of his predicament. "I may not know your situation, but trust me, you do not want to get involved in collecting this bounty with him."

She replied to him in her native tongue, asking why he'd chased after the human if it was such a bad idea.

He looked confused. "I don't know Alflentani, sorry."

What a waste of time, she thought. "I need that coin," she said.

"I can help you get it, but not this way. Trust me."

"Why should I?"

"Because you followed me, a stranger, this far," he said with a snarky smile.

Before she could react, something big came from the rooftop and landed behind the halfr. Llorva noticed the child using the moment of surprise to slip out of his shirt and attempt an escape. Llorva reached for him as he passed her, but the halfr pulled her aside by the arm, making a path for the boy.

"Get your hands off me!" she yelled, pulling away from him. She was about to scold him for the offense but caught sight of the thing fighting with the bounty hunter behind him. It was a beast that stood taller than the human with bluish-green scales covering the body, which was draped in a dark hooded robe. The head was large, with velvety indigo stag horns at the crown behind large, cow-looking ears. White mane hair came from behind the horns and down the neck. It had orange eyes and rows of small spikes on both cheekbones.

The creature grappled with the human and pinned him against the wall with superior strength. Like an animal, it sniffed the human with its short snout and snarled. Not taking its attention from the human, it said in a booming feminine voice, "Do not be afraid. I came for this hunter."

The human screamed. "Put me down! Please! Have mercy, monster!" The creature obliged, dropping him to his knees and she blocked his path.

The halfr stepped forward cautiously and knelt before the cowering human. "Criminal or not, I know the fate of small folk in the hands of people like you," he said self-righteously.

"Who are you to decide such fate?" questioned Llorva. He stood and turned to face her again, his expression unfazed by her objection.

"Barron Von Riker, musician and adventurer," he said to her with a slight grin. He turned his attention to the creature standing over the human.

"What do you want with him?"

"I'm searching for a group I believe he knows," she

said. *Her fiery eyes looked hungry,* Llorva thought.

She was ready to turn and leave when the halfr named Barron Von Riker stepped away from the human. "By all means, have your business. We were just leaving." He stopped when the creature started her questions.

"Where are the Dragon Slayers?" she said with a rumbling growl. The halfr turned to look. His curious eye read that he knew something connecting to the situation.

"Dragon Slayers? There are no dragons here," the human said, struggling to breathe. The creature's grip was so tight against him that Llorva saw his skin bleed from the creature's claws.

"I know they're here. Tell me what I want to know," she threatened, tightening her grip.

"Agh! Agh! Fine! They are here but I don't know where!" "Go on!" she roared.

"They come to buy sea snakes from the fishermen! That's all I know! I swear!" The creature started growling. "They never stay in one place more than once!" he continued, gasping for air. "Soon they will move on to the next city!"

"I think I can help you," said the halfr to Llorva's surprise. "I crossed paths with a poacher claiming to have brought a dragon into the city." The creature released the human, and he wasted no time stumbling out of the alley. Llorva thought to stand in his way but knew better, as he would have easily knocked her over.

"Why did you let him go?" she said, louder than she meant to. "I got all I could from him," the creature said plainly.

"True," the halfr replied, "but now your Dragon Slayers and the entire city will know you're coming for them."

"Not to mention my involvement," included Llorva. "What does this mean?"

"At worst we'll have even more unwanted attention so long we stay in Narabari. At best he won't mention us, but I am sure these Dragon Slayers will know all about you," he said, gently pointing at the creature.

"Then it is a good thing you know where to find them so that I may get to them before they find out," the creature said, stepping up to him. Despite being nearly two feet taller than him, the halfr remained unmoved.

"I said I came across a poacher. I don't know who these Dragon Slayers are, but as a favor for a favor, I will help if you can help me get across the Haran Gulf."

It was an interesting proposition, but what made him think this creature had a boat? Llorva wondered. The creature brought a clawed finger up to her sharp chin.

"If I refuse, you won't take me to this poacher. Am I understanding you?"

"Yes! I see you're catching on!"

"What makes you think I will tolerate this? I could torture what I need from you." This game of bluffing was making Llorva tense. She took a step back, whereas the stupidly brave Barron Von Riker remained planted. "Is this your mate?" she asked, referring to Llorva.

"No!" she and Barron V. Riker exclaimed.

"It would be a shame for her to witness you hurt."

Llorva raised a brow at that. It was the way the creature said it that broke the illusion it was trying to cast on them. She was indeed big and scary, but her demeanor wasn't the same as dealing with the human before. Llorva noticed she was slouching and the once booming voice sounded a bit too performative.

"She and I are strangers, and you may try to harm me if you wish, but hear me now: I don't scare easily."

The creature flared its nostrils with a huff. "I don't have a boat... but I can lead you through the jungle around it. If I can take care of my business here in Narabari, then I'll be free to go anywhere."

"Why do that when a boat is faster?" he retorted.

"Because I can cut through a jungle faster than a horse-drawn carriage on any road. If you help me, I will take you where the rivers meet the Gulf Coast."

Llorva knew these rivers from the maps she'd studied. They met the Haran Gulf in the north, where she knew there would be fishing villages.

If she went with them, she could find a fishing boat that could take her farther north and closer to her destination.

"We accept your offer!" she said before Barron V. Riker could respond.

"Wait, we? Why do you want to come?"

"I need to reach the northern province within a year, and those rivers are my best chance through this province's rainforests."

"What I mean to say is: Why should you come?"

She scowled at him. "You owe me for associating me with the wrong side of that human."

"I did nothing of the sort," he said, laughing. "You followed me here and stayed. You have no one to blame but yourself."

"Stop it!" the creature roared again. "No point in discussing an arrangement without you fulfilling your side of the deal."

"Very well," he agreed, "I show you your man and you help me get across the gulf."

"We go nowhere until I face the Dragon Slayers." "And if you die?

What do we do then?" Llorva added. "I have no plans of dying."

"I have sung countless stories about dead heroes that said the same thing," claimed Barron Von Riker. "But I'm willing to bet your story will be different." He reached over, took the creature's clawed hand, and shook it. "Call me Riker. I much prefer it to my first name. To whom do I owe the pleasure?"

"I have been given the name Vylasgarden," she said.

"A pleasure," he acknowledged before turning to Llorva. "I'm sure your name is just as pleasant."

She gave a forced smile. "Fortunately for me, it isn't necessary for you to know."

"I'm sorry, but an exchange of names is necessary for this little adventure of ours," he said, smiling. He extended his hand to her. "Take my word for it. It builds trust."

She reluctantly shook his calloused hand. "Llorva. My name is Llorva."

"So why do you wish to go north?" Riker asked Llorva sometime later as they walked the streets to meet this poacher he'd promised.

"There's a place there I believe I can call home." The two walked ahead of the creature, who wore its hood over its head and crossed its arms in the sleeves of its robe. Monkeys hissed at it as they passed under a fruit tree at the crossroads.

"Another Land of Elves?"

"Land of Elves? My sisters and I call our home Foss Sergens, in our language anyway…"

"Sisters? So it's true that there are no male elves where you're from.

If it's true, then how do you… you know."

Llorva looked at him curiously. "I don't know what you

mean." "How do the elves (ahem!) grow fruitful?"

An odd question, but Llorva had noticed a while ago, since leaving Foss Sergens, that things worked differently in the human world. "Fruitful... Well, berry buses in particular grow well in the groves back home. As much as I enjoy the strawberries and gooseberries, plum trees are a personal favorite."

Riker seemed displeased with the answer.

"How much farther?" Vylasgarden asked, interrupting the conversation.

"We're almost there," Riker replied graciously.

"Your home. Is it near Foss Sergens?" Llorva continued.

"It isn't far. Maybe a week's travel. I can't say for sure I've never seen your home."

"That's no wonder. We share kin's blood, after all. All ties have their origin," she said nervously. In those early days leaving home, Llorva had noticed that the communities close to Foss Sergens were harboring alfar like her who left their new kingdom. They seemed happy enough, which brought hope to her endeavors, but she also noticed something she thought was unthinkable. Some of the former sisters were carrying babes belonging to human men. Those babes would grow to become halfr like Riker. If they or any former sister were to set foot back into Foss Sergens, the sisterhood would kill them on the spot. Living by those beliefs made sense growing up, but since leaving, she'd found the outside world to be more complex and more accepting in ways that were foreign to her before. "What of your father?" she found herself asking.

"He was a spice merchant," Riker replied. "My mother died giving birth to me, and he died fifteen years after that, so I didn't know either of them. I grew up being told by the neighbors that they loved each other. I hold onto that when I feel alone sometimes." He stopped in front of a building that smelled of hemp and fruit. Vylasgarden came between them to open the front door. "Wait!" said Riker, blocking it. "We can't just go in there like this."

"Why not?" she growled.

He raised a finger. "Tell me if you heard this one: Two elves and a blue beast enter a hookah bar…"

Llorva and Vylasgarden waited for him to finish. "I don't understand," Vylasgarden eventually said.

He shook his head. "Allow me to get the information we need to find the Slayers. I've already met him, so he'll likely spill the location if I pry enough."

"What will you have us do?" Llorva asked, annoyed.

"Keep an eye on the exits. You're looking for a man with a tiger tattoo on his arm." With that, he entered the building. She and Vylasgarden stood there without a word for several minutes as it started to pour rain.

The two huddled under the canopy of the doorway, and Llorva noticed how dazzling Vylasgarden's blue scales

41

were up close. They were like the scales of a shimmering blue carp.

She saw that she was looking down at her. "Excuse me, I don't mean to stare."

"Do I scare you?" Vylasgarden asked.

"Yes. You do scare me." They didn't speak again for a while until a question formed in Llorva's mind. "What did these humans do to you?" Vylasgarden waited to speak and thought about her answer. "They killed people I cared about," she finally said. "My kind of people." Llorva had thought as much. Vylasgarden was so different than when she'd come down on the bounty hunter in the alley. She was calmer and less of a monster standing there with Llorva.

"The Slayers killed them because they believed you all were dragons?" she asked hesitantly.

"My kind are dragons, Llorva," Vylasgarden explained. "We were the descendants of the first children of a tempest dragon and the mountain fairy he fell in love with."

"Mountain fairy?" Llorva questioned.

"You know, the spirit of the mountains taken corporeal form. My people inherited power from both the dragon and our fay grandmother, but when the Slayers came for us, we were too few to defend ourselves. I can still hear the hooves of their horses thundering up the mountain as I was…" She stopped and stared at the ground for a moment. "I shouldn't be alive, but I am, and vengeance is

42

all I live for now."

Llorva felt her heart sink with the setting. She was thinking that when the time came, she didn't want to see what Vylasgarden would do to these Dragon Slayers. Perhaps they very well deserved her vengeance, but for how personal it seemed she felt, it wasn't for Llorva's eyes. Vylasgarden might have noticed her discomfort, because she hesitated to say more.

"How do you think it's going in there?" Llorva said to change the subject.

"I worry that it shouldn't be taking him this long," Vylasgarden replied, looking up at the second story. "Perhaps I should go in there and see for myself —" Right then, Vylasgarden's long ears perked at the sound of a high-pitched noise coming from that second story. What followed was an explosion. Fragments of wood and stone fell on top of them.

Vylasgarden used her body to shield Llorva, and they ran away from the debris as a cloud of dust and a human man came raining down.

He fell into the street face-down. Llorva and Vylasgarden approached.

It was the human Riker had described with the tiger tattoo on his right arm. "What happened in there? Where is he?" Llorva said.

Vylasgarden sniffed the debris in the air. "An explosion, but…"

"But what?"

"I don't smell powder or fire."

"There!" Llorva pointed at what looked like Riker's silhouette. He ran through the front door. His hair and white clothes were covered in dust, but he had a pleased expression on his face. A flute Llorva only then noticed hung from a chain around his neck. He came over and stepped on the human's chest, making him bleed through his gritted teeth.

"I'll ask one last time," Riker threatened in a playful tone of voice.

"The tunnels! The tunnels under the city!" the human cried out. "How do I get there?"

"Why would you want to go there? Weren't you listening? They will kill you!"

"That is the least of your concerns right now. Tell me!" Riker continued. Llorva drew in a breath as she watched him apply pressure to the human's body with his foot. She could hear the man's rib bones cracking as he screamed.

"What are you doing?" she cried.

"He's getting the information I need," said Vylasgarden, crouching down at the human's face. "Tell us what we want to know and this all stops."

"The abandoned salt mine on the beach!" he relented. "It's the only way I know. I swear!"

"Does that satisfy you?" Riker asked Vylasgarden.

44

"What do you know about the Dragon Slayers?" she asked.

"Dragon Slayers? Is that what they call themselves?" The human was groaning and spitting up blood between sentences. "I bring them the sea snakes alive and they pay me. I don't know who they are except they all look like they come from the other provinces."

"What else?" she growled and pressed her clawed hand on Riker's foot.

"Ow! Please… that's all. They don't speak, they just pay me whenever I have what they're looking for."

"We have our location. Let's get going before the city guard shows up," Riker insisted, taking his foot off the human and digging into his pockets. He pulled out a rusty key and put it in his pocket. He walked over to Llorva, who was feeling flushed at that moment, watching the human suffer like an animal. "Are you all right?" he asked.

"No, I'm not all right. I just watched you torture a man."

Riker looked over to the human, whose blood was pooling on the ground.

"Believe me, he was planning worse for me if not for that explosion upstairs. Vylasgarden, it's time to leave!" She was still crouching over the man, reverting to the beast Llorva saw her as before.

"I don't ever want to hear about a human with a tiger

45

tattoo associated with the Slayers again. If I do, I will find you and break so many of your bones you will beg for death." She turned away from him and walked past Llorva and Riker. Llorva was the last to leave, watching the human bleed in the street. She pulled her hood up, and when she noticed the men dressed in armor coming from up the hill, she joined the pair farther down the street.

When she caught up to them, she heard Riker say, "Consider my end of the bargain kept."

Chapter Three
INNKEEPER

RAHUL BAGCHI HAD BEEN the proprietor of the Shells and Block Inn for nearly thirty years when he'd bought it off his late uncle. Usual days and nights featured occasional sailors and merchants wanting a fancier place to rest their heads. He prided himself on his clean establishment and felt blessed that he kept the smell of fish at bay. He laughed at the pun as he sat behind the check-in counter, petting his pet peacock, Daleel. He was anticipating the return of the elf that was staying in his best room. That night was her last night, and he would have refused her before if not for the rare elfish jewelry she offered as payment.

The bell above the door rang, and there she entered with a male elf, which he'd thought didn't exist — and a reptilian beast wearing an ominous cloak. The beast was so tall it bumped its blue horns on the ceiling, startling Daleel. "Stop it right there!" Rahul called out. "This will not be allowed!" He pushed up his weighty glasses from the bridge of his nose.

The elf was too confounded to speak, but her male companion spoke unassumingly. "Good evening, innkeep!

I see you're well-acquainted with my sister. You see, she and I and our, err —" he awkwardly gestured to the beast standing behind them — "bodyguard! Yes! We were to meet here on account of our elfish family reunion."

"An elfish family reunion. Here in the Middle Province?" "Yes, you see, we are a family of explorers!"

"That may be so, but your 'sister' neglected to mention this to me when she rented my room," the innkeeper said, stroking the feathers of his peacock.

The male elf leaned over the counter and whispered, "Ah, yes, she is a bit forgetful, I'm afraid, which is why ole grandma'am has me looking after dear sister."

He's a witty one, this elf, Rahul thought to himself.

"I can make an exception for you, but your... bodyguard cannot stay here."

"Well, she wouldn't be much of a bodyguard if she weren't by our side, would she?"

"I don't want its filth stinking my inn." The creature made a guttural sound, and Rahul held Daleel close. "Get rid of it!"

"I'm afraid that isn't possible."

"Then I suppose you won't be staying here. Bah! What do you take me for, boy? I've played along long enough." He addressed the elfess. "The deal is off! I want you gone as well."

She gasped.

The male stepped into view wearing a mischievous smile while fondling a charmed flute on a necklace. "Dear sir, I do believe you should reconsider." At first, Rahul suspected that he was going to offer the flute as a bribe, but instead, the male elf suddenly began blowing into it. The sound was an uncanny melody that gave Rahul pause. His anger suddenly melted away, and his stiff shoulder began to relax.

"What are you doing?" Rahul said, but it felt as if he had been saying it for hours. "What are you doing to me? Stop! Please!"

The elf kept playing his song, which was slower now. Rahul's eyelids became heavy, and the world around the flute-playing elf became dark. He heard Daleel squawk, which rang in Rahul's ears over and over. He gripped the counter because up, down, and side-to-side were indistinguishable. He closed his eyes, and all became quiet.

Chapter Four

RIKER

"WHAT DID YOU DO TO HIM?" Llorva asked. She looked astounded, her mouth agape. Riker didn't want to reply. He was too focused on improving his next move. He didn't want to let it show how spontaneous all that was. He picked up the unconscious innkeeper and posed him on his stool while the colorful bird pecked at his feet on the floor.

"Could one of you get the bird? It's really pretty and I'd rather not hurt it." As Vylasgarden chased the bird away, Llorva slowly approached Riker, eyes fixed on the flute.

"Where did you get that?" she asked while he admired his work. The innkeeper looked as if he had fallen asleep at the counter. "When were you going to tell us you can cast spells?"

"Keep your voice down, 'less you wake him," he said playfully. "Everything will be fine." He walked over to the front door and locked it. "We will be long gone by the time he wakes up."

"You've done this before?" Llorva continued. He only smiled at her, and she kept her disapproving gaze.

"Look, I took care of the problem. You're welcome, by

the way.

Tonight you keep your bed and we don't have to be on the streets." He made his way to the stairs. "Now may we please continue?"

Llorva hesitantly took the lead up the stairs and to the attic room of the inn. She used a brass key to open the trapdoor, which released the ladder above them. Riker went first and Vylasgarden squeezed through second. The room was more than he'd expected — a wide space and ceiling that sloped with the roof. It featured old, painted furniture, and Riker caught a waft of plum fruit and rose petals over by the bathtub sitting under the window. The window had a spectacular view of the tropical seaside. "My, this must have cost you a small fortune."

"It cost me all I had left," said Llorva, coming in last. She went over to the window and picked up a bar of soap lying next to the bathtub — the source of the sweet smell. Llorva softly cursed in her elf language.

"What is it?"

"I was looking forward to a bath tonight."

Riker sensed a quiver in her voice. "I'm sorry," he said and partially meant it. He didn't like intruding into people's lives; however, he reminded himself that she was the one who came to him in that alley. "Thank you for sharing your room with us."

"It wasn't like I had a choice," she replied contemptuously. "Now you have no choice but to take me with you to the rivers." She brought the soap up to her face and breathed it in, which seemed to relax her a bit.

Then she went to the only bed in the room and tore the sheets from it. She used the clothesline and sheets to create a partition at the room's center. "This side is mine," commanded Llorva from behind it. "The two of you stay over there." Riker and Vylasgarden exchanged a look but said nothing. As he unpacked his belongings and laid his bedroll on the floor, Vylasgarden took a spot in a corner and sat with her burly legs in a meditative position. She removed the wrappings around her feet, which revealed black-clawed appendages. Her eyes darted up at him like she was expecting him to be staring.

"You travel light I see," he said and attempted to seem casual.

The membranes of her reptilian, amber-orange eyes blinked at him. "I need for little," she replied. Seeing her in the dark and as still as she was made Riker uneasy for the first time in her presence. There was something predatory about the way she looked at him. It was as if she were saying, "Don't you betray me." Whatever Vylasgarden was, Riker knew after seeing her in action that she was at least a force of nature.

"When we find the Dragon Slayers tomorrow, what are you prepared to do?" he then asked.

She waited and let the question float for a moment before speaking. "When they came up the mountain that day and into my home — nets, and swords in hand — they shed so much blood that all I can remember is red. I cannot remember the faces of my people without them being in red. So you ask me what am I prepared to do, and I tell you that I am prepared to end their entire bloodline with my rage."

"And only then you will be at peace."

"I will not know peace for the rest of my days, Barron Von Riker. But at least I will have avenged my family."

"Well, that would make for an excellent ballad," he said with a timid laugh. "A hero to your lost people. Just remember when the deed is done-"

"You will have your guide," she interrupted. "So long as you stay out of my way."

Later he was polishing his instruments when he noticed Llorva's silhouette standing behind the curtain sheet. "You're still awake?"

"I wanted to ask you a question. Where did you get that flute? That magick. I know it. The enchantments belong to the alfar."

He put down his lute and faced her. "It doesn't matter what form it takes. Magick belongs to no one. That is what I've learned from my years, and you'd be wise to learn the same if you wish to live in Man's world and away from that place you call a sisterhood."

"Even so," she relented, coming from behind the sheet,

"I was taught that the secret to what you did to that human downstairs isn't supposed to be known outside of the alfar. Is it the flute or is it you?"

Riker twisted a smile. Seeing the desire to know so deeply on her face put him in a mood that had been lacking in the past hours. She came and sat on the floor next to him, still holding that bar of soap. "If you must know, then I shall tell you. The magick and the flute come separate." He pointed with a finger. "This flute, which was a gift, is more sensitive to casting my spells. Enchantment and all that I know came many years ago when I was discovering myself after my father's passing. He left me a home and an inheritance I knew not what to do with except spend it chasing rumors. I learned about a being, a wizard of sound and music called the Ichomancer, who would teach you to play the sound of gods on the fiddle for a price. It turned out he was more aloof than a unicorn, but I found his hiding spot. With some convincing, he agreed to teach me. My fingers bled for months, and I never did see his face or learn his true name."

"He couldn't have been a man."

"No, probably not. I'm almost sure he wasn't."

She nodded. "Thank you. That was interesting to know." She stood and went back behind the curtain sheet. Tired, Riker lay in his bed roll. He relived his memories of the magick stranger and thought of him fondly. The power he possessed, Llorva and Vylasgarden could only imagine.

Llorva got into bed and blew out the flames of the candelabra sitting on the end table. Riker expected the room to go dark but noticed a faint golden glow from her side of the room. He looked over and saw the glow disappeared after Llorva covered herself with her cloak, darkening the room. It dawned on him that perhaps he wasn't the only one holding secrets.

Early the next morning, Riker led the charge to their escape. The plan was simple: they were to quietly make their way to the lobby stairs and have the ladies wait for him at the top so that he could scout the front desk for an angry innkeeper. The sleep spell hadn't failed him before, but magick, like the people it was cast on, was often unpredictable. Since her belongings were already prepped, Llorva had spent the time getting ready, tying her long hair into a messy braid. Vylasgarden didn't have much aside from robe garments. She spent the time stretching and rolling her shoulders after a night of sleeping on the floor. Riker, on the other hand, spent the time repacking his bedroll. "All right. Are we ready?" he said, prepared to open the attic's trapdoor. He looked up for assurance. They each gave him a nervous nod.

He swung the door open, and they each hopped down gently. Though the sun had yet to come up, sweat was already trickling down his neck and back. They snuck to the lobby stairs, and Riker signaled them to wait as he made his way down. He discovered that the innkeeper was not where he'd left him.

He cursed, looked at the front door, and noticed it was unlocked. Riker contemplated the situation and wagered there was still time to escape. The innkeeper may only be moments ahead of them. He turned to signal the ladies but found Vylasgarden already behind him. He nearly fell over in surprise. "What are you — you're supposed to wait for my signal!" She grabbed him by the shoulder and helped him regain his balance. "Where is the innkeeper?"

"I don't know. He woke up sooner than I expected."

Llorva joined them on the stairs. "He could be waiting for us."

"Relax. I have this under control," Riker assured her, but inside he was screaming. She was right. The innkeeper could be waiting outside with an army of city guardsmen or worse. He went down the stairs and searched for an alternative exit. Through the stained window by the front door, he saw silhouettes approaching. The three dove behind the check-in counter at the sound of the jiggling doorknob. With his back against the counter, Riker listened as the door swung open.

He heard metal boots clank and creak against the floorboards.

"Split up and check upstairs," a man said in a Haran accent. Riker fought the urge to look. In his experience, metal boots meant big trouble, and he had a few tricks up his sleeve to get out of this one. Someone started banging on doors, not announcing themselves, which meant to Riker that they weren't dealing with city officials. *Could be good. Could be bad,* he thought. But then he heard a pair of boots staying behind in the lobby. He waited, but the sound got closer, and someone squeezed his arm. It was Llorva, biting her lip in fearful anticipation.

Riker pulled out his flute and gently blew into it, playing a fluttering scale that was heard magickally across the room. As predicted, he heard the boots march in that direction. They only had a few moments. He saw that Vylasgarden was missing. He and Llorva looked over the counter and saw her hunched over an incapacitated Haran man dressed in heavy armor.

Llorva went over and picked up the crossbow from his hand. "Who are they?"

"Not Dragon Slayers," Vylasgarden groaned.

"And not the authorities," Riker added. "Whoever they are, they're no doubt looking for us." He watched Llorva search the drawers and cabinets. "What are you doing? We don't have time for this!"

"I'm looking for the jewels I used to pay for the room," Llorva answered, pulling out a dusty bottle of wine from one of the cabinets. "Or a handful of coins at least."

"Forget it, we need to leave now!"

She gave him an annoyed look and quietly fitted the

bottle of wine in her knapsack. As the search and ruckus continued upstairs, the trio met at the front door. Unprepared for what came next, Riker opened the door to a small group of surprised Haran men standing out front wielding crossbows and swords. Two of the bowmen raised their weapons and fired, and, had it not been for the doorknob in his hand, Riker would not have had the time to slam the door closed, catching the bolts. "Block the door!" he commanded as he swung his lute to the front of his body. Vylasgarden single-handedly held the door as the men on the other side started to ram it and attract attention upstairs. "Take that crossbow and hide behind the counter," he said to Llorva as he tested the lute's strings with his fingers.

"I hope you know what you're doing," said Llorva, running over. "Don't worry. I've done this before," he said unconvincingly to himself. "Vylasgarden, at the start of the third stanza, opened the door."

The sound of boots gathering approached the stairs.

"But I don't know what a stanza is!" she cried, struggling to push against the door.

"It's the part of the song where — you'll know it when you hear it." He started to strum and sing.

O-oh! O-oh!

My friends, are you coming with me?

To the place of gold and charity.

The boots started storming down the stairs, but Riker played on.

Where the wine keeps pouring if you have the fare And the smells of bread and honey are in the air.

He held onto the note until Vylasgarden got the signal and opened the door, letting in half a dozen angry and armed humans.

So come with me friends if you please To the place of gold and charity.

They started to rush him from all sides but came short a few feet. Their confused faces turned soft as Riker swelled the music from his lute.

Oh, won't you be my friend oh won't you please?

The humans all lowered their arms and sheathed their blades.

"Well, hello there. To what do I owe the pleasure, gentlemen?" Riker asked, checking their eyes, which had turned dreamy and unthreatening.

"I... can't remember," said one. His confused face turned into a smile, and he started laughing. "Ha! I simply can't remember!"

"It is good to see you!" exclaimed one of the others.

"Ah! I see," Riker said quickly to get ahead of the conversation. "You're all here for the concert."

"Concert?" asked a third.

"Yes! Me and my lovely assistant are part of the traveling festival." He hastily waved for Llorva to come to his side. She obeyed, hiding the crossbow behind her back and moving a bit too slowly for his comfort. He put his arm around her and looked at her with an obvious raised brow, hoping she understood.

"We thank you for coming!" she said cheerfully with a head tilt. "Yes! We thank you!" echoed Riker. "But it's now time for the next show. We work on rotation. On to the Salty Sea Serpent!" He pushed Llorva through the crowd and discreetly waved for Vylasgarden to follow them out the door. The humans started to follow them. "No, no. You have to stay here for the next performers."

"Ooh!" the humans said in unison.

They moved with haste outside. "That was too close," Llorva said after they got some distance away from the inn. The jungle birds were chirping and cawing, and a morning mist sprinkled their faces. As they walked, Riker took notice of the few people already out on the streets, sleepy vagabonds and early-rising vendors.

"I have to agree," Vylasgarden followed. "If not for your musical magick, we'd likely be in serious trouble."

"We probably wouldn't be in this much trouble if it weren't for him. It keeps getting worse. First the bounty hunter, then the poacher and the innkeeper, and now whatever that was!"

"You can leave at any time," he spat back at her. "No one is keep- ing you here." A thought came to him to abandon them, but he fought against it. Since he'd started the use of his magick, he felt responsible for their well-being, and admittedly he felt responsible for the trouble caused too, but he wouldn't dare say it aloud. "At least I do something when trouble finds us. What's your excuse?" he directed at Llorva. She stopped walking, and her pale face grew red.

"Apologize," she demanded. "You can't be serious. No!"

"I demand an apology!" She came closer to him, raising the crossbow.

Riker slapped the weapon away and pushed her against a nearby wall and smelled the scent of plums and roses on her. "The charm will not hold a group that size for long. We don't have time for this!" The anger in her face melted away, but her pale green eyes remained fixed on him.

"Do you understand the situation we are in?" She nodded, and he gave her space and looked over at Vylasgarden, who was waiting patiently with crossed arms. "You don't know who they were, do you?"

"No, but I know who they weren't."

"Right, but perhaps the Dragon Slayers know we're onto them. It might be best if we find somewhere to hide and wait this out." Riker returned Llorva's crossbow to her.

"I hate to admit it, but I think he's right."

"You can, but I'm going to find the salt mine," Vylasgarden said, marching on ahead. Riker was going to object but was cut off by people shouting behind them. Out of the morning shadow came a group of little folk dressed in dark hoods, and their faces were covered with creepy wooden masks. Riker felt a chill when he caught a glimpse of the small knives they were carrying.

Chapter Five
VYLASGARDEN

RIKER WAS LEADING THEM AWAY from their pursuers. Vylasgarden took up the rear to shield the elves from the volley of knives being thrown at them. Most deflected off her skin, but a few cut her on the arms, back, and shoulder. She stumbled as they ran away, and she started feeling sick.

"Must move faster!" she roared in a strained voice.

"This way!" cried Riker, but he sounded distant despite being right in front of her. If she wanted to, she could surpass him, but that would be pointless without knowing where he was going. Another stumble, and a knife stuck behind her thigh.

"Wait!" This time her voice was unrecognizable, and her vision grew weak. Before she knew it, she was on the ground and caught visions of Riker and Llorva looking back at her.

"Wait! Don't go!" she wanted to say, but her tongue was swelling in her mouth. She attempted to stand but felt her muscles weaken. She fell back to the ground before feeling a strike to the head and darkness taking over.

Vylasgarden was kicked awake. She was colder than she'd ever felt before in a room bathed in shadowy orange light coming from a hole in the ceiling. Her head was throbbing, and she felt her blood draining down her face. Her arms and neck were restrained in an iron pillory that had pressure points digging in her neck. It was held up by chains inside a large iron cage. She was looking down at the floor, where her blood was pooling beneath her. She surmised that she was somewhere underground from hearing distant echoes and feeling faint vibrations from shifting ground nearby. Before her was a light-skinned human standing in an iron cage with her. The human had yellow hair and a red beard and was dressed in familiar dragon's scale mail armor.

"These restraints are typically reserved for something much bigger than you," he said to her in an unrecognizable accent. Vylasgarden wanted to roar but felt a fine pressure against the sides of her neck that made it too uncomfortable.

"See? It's alive. Now are we done here?" came a feminine voice from behind her. "Give me what was promised."

The voice came around into Vylasgarden's view. She was one of the little native folk Vylasgarden had seen before, though this one was

different. Her hair was straight and her eyes were small and brown instead of yellow like the rest.

"You will find your reward with my guild's master," the human said while annoyed by the interruption. "I'm sure he will allow you to keep the trophy you took for yourself." The small woman carried a satchel over her shoulder and patted it with a bloody hand.

Vylasgarden found it within herself to cry out, which caused the small woman to stagger a bit. "I'll be on my way now," she said before leaving the human alone with Vylasgarden in the cage. There was an echo of footsteps and then the opening and closing of a heavy door.

"Come, stop your balling," the human said. "We've only begun your suffering, dragonkin." He unsheathed a dagger from his belt and flashed it before her face.

"M-m-m… monsters!" she said.

The human gasped and dropped the blade. "You can speak?"

"B-b-butcherer!"

"Kazymyr! Kazymyr! Come quick!" He ran out of the cage and made sure to lock it behind him before charging out of the room and slamming the door shut.

Vylasgarden pulled at her restraints to no avail; the poison was not done with her yet. Blood came from her head and speckled on the floor.

"Vylasgarden?" she heard from across the room past the light cast through the hole in the ceiling.

"R-Riker, is that you?" The pressure points on the collar

made it difficult for her to get the words out.

"Vylasgarden. What did they do to you?" "Where is the elfess?

Is she okay?"

He didn't answer right away. "She was hit by one of those knives.

I think she may be in trouble. She's as cold as ice." "I can't see you."

"We're across the room tied together on a post. Listen to me carefully, Vylasgarden. Did he leave the knife lying around you?"

Vylasgarden saw the dagger right below her. It was out of reach, but perhaps her feet could bring it closer. She tried, but it was no use. "I can't get to it."

"Keep trying," he insisted. "You're the only one who can get us out of this."

She reached again and again until she heard the door swinging open again. The human from before was with an older and taller man dressed similarly. "Show him!" he demanded. His companion was brown-haired and was wearing an eyepatch that covered a nasty scar across his right eye. Vylasgarden remained silent.

"I see nothing special here," said Old Eyepatch. His accent was heavier than the other.

"I swear to you, it spoke!"

"It's drugged, boy. You were hearing pitiful cries." Old

Eyepatch started to leave before noticing the dagger on the floor. He picked it up and handed it by the blade to the yellow haired one, who tried taking it, but Old Eyepatch resisted. "Lose this again and I'll use it to cut off your fingers." He released it. "Put it out of its misery and get a few others to help with the elves."

"Don't touch them," Vylasgarden said to him. "See! I told you!" exclaimed yellow hair.

"What is this magick?" questioned Old Eyepatch.

"C-Come closer and f-find out for yourself," she threatened.

"Fascinating," he said, leaning in. "That look in your eye. Have we met before?" Vylasgarden thought back but had no specific memories of the faces who'd torn through her people. "Can't be sure, but I know a Dragon Slayer when I see one."

"Let me guess. Our horses trample your clutch of eggs or something like that?"

"Kazymyr, wait, this is one of those things we found in the mountains of Froisia a few years back. The ones we thought we wiped out."

There was sudden recognition on Old Eyepatch's face. "Ah, yes! Are you the one that got away?" he asked. "That was a hell of a bloodbath. I remember it like yesteryear."

"I'm going to kill you!" Vylasgarden claimed.

"Afraid not, dragonkin," he replied. "Even if you can

breathe fire like your elderkin, you wouldn't so much as puff smoke so long as that collar is around your neck, but I will let you live long enough to tell me your story."

"Let the elves go and I'll tell you anything you want."

He chuckled. "This isn't a negotiation, beastie. Just because I want to hear you speak doesn't mean I see you as my equal. Tell me your story or this all ends now."

With no other option other than giving Riker time to come up with something, she started to tell them her story: how she'd escaped the genocide and how she survived on her own. She told them about her human masters, who showed her the way to speak the common language, and finding strength within herself she then used to get where she was in these chains. She told them about the elves and how they'd offered her help in finding the Slayers in exchange for her help getting them across the gulf. Old Eyepatch scratched his beard. "That is some story, Vylasgarden," he said at the end. "It is a true shame we didn't learn more about your kind. The seeds of potential were there, no doubt."

"We weren't animals!"

"Exactly! An animal can only act on instinct, which then can be exploited, but a dragon has a will of its own. A cunning that starved humanity and once brought us to our knees because they saw a challenge in the way we advanced and organized. You may believe we are the monsters, and after what you've gone through, I would not blame you for seeing it that way, but know that long before today, the blood was on their teeth and claws. So long as there is a drop of dragon's blood left in this world, the Dragon Slayers will do what is necessary to keep humanity safe."

Vylasgarden bared her teeth.

"I will grant you a farewell to your companions, and since you are the last of your kind, I swear to you that what is left of your remains will be respected and given a ceremonial pyre."

Vylasgarden said nothing.

"Myron, collect the elves. Don't take long and come inform me when you are done."

"Yes, Kazymyr."

Vylasgarden made sure to memorize Old Eyepatch's face as he left the room. Myron, the yellow hair, went to fetch the elves from across the room. First, he carried a seemingly unconscious Riker under the skylight and then went back for Llorva. Riker fluttered his eyes open, and he gave Vylasgarden an assuring nod. He then closed his eyes as the Dragon Slayer came up from behind with Llorva in his arms. Her limbs and head swayed lifelessly before he laid her down next to Riker. Her skin was paler than usual.

Yellow hair started tying them together when Riker sprang up, taking the Slayer's dagger from his side and swinging around behind him. "Scream and I will cut your throat," he threatened while pressing the blade against his neck. "Where are we?"

"Underneath Narabari City in the salt mine," he replied in a shaky voice.

"You're going to let us free and maybe, just maybe, my friend in chains over there won't tear you apart. Either way, this is your best choice."

"I won't! Help —" His last words before Riker used the pommel of the blade to strike the Slayer across the head, knocking him unconscious. Riker searched his pockets and found a key he then used to open the cage and set Vylasgarden free.

She rose and put a hand on Riker's shoulder for both support and thanks. "They took your horns," he stated while helping her stand. "How're you doing? We're going to need your strength."

"I will be fine. I think. Go get Llorva," she managed to say, rubbing her throat. Riker obeyed and went to collect the elfess, who was still lying on the floor. She had a gash across her left shoulder and was unresponsive to Riker's coaxing. Her once pale lips were as red as blood, and her mouth was foaming. "Is she breathing?" Vylasgarden asked. Riker brought his ear to her face. His concerned expression supported Vylasgarden's suspicions.

"The poison will kill her if we don't do something," Riker said. "Then you have to find the small woman who brought us here. It's her only chance."

"Right. She can't be too far away."

"I'm too weak to jump, but I can get you through the hole there," she said, pointing to where the firelight was pouring in. Riker set the elfess against a wall and covered her with his bedroll. Vylasgarden noticed that there was a hint of a glowing light that framed her still body. After blocking the door with the post she'd uprooted from the ground and helping him dress in the Slayer's armor, Vylasgarden had Riker climb up on her shoulders. "Be quick," she said to him before giving his feet a push with her clawed hands and shooting him straight up. There was a thud, and bits of salt rained down on her.

"I'm okay," he groaned. "I got this."

Chapter Six

RIKER

THE HOLE WAS IN A WHITE HALLWAY surrounded by mounds of fine salt on either side of Riker. He surveyed the spot and found footprints in the salt on the floor, which led to his right. Following the path and its order of sconces, he likened the yawning tunnel to a portal taking him to hell itself. Eventually he heard echoes of a gathering up ahead. He adjusted his helmet and continued forward cautiously. If not for his quick thinking to play dead after Llorva was struck, they all might not have made it this far. Hopefully (for Llorva's sake) he had enough time to find the ebu-gogo who had been in the room with them earlier, or at least find one of the strangers who had been throwing knives at them before.

He followed the bend of the tunnel and found apertures in the salt walls that gave a view of the level below him. Riker saw folk from around the world gathered there in a market at the center of the salt mine. A ginormous serpent head reared up, frightening Riker as it grew. It was in similar chains to Vylasgarden and was boxed in against the wall Riker was peering over. In front of its cage was a man Riker recognized dressed in bandages and with a tiger tattoo on his right arm. He was addressing other, fairer-skinned men. Their banners were of a dragon's skull, and they were dressed in Slayers' armor. The rest of the grand room was full of barterers at stations of potions and elixirs, animal parts, and even human slaves. That was where Riker found the ebu-gogo woman talking to the old Dragon Slayer who had been in the room with them.

They were surrounded by masked ebu-gogos handling the captives. He made his way to the stairs leading to the room with a plan forming in his mind: somehow he was going to get the ebu-gogo leader alone and force her to give up an antitoxin for Llorva, though he was not yet sure if he would kill for her. He kept his head down and went straight to them. He avoided covering his nose, for the room smelled like death.

Near the stairs, a crowd was starting to form around a bookie who called for entertainment. A man and woman both wearing black leathers started sizing each other up, wielding black blades. Both were nearly as tall as Vylasgarden and just as muscular. "Whosoever wins this duel shall earn favor to Lord Sayavong's contract!" decreed the bookie before signaling for the fight to begin. Riker sped past the crowd and noticed the male fighter looking at him as if seeing through the disguise. The distraction cost the fighter a blow as the female made her first move, producing a violet flame from the leather glove on her free hand and reaching out to burn her opponent's face. The two engaged in swordplay as Riker ducked away to the slavers.

He passed a table with various silver-plated weapons lying on a blue cloth. The Haran vendor waved to anyone nearby. "Silver! Silver here!" he yelled. "Get your silver before the next full moon, just under a month away." Once every full moon, a void called the Dark Realm aligned cosmically with the world. It was a place where disease and demons waited for the crossing to thin upon alignment and haunted the world for a night. Riker had once heard wizards and witches could become their most powerful on a full moon, but most folk reasonably stayed inside, leaving silver talismans on their doors and windows to ward off flesh-eaters and black magick. He planned on being home in Bloowood long before the next full moon. He crossed the way, hid behind some crates, and listened near the old man and ebu-gogo as the clashing of swords rang behind them. "This is not what was agreed upon!" she yelled at the Dragon Slayer.

"If you want the horns, then this is what you get," he replied calmly. "The deal was for the *Skink* to be brought alive and whole."

"Fine! Then I keep the elves."

"I don't think so. Elves are hard to come by. Especially a male one. They stay with us."

The ebu-gogo sighed deeply. "I hope you don't expect them to be alive. The poison in their bodies is strong enough to take down a tiger. They won't last long without my antidote."

The old man chuckled. "My dear, your threats ring hollow. If I wanted them alive, I'd have them treated." The ebu-gogo grimaced and clenched her fists. "You want to attack me, do you? Go ahead. You think you're good with a poison blade? Then try it, you she-runt! I've lived through worse than you; you're nothing more than an ankle-biter to me."

"This won't be good for your reputation, Kazymyr. The other guilds will know of this farce of a deal from here to Shady Foot."

"Ha! How rich! This is all possible because of me and mine. You think you have something to prove because you're a small leader in a gang of fetchers, but let me inform you about your place here. You're just one ant of many on my hill." The old man grew quiet and more serious. "Threaten me again, though, and I will cut your tongue out of that freakish head of yours." Right then, a few of the captives noticed Riker and started calling to him.

The ebu-gogo drew a blade. "Who's there! Show yourself!" Riker remained still and fought against the urge to run as he watched her and the old man come closer to his hiding spot. There was no use. If he didn't run, then they would corner him. Riker ran and threw down the Dragon Slayer helmet. "Stop that elf!" Riker ran straight for the caged serpent as the entire market alerted to his presence. If he were to fail, he would fail unleashing chaos. He looked back, finding the ebu-gogo throwing a knife at his head, which sliced his cheek and knocked him forward, making him fall to the floor. There on the ground, he caught a glimpse of an ax under a table and, without a second thought, he grasped it and sprang up in full sprint, relying on the excitement rushing through his blood to carry him onward. The cage was only a handful of paces ahead. He met eyes with Tiger Tattoo just as his vision blurred and his tongue began to swell.

Tiger Tattoo screamed something Riker couldn't hear over the sound of his own heart beating in his ears, and the man leapt away from Riker, who raised the ax and brought it down on the lock of the cage door while also running hard into the iron bars himself. The next thing he knew, he was lying on the ground, face bleeding, nose probably broken as the cage door flew open and the ginormous, bright red reptilian head came out from within the cage.

"Quick! Stop the wyrm!" someone shouted, and a group of Dragon Slayers rushed the cage. The serpent's red scaly face had long spines all around the head and flexing gills beneath the large webbed ears. From the neck, the scales turned to green all the way down its spiked body to its forked tail, which it used to whip the Dragon Slayers off their feet.

It slithered out of its cage and looked at the people

hungrily. Carnage ensued, and Riker crawled away behind the scenes in hopes of gaining a sense of control as the poison started taking away the use of his legs.

A body crashed on a table he was going to crawl under; then another came and splatted on the wall. Riker mustered some strength and got up to start hobbling — searching for the heavy door so that he could at least free Vylasgarden before he died. He was suddenly knocked over again and found the old man standing over him with a longsword in hand. "I figure Myron is dead. Gods! I gave that boy too many chances." He brought the sword down, and Riker used the Dragon Slayer's gauntlets he was wearing to shield himself. The blade sliced through the scaly hide all the way to his forearms. He screamed. "Stings, yeah? Steel like this is the one of few things that can get through a dragon hide." The old man swung again, this time missing Riker's head and sticking the blade through the floor. When the old man pulled it free, it sliced through Riker's shoulder.

The old man stepped on Riker's chest. "Stop your squirming, boy. I want to make this quick." He held the sword point-down and raised it over his head when someone came from behind him and drove a similar blade through his chest, spraying blood all over Riker as they pulled it free from the old man's body. It was the male fighter from before, shoving the body off to the side. He reached down and picked Riker up by the collar of the dragon armor and threw him over his shoulder. Riker retched and spewed on the stranger's back before he started running as the mayhem continued behind them. The last thing Riker remembered before passing out was the stranger saying, "If you ralph on my jerkin again, I will finish you myself."

Ravens. Raving ravens take flight in a gray sky, Black. Black is her hair like raven's feathers,

Raven!

"Hand me that vial."

Raven feathers and a lyrical hymn, Praise to you, my sweet Raven.

"What is he talking about?"

"It's a side effect. Get ready. Three... two..."

Riker gasped awake, seeing an iron chandelier over him. He was lying on a table surrounded by Vylasgarden, the stranger, and Llorva. "Riker, can you tell me how many fingers I'm holding up?" the stranger asked.

"Eight," he moaned, ignoring the hand and staring up at the ceiling. "Eightlitcandlesinthe chandelier," the stranger finally said after a moment of pause. "That's correct. Praise to your gods, your friends were worried you done killed yourself for them."

"We all would have been dead if not for Zygmund," said Vylasgarden as she helped Riker up off the table. The parts of her head where the ebu-gogo had cut off her horns were bandaged, and he was wearing his old clothes. Zygmund, the stranger, held a syringe in one hand and an empty bottle in the other. "He gave us all a cure to the poison."

"Why?"

"Call it a thanks," Zygmund answered. "That stunt you pulled freeing the wyrm gave me the window I needed to win my contract."

"What's your line of work? Are you some kind of mercenary?"

"Something like that. My work is highly specialized, and my colleagues and I often have to duel for it these days. I knew from the moment I saw you that you didn't belong here."

"How long was I out?" Riker asked.

"A few hours," answered Llorva. She seemed perfectly fine. Even the cut on her shoulder had healed to a scar. "Thank you for risking your life for us."

"You would have done the same for me," Riker replied, knowing better. "Llorva tells me you're in need of a boat. If you're ready, Riker, I can get you on one right now."

"I can manage," Riker said, putting on his bag and strapping his lute to his back. He felt his body ache.

"Then let's not waste any time." Vylasgarden helped Riker walk while Zygmund and Llorva led the way. Blood was everywhere, and not a living soul was around. "That wyrm made getting out of here easy. Stay close."

"Vylasgarden," Riker whispered, "What did you do with that Dragon Slayer?"

Vylasgarden remained silent, not even looking at him.

They found what was left of the serpent flayed and headless on the floor, surrounded by dead men and women. All with various arrangements of injury, from ripped limbs to mangled heads. "I count four dead Dragon Slayers," said Zygmund. "The rest must have killed and taken their trophies from the beast."

"Without their leader, I'm sure they will disband,"Riker stated. Zygmund stopped but kept looking ahead. "This was just the Haran guild of slayers. An organization as ancient as The Dragon Slayers has roots in every corner of the realm." Riker felt Vylasgarden tense up, but she remained silent.

"Zyg… mund," came a voice amidst the bodies on the floor near the stairs.

"Angelika!" Zygmund rushed over to find his opponent, her black leather sticky with congealed blood. He kneeled over her and took her hand in his. "Angelika, I'm here."

She looked at him with familiarity and gripped his hand hard. "To the death… my friend," she said to him.

"Yes, Angelika. To the death." He dispassionately kissed her hand and pulled a knife from her boot. "Please look away," he said to the trio.

Riker stared away before hearing the knife pierce through Angelika, and she gave a final breath. Zygmund took out a reddish-brown substance from his pocket and held it before him. The substance ignited, creating a green flame in his hand. He threw the flame on Angelika's body, and it engulfed her. Zygmund then said something in an unfamiliar language before walking away to the stairs.

He took them to the surface, where the salt mine was hiding inside a beach cave. Salt mixed with sand as they all climbed aboard a sailboat on shore. Riker drifted in and out of sleep as Zygmund guided the boat into open water and took them elsewhere. When they stopped, it was dusk, and Riker saw that they were in a docking area. "Where are we?" Llorva asked.

"A fishing village a little ways north of Narabari. I have a friend here who will take you the rest of the way. Wait here and I'll be back." Zygmund left them on the boat and went over to a building on the pier.

When he was out of sight, Riker spoke up. "All right, let's go before he comes back."

"What? Are you insane?"

"We need to be gone before he's back," he said, slowly standing. "Why would we do that when he's helping us?" asked Vylasgarden. "Because he's not helping us. He's a warlock, a highly skilled, highly dangerous magick wielding mercenary. He wants to sell us to a slavermonger."

"What? That can't be. He healed us."

"Because we're more valuable to him alive. You have to trust me, there isn't much time."

Vylasgarden took him to her side and helped him out of the boat, and then extended a hand to Llorva, who hesitated.

"Don't be a fool, Llorva," Riker said. "If you don't come with us now, your life will be over."

"There are few others I trust more with my life than Riker right now," Vylasgarden added. Llorva took her hand, and the trio disembarked the boat. They frantically moved down the pier and found Harans loading a small cargo ship. They waited until the last crate was loaded, and, while the workers were congregating on the deck, the trio snuck aboard. Llorva found a trapdoor, which led to the hull below deck where the crew was keeping their cargo. They descended into the cramped space full of crates and barrels and settled in for the night.

"Do you think he will find us?" asked Llorva.

"No," said Riker, but he was not sure himself. He just hoped that they would be long gone before Zygmund could track them there on the pier. Riker found a spot to put aside his bag and lute, and he stretched before joining Llorva and Vylasgarden at the center of the boat. Fatigue still had a grip on him.

"Where do you think it's going?" asked Vylasgarden as they got comfortable in their new surroundings.

"Best we worry about that when we get there," Riker said. "I don't care where we end up so long as it takes us east."

"What awaits you there?" Llorva asked. She too looked exhausted.

"There's someone I hope to reunite with."

Vylasgarden snorted at that.

"What?" he asked suspiciously.

"Nothing," she answered.

It was the way she said it that made Llorva arch her brow. "Am I missing something?" she asked. Both Riker and Vylasgarden said nothing. "Come on, you two, tell me. I almost died today, so you have to tell me."

"It's someone dear to me," Riker finally said. "Her name is Raven, and we met at the bard's college in my hometown. She's a harpist."

"Elf or human?" Llorva asked seriously.

"Halfr, like me. She and I were inseparable until she was invited to join the Elves' Festival Orchestra. They travel the continent sharing elf music and culture with the world." Riker sensed Llorva's discomfort, but she said nothing. "It was her dream to join them, and I didn't want to make her choose me over it. But now, after so many years, I have to tell her I want her in my life. That ever since she went away, I've been trying to fill the void she left in me."

Llorva blushed. "Oh my…"

"How do you know she will be there?" Vylasgarden asked.

"I don't know, but it'll be where I start, and I don't care how long it takes me to find her."

"Well, I hope you're wrong," said Llorva. "I hope it takes us north where the rivers are so that I can get closer to my new home." Riker rolled his eyes and felt the boat shift and lurch forward.

Chapter Seven
LLORVA

ZYGMUND'S MEDICINE HEALED HER surprisingly quickly. She once thought she had never known sickness but was told later in life by the sisters that fever nearly killed her in infancy. She was told that the alfar were not made for this world and that sickness was their bodies fighting away the impurities this new world had to offer. She started noticing a looming darkness creeping into the hull. The night was upon them. Llorva searched through her bag, quickly pulled out her cloak, and covered herself with it.

"What's wrong?"

"The dark. I can't be in the dark," she said, folding her arms and hands inside the cloak.

"Your skin is…glowing," Vylasgarden said, approaching Llorva. From her white hair to her fingertips, Llorva was shining a bright light in the dark.

"Vylasgarden, quick, find something to cover her with," Riker said, looking to see if they would be spotted from the deck. "Is this… normal?" he asked her.

"Yes, pure blooded alfar glow in the dark, okay? I

thought I could keep it hidden." Vylasgarden brought over a tarp and covered her with it. That night Llorva didn't fight the drowsiness that was taking over her body, and, to her own surprise, she slept a whole day out at sea. Like her, Riker mostly slept, but eventually hunger kept them awake. With no food around, she amused herself by searching through the cargo and finding odd trinkets and wears. Eventually growing tired of the rummaging and too hungry to bear it, she threw open her bag and pulled out the bottle of wine she had taken from the inn a couple of days ago. "I was going to wait until much later, but what better way to pass the time?" She struggled to twist the cork free and offered it to Riker for help.

"Do you have wine in Foss Sergens?" he asked. He too struggled and then passed the bottle off to Vylasgarden, who effortlessly pulled it free with a single claw and gave it back to Llorva.

"No, but we have a tea we drink, using honey and fruits native to our home realm." She took a sip and tasted the dry burn. "Still don't know what is in this," she surmised, and handed the bottle to Riker.

"Grapes, believe it or not," he replied, and took a sip of his own.

He seemed to enjoy the drink more than she had. "Grapes. Is that a kind of fruit?"

"Yes. They're these reddish-purple bunch of berry-looking fruits that grow on vines. They taste much better that way, if you can believe it." Llorva tried sharing the bottle with Vylasgarden, but she refused it. It would have been interesting to see her try to wrap her stiff, scaly lips around the neck of the bottle. And so only she and Riker sat drinking while Vylasgarden went off to a corner.

"Well, as fermented fruits go, I'd say this was a welcoming luxury," she said in a raspy voice. The wine had parched her mouth.

"Tell me more about this place you're going to in the north province," Riker said, accepting the bottle from Llorva. "Tell why you want to go there so badly."

She reflected, looking down for a moment, and took the bottle back after he drank from it. "Growing up, I learned about our wars with humans when we first came to this world and how the few of us that survived started fighting amongst ourselves over who would rule I suppose. There was a third group from both sides who left Foss Sergens in protest to the wars and made a home somewhere in the northern province."

"The hidden folk," Riker said before taking another drink.

"What?"

"Northerners call them the hidden folk, because they live secretly amongst the forest villages in the area. Stories and song say that they only reveal themselves to the forest creatures and beings of pure heart. The northerners say the hidden folk protects them from blizzards brought on by magick wielding trolls in their mountains. What makes you think they would take you in if they refuse the very people they protect?"

She paused thoughtfully. "We share a past and an ancestry. They would have to accept me," she said sternly.

Riker narrowed his eyes suspiciously. "I share that same blood, yet you see me as different than you."

"I don't expect you to understand. My blood is pure and yours is not. That is the difference," she said. She stood but then fell over from the drinking and the boat rocking. "At least that was what I was raised to believe. Seeing how different the world is, I'm not so sure that is a bad thing now." Riker kept his attention on her. "I was born after my people settled and fought to stay here – supposedly the only birth of pure blood since – and instead of embracing what made this world different from what they knew before, we remain stuck in a tradition belonging elsewhere. As the years went on, I felt like a stranger to my own kind."

"Despite this you seek a group of elves with similar ideals. You're not from where they came from. Do you really think living with them would be any different from where you came?"

"I have to find out for myself. The alfar are all that I know."

Another few days passed with not much speaking among them. Thankfully, they got plenty to drink from the water that came through the deck from the constant rain outside. By then, nothing they had was dry, and Llorva noticed Riker's instruments would sometimes hum and vibrate on their own. "Is that supposed to happen?" she asked while he studied his flute, which was jumping around in his hands.

"I think it's the storm," he said, sounding tired. "There are places where a wild magick the sorcerers call the Primordial Power moves and gathers, forming literal magick storms. Though my instruments weren't the source of my magick, my former mentor who gave them to me said he crafted them using the same primordial magick. Maybe that is why they are misbehaving."

"Misbehaving? Should we worry?" asked Vylasgarden, who seemed to be handling hunger the best.

"No, I can't imagine something more severe than this occurring. Say, Vylasgarden, can you breathe fire?" Riker asked to change the subject.

"No."

"The old Dragon Slayer seemed to think you could."

"Breath of fire and magick were rare among my people. Few of us could control the sky and even command lightning inherently. The power died with my people. I never could."

"It's an honest wonder I never heard of your race before. One would think a book would have been written, or a song at least."

"We were never meant to be found, Riker. Because of the Slayers we were made to preserve and hide what was left of dragon bloodlines."

"Well, perhaps we found you so that you and I can tell your story to the world."

Vylasgarden huffed. "Yes, maybe you're right. What does it matter now?"

Llorva woke late the next day to the sound of screeching seagulls.

She crawled out of the crate she was using to conceal her light during the nights and found Riker and Vylasgarden huddling around the front end of the boat. When she approached, she noticed that they were peering through a hole Vylasgarden seemed to have made with one of her claws.

"I think we may be close to one of the river mouths. Hopefully today is the day we pull in somewhere."

"What of the storm?" she asked, rubbing the sleep from her eyes.

"Take a look for yourself," Riker said, making room for her to see. He looked awful. There were rings of purple around his eyes, and his skin was nearly as pale as hers.

She looked through the hole and saw a land mass ahead of a lush, mountainous jungle and a thunderstorm hanging low above the trees.

"Wait, something isn't right about that storm," she said. Its shape looked too perfectly round, and the flashes of lighting in the black clouds were green and not of the natural variety of white, blues, or violently bright violets.

"That's exactly what I was talking about before," said Riker. "I wouldn't be surprised if a cabal of sorcerers were plotting somewhere around there." Llorva remembered the instruments and how they were "misbehaving" a few days back. She started to ask about them when she noticed a crackling sound that grew louder and louder. All three of them saw Riker's lute sparking with green energy. "I'm not doing that," he said, noticing the energy was flying off the lute's string and catching green fire on the hull's wood floor. Riker and Llorva ran over and tried putting the fire out with the linen, which only caught fire as well. A lump started to form in Llorva's throat as she tried to swallow the panic building within her.

"Riker, your flute!" she cried, pointing at his chest. The runes on the flute were glowing bright green and began sparking the energy as well. Riker threw the necklace off, and the flute jumped around in the fire before exploding at the back of the boat. Llorva crashed hard against the floor and felt cold water seeping beneath her. When she recovered from the dizziness, she saw that the ocean was flooding inside the hull of the boat. Then she noticed that the explosion had deafened her. She didn't even hear the green lightning bolt coming from above and striking Riker's lute, which blew apart the rest of the boat.

The chill from the water shocked her awake as her body plunged into the depths. She tried swimming to the surface, but her leg was yanked down by a sharp grip. Llorva saw the shape of a sizable fish pulling at her ankle. She reached down and clawed at it, but it only sank its teeth deeper into her. With the last of her fleeting strength, she ripped at the fish's gills, which made it release her. When she broke the surface, she spewed salt water from her mouth and frantically searched for land. Disoriented from her lack of hearing, she relied on the flashes of green lightning and swirling clouds as a beacon to shore. She about jumped out of her skin when something else touched her. It was Riker, and he was trying to tell her something. He pointed in a direction, and after the waves dipped, she finally saw that land was close.

They came into an estuary, where they found the boat's crew escaping the rough water. The ripping winds made it difficult to wade through the mud, but with Riker's help she found solid ground. Llorva shivered in her cloak as the rain and wind beat down on them. The air felt strange, like there was a force pushing against her, and her ears started to ring and ache. She looked up, and the gray sky was swirling about with moments of green light to illuminate her surroundings. She viewed the area for Vylasgarden, but she was not in sight. The crewmen were standing around by then, sorting what was found on shore and tending to each other's wounds. Llorva could make out muffled speeches, and it seemed as though Riker's hearing wasn't any better than hers. Riker helped Llorva stand and covered her glowing head with her soaked cloak as the two marched toward the trees; some movement in the brush alerted Llorva, and she stopped him with her arm. A monster raised its long, goosey neck into view. It had the head of a rooster with a comb and crop as red as blood. It crowded when it saw them and emerged from the trees. It was ostrich-sized with long meaty legs and was covered in deep blue feathers. Its eight-foot tail curled and twisted as the creature studied them curiously. One of the human sailors made a sudden move, and the creature leapt up at them. Feathers flying everywhere. Llorva reflexively shot down to the ground, and the bird reared in the air and viciously came down spurring at the Haran man. The man fell over and contorted in the sand until life drained from his frightened eyes. He gave a final exhale, and his crooked body froze stiff.

Fear surged through Llorva, and she pulled Riker to his feet. She ignored the pain in her ankle and dragged him away as the bird attacked Haran sailors all around them. The only place to go was into the unforeseeable jungle. Where was Vylasgarden? Could she be dead? No, she was much too resilient to drown out there, were the thoughts in her head while ringing continued in her ears. The two hastened in whichever way that wasn't blocking their path with as much vegetation; roots in the loose soil caught on her feet, and vines in the violent wind roped around her neck and limbs. After some distance, they crouched behind a fallen tree in a tall grass clearing.

Llorva thought she heard screaming in the wind behind them. The rain and fog made it difficult for her to survey the scene; all seemed still, and the screams were no more. She checked on Riker, who was looking more and more like dead weight at that point. Zygmund's medicine was still working on him, and hunger left him slow to react. Despite this, she couldn't bring herself to abandon him, not after he'd nearly died saving her life. "Can you hear?" she asked him, and he nodded slightly. They both sat back against the fallen tree and waited. Vylasgarden couldn't be far behind.

They exchanged looks while Riker kept watch, and she examined the bite on her ankle with trembling hands. When she was sure she would be fine, she noticed her hearing was slowly returning to her. That was when she noticed the rustling in the grass. She looked over at Riker, and he was holding a branch in his hands, barely alert. Zygmund's medicine was forcing him into another sleep. She peered over the tree, and her eyes were met by the beak of the monster. It crowd, spaying painful droplets on her face. Llorva recoiled and fell over while Riker started swinging the branch at the monster. She felt her face run cold and stiffened like a layer of skin was hardening. She couldn't see what was happening, but she heard Riker's muffled yelling and felt small tremors on the ground as she tried crawling away in the grass.

She dared open her eyes, and an image formed of orange f ire on torches running across the grass. There were yells and screams as figures from the fog passed her and surrounded Riker and the monster. With torches in one hand and swords in the other, a trio of strangers started cleaving the monster and burning it with the fire. Llorva shielded herself from the clouds of embers as the monster squawked painfully. She stood and witnessed one of the strangers, a brute, decapitating the monster with the swing of his sword.

"Don't touch its blood!" she heard another say. They all turned their attention to her and Riker. They were youthful human males, but unlike the dark-skinned Harans from before, they were taller and of a fairer dark complexion. One pointed at her. "Holy hell, Jared! They're elves."

The brute stepped forward and sheathed his blade. "Do you understand me?" She nodded, wearily. Riker fell over beside her, and she went to support him back to his feet. He was heavier than she'd imagined. "Let me help you." The brute brought them over to the fallen tree while the other two stayed behind with the dead monster. Llorva watched one of them carefully cut off the plumage of its tail, and together they drained the monster's blood from its head into a jar. The brute sat Riker on the tree. "What happened to him?"

Llorva didn't speak for a reason she didn't understand. It made her think of Zygmund, and she wondered if Riker was coherent enough to signal to her whether talking to this man was a good idea.

"Hey! Can you speak?" the brute said.

"It was a warlock's medicine," Riker managed to say.

"A warlock?" Riker lifted his shirt and revealed where the warlock had stuck him with his tool. The brute softened his face. "Where did you come from?" The others came over. One leaned on his sword in the ground like a cane, and the other Llorva noticed was leering at her. She noticed something across the way in the trees. It was Vylasgarden watching them.

Llorva breathed a sigh of relief. "Can you help him?" she asked.

"I'm not sure," answered the brute. "Before I try, you're going to have to answer my questions. What are two elves doing this far from Southaven?" Llorva looked at Riker, and he seemed equally conflicted about speaking.

"Brother, let's bring them back with us," suggested the one leaning on his sword. "Perhaps some food and kindness will yield better results."

The brute rolled his eyes and helped support Riker to

his feet. "Come on then." He walked with Riker, with Sword Leaner following behind. The third stood in Llorva's way and looked her up and down. She was about to ask him to move when he lunged at her, reaching for her arms.

"Gideon! What are you doing?" said the brute.

"Making sure she doesn't have any weapons on her," replied Gideon deviously.

"She's in no state to try something. Now let's get out of this storm." He waited for Gideon to move before turning back at the head of the group. Llorva tracked Vylasgarden in the trees before she brought up the rear. A weight was lifted off Llorva knowing that Vylasgarden was keeping watch. The brute led them a mile upstream where the past-noon sun met the eye of the storm; where there was no wind or rain, no strange feeling in the air, and a sunny twilight came through the open sky. They took them to a fire under an alcove, where Llorva was surprised to see a young boy cooking a boar over the flames. He was blond, blue-eyed, and of lighter skin than the older humans. "This is Perry, our squire."

"A great pleasure," said the boy. "I didn't expect you would bring elves back with you."

"Nor did we," said Sword Leaner, throwing the monster's severed head aside. "We found them being attacked by the predator. Turns out all that cock-a-doodle-dooing we've been hearing really was a cockatrice. We shouldn't have doubted you."

Perry grinned and went over to the head of the beast and poked it with a stick. The brute sat Riker down in the middle of the alcove while Sword Leaner cleared a spot for Llorva to sit near the fire. "Milady, elfess." She sat, and the Leerer offered her and Riker meat from the roasting wild pig.

"Perry, pour our guests some ale," ordered the brute. The boy went and drained a liquid from a small cask into a pair of mugs and then offered it to the two elves.

Llorva sniffed at it and curled her lip. "What is this?"

"That there is a fine ale," replied the brute. "It's good for countering a powerful elixir. Consider it an offer of goodwill." She looked at Riker for reassurance, and he was already halfway down his drink. She pinched her nose and took in a mouthful of it. She had to stop herself from gagging before gulping it down.

"Ick! That is…different," she concluded with a sour look on her face. The men erupted in laughter. "Will this help him feel better?"

"Absolutely!" Riker answered. "Thank you for helping us and all the hospitality."

"You can repay us by telling me why you were out here."

"Me and my sister were coming in from the sea in hopes the river would take us north. But then the storm struck our boat and left us stranded here."

Llorva furrowed her brows at that but remained silent to see where he was going with it.

"What about the Harans we found on the beach?" the brute asked suspiciously.

"It was their boat, of course," answered Riker. "We paid for passage." The brute scratched his beard and stared at Riker for a moment as Riker continued to sip his drink.

"What's waiting for you at the end of the river?" asked the Leerer. "We're visiting the hidden folk in the north province," answered Riker.

"Don't waste your time. The hidden folk aren't real," said Perry softly. His expression turned to a mournful frown.

"What do you mean?" asked Llorva. "Are you from there?"

"Yes, but I never saw them or my gods for that matter. The northmen believed that the elves were there watching over us, but when the seafarers came and burned our homes down, the hidden folk didn't come and use their magick to help us."

"He wouldn't have believed that the south elves to be real either if not for us finding you two," said the brute. "A few years ago, my brothers and I found him in a cellar after his village was pillaged. He was the only survivor, hiding with a bunch of books and scrolls. We took him in, and the rest is history."

"Who are you exactly?" asked Riker.

"We're travelers," answered the Sword Leaner. "Myself is Asghar. The big one is our leader, Jared, and that is Gideon," he said, pointing at the Leerer. "We pick up the pieces after a conflicts and go where few are willing."

"What brought you to this jungle?" Llorva asked after her second attempt at drinking the strange liquid.

Jared the brute stood and pointed in the distance. Across from the alcove was the river, and between the trees Llorva could see a building with a great water wheel and a tower. "We came looking for that. Where there are Sorcerer Storms, there are magick secrets to be found. Or so we thought, because the place was abandoned and already ransacked when we arrived."

"I told you it was a wizard's tower," Perry interrupted. "Though the phenomenon is called a Sorcerer Storm, it is the witches and wizards who need to take from its concentrated Primeval Power, because it is they who do not have the Primeval Powers within them."

"The boy fancies himself a scholar on magick," Asghar followed.

"Whatever," sneered Jared. "No wizard, no sorcerer, and no loot or magick was found; so tomorrow we continue the way up the river and find a settlement before the next full moon." Llorva's ears perked at that. Since leaving Foss Sergens, she had heard of living nightmares that would haunt the lands once a month when the divide between the natural world and the otherworldly blurred at the cosmic alignment of a full moon.

"You wouldn't want to get caught in the wilds under a full moon. Why don't you two join us and we see you to a safe place before we part ways?" insisted Gideon, his attention lingering on Llorva.

"There is a fishing village we're heading into in the marshland a few days north of here," declared Perry, looking at a scrolled map he kept in his travel bag.

"Excellent idea," agreed Riker. Llorva remained silent, as she hadn't spoken with Riker yet about Vylasgarden lurking in the trees. Vylasgarden had once said she could lead them through the jungle across the gulf, and Llorva would rather keep it that way.

"A generous offer," she finally said. "Allow me to speak alone with my brother, and we will be back with a definitive answer." She and Riker got up and trailed to the river as the stars came out. They didn't say a word until Llorva's skin was in full luminance and they arrived at the abandoned wizard's tower. Riker held the door open, and she went inside the mill, which was full of abandoned benches and turning cogs that, with the help of the river, moved a long part that went up the tower. They followed it up the stairs and found the door to the room at the top. Inside was a green light coming from a rod in a glass case. "Have you seen anything like it?" she asked Riker.

"We're inside a real wizard's tower," he said as he walked about the room. The laboratory had been scavenged many times over. If there was anything valuable there, it had long been taken away. "Look at this." He showed her what looked like a calendar paired with pages of constellations.

"What do you make of it?"

"Wizard stuff," he replied, shrugging. He put the papers down. "I think we're free enough to talk here. Without my magick, their swords are our best defense against the next monster that may come our way."

"I have no doubts," Llorva agreed, "but what about Vylasgarden? I saw her in the trees waiting for us. She said back in Narabari that she knows the way through this area. We should regroup with her and stick to the original plan."

"Even so, we can't rely on her to protect us. She is just one, and they are three with swords. You saw what they could do. We watched them kill a giant bird. Trust me, this is the right move."

Gideon's disgusting grin came to Llorva's mind. "I don't trust them. They're just as dangerous as Zygmund would have been."

Riker stood quietly for a moment, taking in what she'd said. "I have a compromise. If we can convince them to take us back to the beach, then I may be able to recover my instruments."

"That won't be necessary," came Vylasgarden's voice.

She jumped down onto the window's ledge from the roof of the tower. She handed Riker his flute, which was fractured in a few places.

Riker's eyes widened. "Vylasgarden, I could kiss you!"

"Will it still work?" she asked him.

"As long as the conduit is whole, it should work."

"Now we go our own way," Llorva insisted.

Vylasgarden shrugged. "I happen to agree with Riker. If they're offering you help, you should take it. I'll follow behind in case something happens."

"So we're going to keep on this act with them?" Llorva asked tiredly.

"For now," Riker answered, examining the instrument's cracks. "I think finding a settlement farther up the river would be a good place for the three of us to catch our bearings, learn where the nearest road is, and perhaps go our own separate ways." There was a pause in the conversation. "We shouldn't keep them waiting."

Llorva found herself hugging Vylasgarden, and when she realized what she was doing, she quickly stepped away. "I — I'm glad you're okay." Vylasgarden had a new expression on her face that Llorva couldn't make out clearly in the dark. It was something between surprise and gratitude.

"I was afraid you two drowned. Go back to the fire and keep your wits about you. I won't be far. I promise."

Llorva and Riker trekked back to the alcove while Vylasgarden stayed behind alone and in the solar of the tower.

Chapter Eight
JARED

BY MORNING, the storm had waned to a clearer sky and low winds. Jared led the way up the river as they all spent the better part of the first day trekking upstream and taking breaks to fish whenever he found a good spot. They eventually found the cockatrice's lair: a mass of grasses and branches made up the nest, and an arching canopy of jungle leaves made up the roof. "This is what we were hoping to find going after your monster," he told them and dug his hands in the dead grass. He reached around a bit and pulled out a shiny object.

"Cockatrices love collecting gold and shinies," Gideon said.

"Other than dwarves, leprechauns, and dragons, you'll never find a better horde of treasures," added Perry before practically jumping into the nest head first. The brothers and Perry took what they could carry, and Gideon offered Llorva some jewels, which she begrudgingly took. After meeting the elves the night before, Jared was concerned they may not be able to keep up, but with some food in him, Riker woke the next day like new, and the female, Llorva, was in a far better mood. During one of their excursions on the river, Llorva went alone and sat on the bank while Riker sat with Perry on some rocks, looking at Perry's books and talking with him about magick. Jared felt both relieved and a twinge of jealousy that the boy had someone else to talk to, especially about magick.

Jared was less concerned about where magick came from and cared more about where he could find it so that he could either use it for himself or sell it for a good bit of coin. Ever since taking the boy in, Jared's knowledge of the world grew greater just from listening to him go on for hours. It grew annoying quickly, but he would be remiss if the boy's knowledge didn't save them from a troll's wrath or the wrong end of a tomb's trap. As he tried to net more fish, Jared's concentration was broken by Asghar and Gideon whispering close by. Instead of fishing, they were wading in the water half dressed and staring at Llorva, who was barefoot on the bank, feeding her share of fish to a few river dolphins that came up to her. "I don't believe what I'm seeing," he said to them, garnering their attention. "My brothers are reduced to snickering boys. If she were human, you'd have already attempted your way with her."

"When was the last time you saw an elf, Jared?" asked Gideon. "A true female elf."

He had to think for a moment. "We were in Southaven."

"We were boys then," said Asghar. "Don't you remember? It was our first adventure after escaping that horrid orphanage and you wanted us to walk all the way to Southaven so that we could prove ourselves the men of men and lay for the first time with elf women."

"A boys' dream for sure," Jared said, pulling up his net. He had caught a large catfish, which was more than enough for the day. "If memory serves, we did become men on that first adventure."

"We did in town but not with an elf," Gideon said, smirking and staring in Llorva's direction. Jared considered her, and yes, she was beautiful. He had no doubt a man couldn't resist her if she had a chance to clean the dirt from her hair and skin.

"I'm sure her brother would have none of that, Gideon."

"Something isn't right about the brother," Gideon answered. "They look nothing alike. And didn't all the elf men die off when they came to this world? Given how he looks, I wouldn't be surprised if he is actually a she."

"He's a half-blood."

"At least he's proof that it's possible to bed an elf."

"No one is bedding any of these elves,"Jared interrupted."Need I remind you that they could be playing their own game? Ever since we left the tower this morning, I've had that feeling in my stomach again."

"Oh no, the feeling is back," Asghar mocked.

"I'm never wrong. When have I ever been wrong?"

"Sometimes you're right, sometimes you're wrong."

Sometimes I'm almost certain it's just gas and you need to let one out." Asghar and Gideon started laughing and splashing in the water. Jared crossed his arms and almost lost the fish he'd just caught.

"Just be prepared to draw your blade on the ready." When Jared felt this way, he was almost never wrong. Those elves were up to something, and he wasn't going to let his guard down. As he prepared to return to shore, a memory came to him. "We went to a brothel to celebrate after killing our first monster back then."

Asghar winced. "Our first 'monster' was a fox that was eating up all the chickens on a farm. We were so desperate that we spent all we had on one girl because killing a fox didn't pay for more."

Jared put his face in his hand. "Oh, right."

"Good memories," said Gideon plainly.

Continuing the day up the river, Jared had a growing suspicion that they were being followed, but every time he looked around, he only saw the greenery and heard the ambiance. The farther they went from the coast, the tighter the greenery became as they tried following the river. Soon they were forced inland and had to traverse in the trees, where they came across a yellow long-leg spider hiding in the canopy. Its web was so large that monkeys were caught and bound in it. "Stay calm," said Jared. "Just move slowly and do not turn your back to it." The Spider's many red eyes followed them as they crossed its territory. During one of their breaks for water where Asghar cut open some vines for everyone, Jared noticed Riker inspecting something. From a distance, it looked like an old flute. Jared saw it had etchings on it, and when Perry came to show Riker something, Riker quickly hid it away.

A day later, Jared was still curious as to what Riker was hiding. Was it a treasure? Was it magick? Whatever it was made him more suspicious about the elves. They rarely spoke to each other, and the feeling Jared had didn't go away. That night at camp under the wispy moss trees where the jungle's river met the wetland delta, Jared confronted Riker alone during his watch. "What are you hiding?"

"Hiding? I don't know what you're talking about."

"Listen to me. My brothers mean everything to me; even the boy I would guard him with my own life. Ever since I met you two, I've had a growing suspicion that something is going on that I need to know about." Riker stared at him for a moment, unfazed and tired. "Tell me what's going on so we both can put this behind us."

"It's like I said. We're on a pilgrimage to the north. Nothing more."

Jared shifted his stance and tried not letting it show that Riker's dismissal bothered him. He got closer to him and said in a low voice, "You're not as sneaky as you think. Whatever it is, don't make me regret bringing you along, because I could just as easily leave you two for the crocs and snakes."

Riker smirked. "It won't come to that, but it's good to know the conditions of your charity." They held their gazes, and, despite being bigger and taller than Riker, Jared was flustered and somewhat confused by the conversation.

"Take a rest."

"But it's my shift."

"I got it."

Riker smiled and went to lie by the fire.

The next morning, Jared checked the map with Perry and announced that they would be arriving at the marked settlement. "Just around this riverbend we should see it on the horizon. We will be there before long."

"And weeks before the full moon!" followed Perry. He was more cheery than usual.

"I can almost feel the warm bath coming," said Llorva.

"You don't have money for a bath," Riker said.

"I'd gladly give my share of treasure for just one."

Gideon snickered. "I have a few coins. How much for your skirt and blouse?"

"Leave the poor girl alone, Gideon," came Asghar. "If she wasn't interested before, she wouldn't be now."

"That's what you think," Gideon continued. "Elf or lady, everyone knows the key to her heart is the ringing call of unshakable longing."

Riker laughed. "Only your call is more like the sound a dog makes when it puts its nose in the backside of a porcupine. Pitiful and needlessly naive." All but Gideon erupted in laughter. "Perhaps leave the metaphors and simile to the experts."

"That's quite the tongue you have," Gideon replied coarsely.

Riker vaulted a large and mossy tree root. "Stick around, Gideon. You will find that there is more where that came from."

Jared sensed Gideon was about to argue and turned to intervene but was confused to see everyone staring up at the sky. He followed their eyes and noticed a column of black smoke coming over the trees in the distance. "That's the village!" They quickened their pace, and when they came around the river, they found what would be their salvation on the horizon in flames.

"What happened?"

"Who would attack a poor fishing village?"

Jared crouched and put his hands in his hair. "Perry, how far are we from the next settlement on the map?"

"The only marked settlement is our destination," the boy answered.

"What's your destination?" Riker asked.

"We're due in a city northeast across the border in Pryden Province," Asghar answered. "The problem is that there are no marked cities or towns between here and there," Gideon continued in a panic. "Once we cross the border, there's nothing but a road and untamed wilderness to go through." Perry started to reassure everyone that the map he had was outdated and that new settlements could have been built, but all Jared could hear were the thoughts he was having about the full moon and the monsters and horrors they would face if they did not find walls to hide behind in the coming weeks.

"Show me the map." There was a mountain range directly north of their position. The original plan was to wait out the moon and spend the next month going around the mountains and following the road up through Pryden. "This is what we will do. We take a shortcut through the Thundering Mountains. If done quickly, we save some time getting to Zilsa City."

"We've never gone through these mountains before. Maybe if we keep towards the road, we will find a new town like Perry said," suggested Asghar.

"If we're wrong, we've wasted time and will be dead in a few weeks," Gideon refuted. "Torn apart by a random pack of Dark Realm werewolves."

"What about us?" Llorva interrupted. "We didn't sign up for this." Jared stepped right up to her and imposed his size against her, pointing at the burning village ahead of them.

"That was your chance to go your own way. It still is.

Plainly, I don't want you and brother around my brothers anymore, but since I'm not yet in the mood to feed you to the wild, I will allow you to come with us until you find a place you'd rather be." Llorva scowled and said nothing, and Riker was about to intervene but was interrupted by Gideon's whistling. He called them over to the brush and pointed at something beyond the vines and mosses.

Jared wasn't sure what it was until they got closer and found a dead Haran man tied to a rotting tree stump by the wrists with rope made of strange hair. "I recognize him," Riker said. "He was one of the sailors we came here with." Jared examined the body. The man's head was scalped, and he had been impaled in the stomach, presumably before death.

"That smell," Llorva gagged. "Who would do this?"

"I don't know. Anything in your books say something about what would do this?" Jared asked Perry.

"We should turn back," the boy insisted with fear infecting his voice. "One thing I'm certain about is that we don't belong here."

"No," said Jared. "There isn't time. We keep going. This man didn't have a chance. If whatever did this shows itself, it will taste our steel." He knew his brothers wouldn't challenge him, but he didn't give Riker or Llorva a chance to debate. He walked past the corpse and continued to the village, sword in hand.

A little later, Riker approached Jared at the front of the

line. He was silent for a moment before speaking. "I understand your confidence given your experience, but I worry that Llorva and I may be a liability if the time comes."

"That may be true," Jared replied plainly, "but my brothers and I can't waste the days. Now might be a good time for you to start telling me the truth."

"Are you threatening me?"

"We will protect you like we did before," Jared assured him, using his sword to cut vines out of their path, "if you tell me what you're hiding."

"There is nothing to hide that is in conflict with you!" Riker reached for Jared's shoulder, and Jared shoved him aside. Riker fell in the mud, surprised and surely embarrassed. Llorva came and helped him up.

"What's gotten into you?" Asghar demanded. Jared stopped in his tracks and faced his younger brother. "Something is bothering you, brother. Let's not get reckless," he reasoned.

"The elves are hiding something."

"What?"

"He's got something in his bag. Something important."

"Let's have a look-see then," Gideon said, approaching the elves. "Stay away from us!" Llorva warned, picking up a dead branch off the ground.

"Whoa! Don't hurt yourself," came Asghar. "Just show

us what it is so we can move on."

Riker looked Jared in the eye and said, "No."

"You mutt." Jared charged toward Riker, and, after a few steps, he heard a plopping sound. He saw that Gideon was kneeling with his left leg thigh deep in the mud.

"I'm stuck!" Gideon announced, and Perry and Asghar came to him, trying to pull him out. Jared rushed to his brother's side but stopped when he saw that the trees surrounding them all were shaking. Little hairy men with clawed hands resembling ebu-gogos emerged from the swamp's shadows and surrounded them, aggressively cooing. When Jared and Asghar drew their weapons, the visitors' coos turned to screeches and howls. One dared jump down from a tree and charged toward them. Jared cut the short savage in half with his blade, which sent the rest of them into a frenzy.

Chapter Nine

RIKER

"PLEASE TELL ME you got him out of that hole," Riker shouted as he, Jared, and Asghar fought off naked and hairy little men and Llorva and Perry struggled to pull Gideon free.

"We leave him," Llorva suggested in a panic. "You faithless shrew!" Gideon shouted.

"I refuse to die with you!" she shouted back. "They would have done the same," she reasoned to Riker. It was probably true, but they had little time before the ferals were on them too. He figured it was best to leave no man behind.

"No! We stick together. Hurry up and get him out of that hole!"

The ferals in the trees started throwing rocks at them as the horde closed in on the ground. Just when Riker was starting to lose hope, a roar brought the fighting to a halt. "What the hell was that?" A smile crept on Riker's face as a body of familiar blueish-green scales emerged from out of nowhere and knocked over dozens of attackers. Vylasgarden ripped and threw aside the ferals, making a path for the rest of them.

"Now is the time!" announced Riker, and Jared and Asghar assisted in getting Gideon. With a final pull, he was free minus his boot. Vylasgarden led the way through the swamp, where a low hanging fog crept in all sides of the fray. Behind Riker was Jared's group, floundering in the mud with the ferals closing in behind. Vylasgarden stopped and encouraged Riker and Llorva to keep going. "What are you doing?" Riker said.

"Just go!" she roared. Without hesitation, he took Llorva by the hand and kept running. He could hear Vylasgarden roaring behind them and the slashing of blades on flesh. He hoped that it was not her they were fighting. He and Llorva were far ahead when the clashing and screeching stopped. When the fog grew so high and dense that they could not see in front of them, they stopped running. The silence was deafening.

"We have to go back," said Llorva.

Riker stopped her. "Just wait." Soon the screeching and cooing started up again, and Riker could make out shapes in the fog. He reached into his bag and readied his flute.

"Will it work?"

"Only one way to find out." He pursed his lips together to blow into the instrument but saw that it was Jared, Gideon, and Asghar coming towards them. The horde was fast approaching behind them. Riker readied himself but then saw Vylasgarden charging behind them all, carrying

Perry in her arms. "Everyone get behind me," Riker commanded. He took a deep breath and thought of the spell he was going to manifest.

Something that would be a convincing enough bluff but then something strange happened. The feral folk suddenly stopped in a uniform line before them, staring at the group with their wild yellow eyes. No howling or cooing, but a haunting silence with murder in their eyes.

"Why did they stop?" Gideon asked, catching his breath.

"We made it out of their territory," Perry suggested.

"No, this is something else," Riker insisted. "This is magick." He cautiously approached the invisible line.

"Riker, get back here!" Llorva demanded, but he ignored her and got closer, almost touching one of them. "A ward spell," he said under his breath. "None will pass this point." He returned to the group. "It's over now. We're safe."

"How do you know that?" Asghar asked him accusingly. Riker noticed Jared was looking down at the hand that was holding his flute.

"I recognize the ward spell affecting them. Someone very powerful wants to keep them out."

"Will it hold?" asked Vylasgarden.

Gideon swore. "It can talk!" he cried.

"It will hold so long as whatever conduit the spell is

casted from holds it in place."

"Let's keep moving then," said Jared. And the group plus Vylasgarden and minus Gideon's left boot walked away and continued north.

"Your people were also killed?" Perry asked Vylasgarden. They were just behind Riker as he kept his pace with Jared at the front of the group. She and the boy went on about their experiences with their people's genocides while Riker took a moment to check on Llorva.

"How are you doing?" he asked her.

"I'm tired, haven't had a proper meal or bath in over a week, and almost died again. Aside from that I'm fine." He saw that she recognized how serious he was being and softened her expression. "How are you doing?"

"Same as you, but I worry we may have other problems. The cat is out of the bag regarding my magick."

"Has he said anything?"

"No. None of them have said a word since we left the swamp. Now that Vylasgarden is with us, the only trick up our sleeve is her."

"Something isn't right."

"True. I don't like how quiet they've been."

"No, Riker. Something is wrong here. Have you noticed we've been walking for hours and the fog hasn't gone away?"

"Probably an effect of the ward spell."

"But how do we know we've gone anywhere?"

Riker stopped in his tracks. They both looked around for anything inconsistent with the landscape but could see nothing but soft ground under their feet.

"What is it?" asked Asghar.

"We might be in an illusion," Riker told him.

"What are you saying?" Jared said.

"I'm saying someone is playing a trick on us. We've been walking in place for hours."

"No. It can't be."

"How do you know? We can't see anything in front of us. We're lucky we're all still together."

"What do we do?" asked Perry.

"I think I know how to get us out of this, but I can't be the one to lead us."

"What do you need?"

"Vylasgarden. You have the best nose. Is there anything you can smell that will make a path?"

She closed her eyes and flared her nostrils. Minutes passed and nothing changed.

"This is hopeless!" cried Gideon. "We're done for."

"No, wait," she finally said. "I smell something…wood. Something burning."

"The fishing village," said Jared.

"Follow me," she said before taking a step, her snout in

the air. Eventually they found what was left of the fishing village. It was all burned to smolders. They started exploring and all came to a hut at the center of the village. Llorva picked up something from the ground. It was a human-shaped wood carving with pegs in it.

"What is it?"

"I don't know."

They came up to Perry, who was standing in front of the hut holding out one of his books. The page he was on had an illustration of a shaman in it. "Who lived here?" Jared asked.

"This wasn't a home," Perry answered. "This was a witch's hut."

"Would make sense," Riker replied. He stood before its sunken doorway and stared into the dark void within. "If this is her hut, then where is the witch?"

"Here," Vylasgarden said from behind the building. When they came around to the back, they saw a skewed pike in the ground with a charred female corpse tied to it and three human men standing around it. Jared attempted to unsheathe his weapons, but Vylasgarden stopped him.

"Don't."

To Riker, these humans looked ill from that distance. Their dark skin stretched across their gaunt frames. "Why are they standing there?" Perry asked.

"Because they're puppets waiting for a dead master,"

Vylasgarden finally said. Riker walked up to the men, who remained standing around the pike, slouched and near motionless. He then looked up at the hanging corpse. "I've heard of witches like this. A woman with power that could heal the sick but also inflict hexes upon you using magick sourced from the Dark Realm."

"Dark magick..." Perry said under his breath in awe. "She possessed a connection with the Primeval Power. She wasn't a witch, Riker. She was a sorceress."

"What's the difference?" Llorva asked.

"Witches and wizards bend the forces of nature to their will using magick sensitive crafts and their intellect. Sorcerers have the Primeval Power within them innately as if their own bodies draw in raw power. I believe she was a necromancer."

"I can see how that would create enemies," said Jared, cutting the body down from the post. "But you said sorcerers have an innate connection with the Primeval Power." He reached down and grasped at a necklace around the dead woman's neck. "Explain this."

"What are you doing? Stop!" Vylasgarden warned, but Jared clenched and pulled the necklace free from the corpse. The undead snapped their heads at him and moaned.

"Jared. Put the necklace back," said Riker. "There may be a curse in play here." Jared stared at the small amulet on the necklace and rubbed away the soot covering it, revealing a bone carving in the shape of a skull. "She was in fact a witch," he said, "and someone wanted her dead."

With his sword in one hand and the pendant in the other, Jared stepped away from the corpse only for the puppets to seize him to the ground. Vylasgarden tried pulling them off, but they effortlessly tossed her aside. They dragged him to the water in a flooded area and buried his face in the mud. All the while the group tried fighting them off. One of the puppets put its hands around Jared's throat as they held him. Only when Llorva beat their heads with a piece of wood from the hut did the puppets relent. Jared shot his head up for air. The three bodies lay motionless around him.

"Was it worth it?" Riker asked him.

Jared rubbed his throat. In his other hand, he rubbed his thumb across the pendant. "I would do it all again for this hunk of bone. Rarely does a mortal carry power such as this. Perry. Tell them what this is."

"It's a witch's pendent. Without it her magick words have nothing to draw from."

They stopped a few miles north of the marsh on more solid ground, and the night sky could be seen past the fog. The surrounding mugginess prevented a fire, so they shared and huddled around the last of their torches for warmth. In the dark, Riker noticed the absence of Llorva's familiar glow but found her hiding behind a large rock formation. "I bring a torch," he said, approaching. She was cradling herself against the rock. "What are you doing over here by yourself?"

"I needed to be alone to think," she replied, accepting the torch. Her body's luminescence faded in the fire's light. "We almost died again."

"We did," he said, sitting next to her and reflecting on the events. He thought about how ready he was to leave them all behind and how tiring the journey had been thus far; yet he was not any closer to getting home or to Raven. They sat in silence for a while, listening to the wilderness. "We have to keep going with them," he finally said. "You know that, right?"

"Just when I think I'm done with you, there's more steps to take together."

"I'm sure you're beyond tired of me now."

"I wish I could say that is true," she said in a whisper. "The truth is I can't imagine going north without you and Vylasgarden now." Riker fought a smile.

"Oh, now you've done it! I take it back!" she said half angrily.

"No, no! You can't take it back. Why are you upset then?"

"Because I wanted to stay away for a reason. I never wanted your companionship, Riker!"

The words stunned him. "I understand."

"You do?"

"Yeah, you think by shutting the world out that you're keeping yourself safe, but I'm sure you didn't realize that closing yourself off from having friends makes you no different from the sisterhood you left behind." She only stared at him. "Tell you what, Llorva. Let's go with them and find someplace to rest before the next full moon. Then the three of us talk about going our separate ways once we're safe. I'm fortunate to have met you two," he said, glancing at the ground. Llorva looked at him skeptically. "It's true. I see how we affect each other. I think Vylasgarden would have been dead chasing the Dragon Slayers. In a way, she seems more whole with us."

"Are we keeping her whole or are we holding her back?" she argued.

"Don't say that. You know it's true. She cares about us, and that helps fade the memories that have been tormenting her." Llorva stayed quiet after that, and Riker didn't get the sense he had convinced her. "What?" he asked.

"Nothing. I'm just tired. We should sleep."

"Right. Come with me back to the group around the fire."

"No, I'll stay here for a bit longer," she said. "The torch will keep me warm."

"Okay." She seemed distant in a different way then, but Riker knew not to pry further. He returned to camp, and, with flute in hand, he steadily fell asleep.

In what seemed like five minutes to him, a firm hand shook him awake. It was Vylasgarden. Her nostrils exhaled over his face, and he squinted at the morning sun. "Why didn't anyone wake me for my shift?"

"Llorva is gone," Vylasgarden said.

He sat up and looked over at Llorva's sleeping spot. She wasn't there.

Jared's group approached. "Did you see anything last night? Riker asked them.

"No. Nothing after the argument you two had," Jared admitted. "She must not have liked what you said to her."

Riker ignored that. "We have to go after her. Vylasgarden, can you track her?"

"I already tried, but her trail is short. She hid her tracks in the flooded areas, and her scent is somehow masked."

"Forget the shrew," Gideon blurted out. "She'll soon regret it. The wilderness is full of monsters and probably more of those savages."

"You know we don't have time to go after her," Jared said. "She made her choice."

"I know," Riker admitted. In the distance to their north was a range of mountains taller than he had ever seen. He looked around for where Llorva might have gone and felt a creeping concern for her.

Chapter Ten

LLORVA

LLORVA AWOKE TO A STRANGE SMELLL and found herself lying on a cot in a white canvassed room. It had been another two days since she'd left on her own. Since then, she had strange sensations after leaving the wetlands and trekking northwest. She felt hot and her heart was pounding in her head. Anything she deemed edible she couldn't keep down, and she eventually collapsed somewhere in the grasses. She had been sure she'd die, but there she was in this strange room. A burning brazier hung from the wooden post at the room's center. There was a strange stank of rotting herbs and substances. Llorva tried sitting up, but a painful beat in her head forced her to lie back down. "Where am I?" her voice croaked.

"You're in our care," she heard from across the room. It was an old, dark-skinned human woman with a strange accent who spoke. She was doing something hunched over a simple table while a younger-looking woman standing behind her detangled the older woman's black and gray hair. The younger looking woman was watching Llorva from the corner of her eye.

"Sister, she is rather lucid now," she said.

"Who are you? Why am I here?" Llorva asked. Each question was more frantic than the last but neither of the women answered one. She surveyed the room and found a spear leaning against the post.

"Don't," the younger woman warned, but Llorva had leapt from the cot and ran over to the spear despite her fatigue and pain. "You'll regret that, my dear," she said playfully.

"What did you do to me?" Llorva demanded, pointing the spear at the women. The elder of the two slowly turned to face her. Her face was scarred from burns, and her left eye was gone from the socket. She wore a charm around her neck similar to the dead witch Llorva had seen in the swamp.

"We saved you, Azariah," the older woman said. "Don't be afraid of us."

"Where did you learn that name?" Llorva demanded again.

"It is your true name. The name you try to forget," the younger one said. "I saw it in your dreams, dear."

"I won't ask again. Who are you and how do you know my name?"

The room began spinning then and the older woman flicked her wrist saying, "*Magas alture, daemon,*" to which the spear began to warm in Llorva's hands and quickly wrapped itself around her, transforming into a hissing snake.

"Azariah, this is Mlezi," the old woman said, referring to the snake tightly wrapping itself around her body. The snake flicked its forked tongue in her face. "You may call me Sabba. I am a practicing witch. My older sister is Shanani." She said, referring to the one that looked much younger than herself. "She is a sorceress."

"What do you want from me?" Llorva replied, panting. Her restrained body began to ache and shiver. "I have nothing worth anything to you."

"Not true," replied Shanani. "You are more valuable than you realize, Azariah."

"What you need to know now is that we found you wandering in the wilderness all alone," Sabba followed. "You are very sick, and I am the only one who can help you." She returned her attention to the table and finished preparing a substance she poured in a bowl. "I will help you gain your strength back, but I expect you to help me in exchange."

"What do you want?"

"We can discuss that later. Now you rest," said Shanani.

"I don't trust you," replied Llorva.

Sabba turned to face her again, looking more serious. "My dear, you don't have a choice."

PART TWO

The Thundering Mountains & the Sea of Sand

Chapter Eleven
VYLASGARDEN

A WEEK AND TWO DAYS had passed when the group found themselves in a montane forest of the new province's southern mountain range. The range was surrounded by flat plains to its east and west and presumably sandy deserts to the north. That was where Jared insisted they would best find a road to the nearest cities and beat the haunt of the full moon soon to come. Vylasgarden's agility made her the leader coming up the woodland slopes. The mountain's rocky plateaus supplied them with basins of water, which was the only time Jared would pocket his dragon bone pendant and reference his map with the boy, Perry, and make sure they were meeting the marks on time.

It was on one of these peaks where they came face-to-face with the largest bird nest Vylasgarden had ever seen. It was twenty feet tall and made with broken carriages and whole uprooted trees. Jared bent his head all the way back. "What is this?"

"I've never seen anything like it," someone else said.

"Perry, what made this?" Vylasgarden asked.

"Maybe it belonged to a dragon a long time ago."

"Impossible," stated Jared, "the branches are too fresh. Also, it smells like there has been a recent kill." Vylasgarden had noticed the smell miles back but didn't think it would lead them to a nest the size of a small village home."We better go before —" Jared was interrupted by a sound from within the nest like the low trumpeting of an elephant. Suddenly, the sun had gone behind a great shadow, and they looked up to see a great bird large enough to block out the sun. "Hide!"

Everyone scattered in different directions as the bird descended, flapping its powerful wings, which knocked Vylasgarden over the cliff. She dug her claws in and caught herself on the ledge. When she pulled herself up, she came face-to-face with a titan of a bird. It was as black as a raven, but its face and hooked beak were bathed in blood.

It stared at her for a bit before returning to its meal. Eventually the others came out and slowly joined her on the other side of the nest, where a tattered banner on a post was waiting for them. It was erected askew and featured a golden sun with reaching rays and an elegant bird at the sun's center.

"What a welcome," claimed Riker. "Doesn't that look familiar."

They didn't see another bird like that again for the rest of the journey. They did see wild goats and hunted them for their meat. When they reached the summit at the middle of the range, Vylasgarden noticed a pungent, earthy smell while Riker and the humans surveyed the area ahead of them. The smell led her to the ledge, where she saw that the peak of the adjacent mountain had been flattened. The surface was black as coal, and there was a disarray of rusted metal contraptions in its wake. "What did you find?" Riker said behind her. Perry came up excitedly and crouched on the ledge. "Wow! Have you seen anything like it?" he said, bringing his hand above his eyes.

"Probably an old dwarf mine?" Perry suggested.

"You know why the Prydens call these the Thundering Mountains?" Jared asked no one in particular. Vylasgarden remained silent, looking out to the wasteland of metal. "It's because long ago when the dwarves inhabited these mountains, their mining would sound like thunderstorms on days with clear skies."

"I've read memoirs about adventurers who saw the dwarves of Pryden up close," Perry said. "They say that the dwarves called themselves the Iron Clan. One tome I've read described their machines as metal demons that billowed fire and smoke like a dragon."

"Is it true about them being short with stout bodies?" Riker asked smiling.

Perry was about to speak, but Jared gently pushed him aside. "We've met dwarves, and they're every bit like what you imagine."

"Where are the dwarves now?" Vylasgarden asked. "This place has been abandoned for some time."

"Many folks have ideas —"

"But no one agrees what happened to them," Asghar interrupted.

"Merchants believe the king of kings slaughtered them all because they refused to pay tribute and then took all their treasures," said Perry.

"There are those who will say that's the end of it," added Gideon, catching up to the group on a limp. "I believe no human force can truly wipe out a race of dwarves. No, they still inhabit the mountains in secret or migrated away because they tapped its resources dry like a plague of locusts."

"Hey! Come look!" Asghar shouted from the other side of the summit. His voice was echoing throughout the range.

"What did you find?" Jared asked his excited brother. Asghar pointed down the underpass, where an animant flame was hovering in the air, burning on nothing.

Chapter Twelve

JARED

THIS FLAME WAS FIXED IN THE AIR as if an invisible force were carrying it. Its orange glow illuminated the entrance to the gray shale of an underpass. "Hmm," Riker pondered aloud, "I suspect an illusion. Perry, could this be the dwarves making contact?"

The boy shrugged. "Could be some kind of mountain spirit," Perry replied in a squeaky voice.

"Whatever it is, it's in our way," Jared said, slowly approaching it. "And I don't scare easily." He brandished his sword at the flame, and it ascended above him and began bobbing around the group, changing color and giggling like a child.

"Perhaps it's our welcomer," Riker said as the light made a second round to him. He cupped his hands, and the flame stopped in the cradle.

"There isn't a warmth coming from it."

"What do you think it is?" Vylasgarden asked Riker.

"If it's an illusion, it's a damn good one, but Perry's guess is as good as mine."

"What do you know of magick and illusions?" asked

Jared suspiciously.

"No more than the next, Jared."

At that, the light changed its color from orange to a bright white, which made the group shield their eyes. It hovered over to the underpass again and made a long calling sound that rang through the underpass.

Across the way on the next mountain, a sudden trail of lights flickered in the growing darkness as the sun disappeared behind the peaks in the west. Jared felt the hairs on the back of his neck stand up. "What's wrong, Jared?" Asghar asked, grabbing his shoulders. "You have that look on your face."

"Something doesn't feel right. We should find another way."

"It will cost us a day to backtrack the way we came," said Vylasgarden. They all collectively sighed.

"Damn! We don't have a day to waste. We have a week before the full moon."

"Then we continue our path with our guards up," suggested Riker. "What other choice do we have?"

"Fine," Jared snorted, "but we set up camp before it gets too close to the witching hour." As they walked, he kept one hand on the hilt of his sword and a watchful eye on their surroundings. In the dark, the mountain peaks resembled gargantuan teeth, and the valleys between them looked like great abysses. Whatever was awaiting them,

Jared was eager and ready to face it. The line of lights led them through the mining graveyard and into a heap of stone rubble that Perry called a valley fill, and across the way was the east mountain. As they crossed, the rubble turned to gravel and the gravel turned to silt as the lit path sloped downward into a cavern on the face of the east mountain. The lights gathered in front of this cavern and all at once snuffed into nothingness. "This is what I was worried about," said Jared, lighting a torch with tinder and throwing it into the darkness. Its descent revealed the slope continuing downward, where it hit an edge before a straight drop.

"What could be down there?" Perry whispered.

"This doesn't feel right. We turn back," Jared announced, but when he turned around, he caught a glimpse of one of the lights above them in the rubble. It snuffed into smoke and revealed a creature in its place. It was child-shaped with a bulbous nose and sunken eyes that showed off black masses in its gaunt, yellow face. The creature grinned and started kicking boulders into the slope.

"Watch out!"

They all leapt into the cavern as the boulders tumbled after them, causing an avalanche. in the cave. Jared took his sword and dug it and his knees and feet into the silt. He slowed soon enough not to fall into the drop but witnessed the silhouette of a body falling over the edge. He dared peer over but only saw darkness. He heard a male scream descend until it was cut off by the sound of impalement.

"Who? … Who!?" Jared called out into the dark. "I can't see a damn thing! Gideon! Asghar! Are you there? What do you see?"

No one spoke. He was alone, but the silence was broken by the moaning coming from below. "We're coming to get you!" Vylasgarden shouted to Jared's right. From the mouth of the cave came a swarm of flickering fire lights. They rushed down into the drop, and their collective light illuminated the scene. There, some sixty feet below the ledge, was Asghar, impaled by blood-soaked pikes. His mouth pooled with blood as the lights swarmed him like flies on a dying animal. Their orange light grew into a bright red as Asghar's moans turned to suffering screams.

"What are they doing?" Perry said.

"Perry, look away," said Vylasgarden, and through teary eyes Jared watched the life fade from his brother body. A sudden collection of chattering erupted all around them. Dozens of those child-sized creatures began dropping from stalactites on the ceiling. "Hurry! To the right," Vylasgarden yelled as the creatures closed in on them. Jared quickly shambled to his right and blindly ran for his life as what was left of the group continued deeper in the caverns.

His path became lit when some of the creatures in candle-light form surrounded the group as they ran. Their once sensationless touch felt like venomous stings on Jared's skin. Gideon shoved Jared out the way as one of the

146

creatures tried to drop a minecart on top of him from the levels above. With their path blocked, the creatures chasing them caught up and pounced on the brothers. Their numbers overwhelmed Jared as his knees buckled under their weight. As a last-ditch effort, Jared grabbed the bone pendant around his neck and squeezed it. "Do something, damn you!"

Suddenly the mass of bodies piled on top of them melted away, and what remained were withered masses of dead skin and bone. Jared's hand grasping the pendant ached terribly, but he wasted no time acknowledging it. Just when more of the creatures were upon them, Riker ran to their side, facing the oncoming horde. He took out his flute and played a high pitched note.

The resounding echo made the cave rumble, and to Jared's amazement he witnessed a blast of magickal energy rupture from Riker's instrument, which blew apart the cave walls and ceiling. *Let's go,* Jared saw Riker shouting but couldn't hear. The three of them turned heel and ran as the cave came apart around them.

Ahead were Vylasgarden and Perry in front of large double iron doors. "Hurry! Hurry!" she cried. When they joined them at the end of the cave, Vylasgarden swung the doors open by herself. As they entered, a few dozen of the creatures made it inside after them before the cave fully collapsed. Fatigue started to possess Jared as he fell behind. He grasped the pendant one more time but ran through a rotted wooden beam while distracted. They were at a forked path, and everyone had gone left. Behind him, the collective chatter drew closer, ready to take him, but someone was on their way back to him. He was expecting Gideon and Perry, but instead it was Riker reaching for him.

"I will lead them in the other direction," he said. "Go! Join the others!" He started banging the flute on the walls. With each slam, the wall fissured and the damaged instrument permeated with magickal energy. "Come and get it!"

As Riker stood his ground, Jared started to run to the left, but part of him wanted to make himself stay. He hated his cravenness but could not bring himself to do it. What bravery he'd had before died with Asghar that night. Jared ran after the group to the left.

Chapter Thirteen

RIKER

AS SOON AS THE HORDE REVEALED ITSELF, Riker turned heel and sprinted down the right corridor. It felt as if their chattering teeth were inches from the nape of his neck as he aimlessly followed the winding cart tracks and lowering ceilings. Just when he felt he had no breath left to continue, he saw the end where the tracks met a boarded threshold. Riker gave all he had to rush the barricade and crash through it, dropping several feet into a mining chamber. With the wind knocked out of him, he fought to stand before the cave dwellers were on him. If he were to die, then he would rather be standing.

As the chattering grew closer, he looked at his flute. The once lustrous runes inscribed on it were dulled, but he saw a hint of fluorescent static from its cracks glow in the dark. "It's been an honor, old friend," he said before beating his flute against a rusty beam beside him. With each whack, he felt the power within the instrument lift the sound into a swelling vibrato that shook the room. He felt he could bring the roof down on him and the little monsters.

The cracks fissured more, and the instrument grew hot in his palm to the point he could not hold it any longer. He threw it up at the entrance just as the cave dwellers were crawling into the chamber. Flashing light and a roll of thundering explosions quaked the room and knocked Riker over followed by the threshold's supports collapsing and the ceiling coming down. Riker scooted away as rock, dirt, and metal beams piled before him, almost catching his feet and legs. He was halfway across the room when it stopped. As the dust and avalanche noise cleared, Riker could hear the cave dwellers' muffled moans underneath the rocks.

Their moans turned to shrieks and screams when he noticed the familiar haunting fire-like glow shine between the gaps. They were eating each other. Then came a great roar that rumbled into the chamber, dulling the sounds of the cave dwellers' suffering. Riker shuddered as the walls shook against the power behind the roaring.

What was that?

As he got his bearings, he noticed a white light fading in through the coal dust behind him. The light came from the top of a long stick carried by the shape of a hunched human figure. The individual had the stick in one hand and a thin bladed rapier by the hilt in the other. He stopped short of ten feet and used the light to illuminate Riker's presence. He himself was a stocky old human with an unkempt beard and long, greasy brown hair. His fair skin was covered in soot and his eyes were of two colors, one brown and the other blue. He wore an amulet around his neck over a mix of rags and animal skins and a rusty belt buckle on his waist.

The unimpressed grimace on his face and the way he wielded the rapier admittedly intimidated Riker. "Who are you?" he asked.

"Who am I? Who are you and what are you doing in my mountain?" the stranger replied in a gravelly voice.

Riker dusted himself off. "I'm lost."

"No doubt about that. Surprise me with something I don't know." Riker scratched his head. "My name is Barron Von Riker. I got separated from my companions. We were passing through on the outside. Did you hear that roaring just now?"

"Why, yes I did," said the stranger, staring up and around. "I also heard the mess you made." The stranger passed Riker and crouched down, examining the cave-in. "*Magas a la oculus!*" The light coming from his staff turned blue, and Riker could make out the image of an eye at its center. "Behave yourself, Barron Riker."

"You're a wizard! Aren't you supposed to be advising kings or something like that?"

The stranger pinched at the dirt and rubbed it between his fingers. "An answer for an answer. You shattered something here. I think it was a magick conduit."

"It was a flute gifted to me. It was broken, so I had to...improvise."

"You are either an amateur at best or a fool at worst.

151

Take better care of your things," he stated after turning around. His blue eye was shining with the same light that was coming from the staff. He sheathed the rapier and said, "*Magas abjure*," while throwing up a gesture with his free hand. The light turned white again, and his eye stopped shining.

"Yeah, well, perhaps it was for the best. It was already broken after being supercharged by a storm." Riker showed the wizard the scars across his fingers. "Besides, the real magick is in my hands."

The wizard gave the hands a passing glance and scoffed. "I'm not impressed. You've overstayed thy welcome, elf. Come, I'll see you out." Riker followed the wizard the way he had come, through a narrow passage. "We aren't alone in these caves, so do as I say and stay quiet."

"Speaking of which, I didn't learn your name."

"My name is Kruzco."

"Kruzco the wizard. Interesting, I would have guessed something with a bit more flare."

The wizard smirked. "What kind of name is Barron Von Riker?"

"It's a bard's name actually." He puffed his chest. "Barron von Riker, storyteller of the Southern Seas. Perhaps you've heard of me?"

"No," the wizard said plainly.

"Well, I'm not surprised. You seem to be a bit of a

hermit, my friend." The wizard didn't reply, and Riker wringed his hands as they walked farther into the dark mine shafts. "You said we weren't alone here," he said in his softest voice. "Do you mean the dwarves? I haven't seen a one since entering these mountains."

"They aren't here anymore," the wizard replied, stopping in front of a wall. He tapped the end of his staff against a bulging part of it, and the bulge pushed in, revealing a secret room. "Yes, no more dwarves. Only what they left behind." He handed Riker his staff, which Riker felt pulse with magick. Kruzco pulled out what looked like a tinder-box from a fur pocket. With the tools inside, he lit a match with one hand and slowly spread the fingers of the other over the flame. "When you've been alone for as long as I have, you learn to get by with what little you have." He positioned the index finger with his thumb and ring finger, with the little one and the middle finger alone pointed forward. He said, "*Abraigni triradi*," and three small rays of fire flew from the match and landed on the wicks of three lanterns in the room.

Riker looked around and found that it was a cozy space. There was a pile of animal skins in a corner, a stack of slab rocks made into a work benchnear the secret door, and various bottles and tools lying about. "You've lived here for how long?" Riker asked, picking up a bottle. There was a white powder inside it. The wizard snatched it from his hands.

"Mind your manners, elf." He put the bottle of powder in one of his fur pockets. "I've lived in this mountain for a long time. How long, I could not tell you. Maybe five or ten years. When you can't see the sun, one loses track of the days, let alone the years."

"Why are you staying here then?"

"That is not for you to know," he replied. "I've answered enough of your questions, Barron Von Riker. I want to know why you and your friends came up here. This place is mostly desolate. Did you think you'd find the dwarves' gold like everyone else?"

"We thought going through the mountains would get us to civilization faster than going around it. I had no idea what was waiting for us…" Riker noticed the wizard's rapier leaning against the wall near the pile of animal skins and casually walked in its direction as if interested in the pile on the floor. "One of us died to those things," he continued with his back turned to the wizard. "I got separated from them after that, and before meeting you I heard that roar echoing in the mine." He retrieved the weapon and pointed it at the wizard. "You know what it is. Tell me, please."

The wizard's face was unsurprised. He presented a lit match in the fingers of one hand over red and gray powder in his other. Before Riker could act, he dropped the match in the powder and spoke. *Abraingis et metallis.* The powder combusted, and he threw it at Riker, who shielded his face with the blade, which grew hot in his hand. It glowed red and became so hot Riker threw it down. "Who do you think you are, commanding me? I am trying to help you!"

"How am I to trust you if you can't answer a simple question?"

Riker's hand had blistered. Kruzco sighed, went over to the pile of skins, and pulled from it a leather satchel that had glass that clanked and scratched inside. "Here." He gave Riker a bottle wrapped in cloth. "It's a salve for your hand."

"What was that roar I heard earlier?" Riker persisted. Inside the bottle was a clear and viscous liquid.

"That roar is the reason you must leave, and that is as much as I will say about it. Now don't get comfortable. We aren't staying here." He sheathed the rapier and handed Riker one of the lanterns. "Stay close and —"

"I know... keep quiet."

As the two ducked through another shaft, the wizard's staff light refracted off the deposits of minerals on the walls. If there were more light in the mine, Riker was certain he'd be more at awe at all that he didn't see. The shaft had ended on an overhang in a large pit, and he feared how deep it went. Across the way was a line of broken posts that would have been a part of a bridge to the other side. He was about to lean over for a better look below, but the wizard blocked him. A large creature flew up, screeching at them as it went higher. Riker followed it with his eyes and saw that it was, in fact, a bat the size of a man. Riker measured it to have a twenty-foot wingspan. The beast grappled onto a stalactite on the ceiling, where Riker noticed there were more staring back at him from above.

"Umm."

"Don't panic and don't stare at them," said Kruzco. He banged the heel of his staff against the floor and said, *"Abrafonslux monradi!"* There was a static sound, and the white light from the staff shot up to the ceiling and bathed the creatures in its radiance.

Riker saw them more clearly then. They were all grotesque looking, like gargoyles with uneven, sharp teeth. They collectively hissed and took flight; some dropped bodies of those things that had chased him earlier.

"Great vampire bats," Kruzco remarked. He manifested another ball of light on the staff, which shielded them from the flying creatures fleeing to the darker spaces inside the mountain.

"Those were vampires?"

"No, vampire bats. No amount of silver or holy water will keep these away." Kruzco produced a jar with bird feathers in it and a compass from his clothing.

"What is that for?"

"I need them for a complex spell. Feathers sprinkled in pixie dust." He used the compass to determine the direction of the other side. He then opened the jar and took out two feathers, giving Riker one of them. "It is more ethical than taking a pixie's wings. Repeat after me and be sure to match my pitch and resonance. You're a bard, so it shouldn't be that hard."

Ignoring the mocking, Riker felt a wave of excitement. He had never cast a spell without his instruments before, nor did he think it was possible. *"Valor supre!"* Riker repeated the magick word the same as the wizard, and the two feathers illuminated before disintegrating in their fingers. He suddenly felt lighter and noticed he was gradually levitating off the ground.

"Focus!" Kruzco demanded. "The slightest distraction will send you to the vampires above us. Take my hand." Riker reached out for his hand and nearly turned himself upside-down. *"En cronosa!"* The crystal inside his amulet glowed, and Riker suddenly found himself in strange surroundings. There in the air, all was still, and in every direction he looked, he saw infinities of himself and the wizard. It was like being in a surreal dream. *"Nord-esta!"* all infinity of Kruzco said. They were pulled along a trail of themselves that took them across the gap and to the other side. *"Cronosa abjure!"*

Riker tumbled back into a reality that made more sense, though his vision was swimming. The wizard looked down at Riker, grunted, and reached down and took him by the hand. It was a strong grip, leaving Riker's already burned hand aching. He struggled for balance while Kruzco offered him his staff. "First time in a higher dimension?"

"Where were we?"

"The fourth. Better known as the Dimension of Space-time."

"I think I'm going to be sick…"

"Save it for later. We're not done yet." They continued on by squeezing their way into a room made up of a web of metal beams, cylinders, and toothed wheels ranging from as small as Riker's hand to large enough to stand on. They climbed across the rusty wheels on the floor and weaved past metal structures.

"What was the purpose of all this?"

"It was the greatest smelter in the world," said the wizard.

"This room?"

"The entire mountain." He led Riker to a tall corridor and abruptly stopped. Before them the path was blocked by a collection of stone boulders. The old man stared at the mound for a moment and said, "This was the way out. He must be angry."

"Who is angry?"

"Before you and your friends can truly be free from these mountains, you must meet my master. Pray to your gods he isn't in too bad of a mood." He took out a handful of what looked like shedded lizard skin and the scroll he'd had from before.

"What is that?"

"The questions never end," he said unrolling the scroll before presumably reading the magick words written on it.

"*Abracronosa-con-coro a la dracon!*"

"Wait, who is your master?" The shed skin burned up, and Riker found that its embers were flying up behind him, where a fiery gate manifested.

Kruzco shoved him through to the other side, which was near the top of what Riker assumed was the same mountain. Kruzco closed the parchment, and the portal closed in a huff of smoke behind them. As Riker took in the view, he wondered if the others were okay and found himself thinking of Llorva, hoping that she was all right. The plateau they stood on was several hundreds of feet higher than the surrounding mountains. "Your master, why would he be angry?" Riker asked Kruzco.

The air was thin and tainted with the smell of brimstone.

"He doesn't like intruders," he replied. "My job is to get rid of them, but he sealed off the exit." They carried on to the peak, where the winds were stronger and brimstone was all Riker could taste between gasps of air.

Seeing that the air was choking Riker, Kruzco forcefully planted his staff into the stone ground and performed a short ritual of incantation chants and somatic movements that created a bubble around them. "Catch your breath. We have a ways to go."

"Why are we doing this?" Riker asked after dry-heaving on the ground. "What's going to happen when we get to the top of this mountain?"

"We will likely make a plea for you and your friends' freedom."

"And if that doesn't work?"

"You and I will die."

"Well, we best not keep destiny waiting," Riker said, straightening his posture and giving Kruzco a nod. The magick bubble came undone, and it started to become difficult to breathe once more. Fortunately, a tall but narrow cavernous opening was not far ahead. Once inside the golden brown cave, Riker immediately noticed the change in the atmosphere. The dry heat weighed on him. He leaned against a wall to catch his breath but found it scorching to the touch.

"Move quickly. He knows we are here," Kruzco's voice echoed before him as the wizard led the way past the heat hazes. They turned a corner and found an area with an unknowable ceiling but a floor vast with wealth. "If you value your life, do not touch anything," said Kruzco. Riker saw scattered golden statues of animals and men alike, flawless jewel-encrusted weapons sticking from endless mounds of coins, and remnants from the dwarves that had once ruled these mountains.

Riker wiped his brow as they ventured deeper through a

narrow path among the hordes of gold. In the distance, he saw scratches on the walls that only a creature with claws strong enough to crush stone could make. When they reached the back of the cave, Riker's nose was assaulted by the stench of spoiled meat and decay. There was an array of various charred animal carcasses upon the floor; with them Riker recognized bodiless armor strewn about with the Dragon Slayer badge on them. He imagined them eaten whole with nothing but their armor spat out after the stomach churned and crushed them.

His daze was interrupted when the coins from the heap behind them started sliding down the mound. Riker turned around slowly to see a serpentine neck writhe up and over the gold. The head staring down at them was narrow, with two devilish curved horns upon the crown and fine spikes upon the cheeks and sharp jaws. The body crawled over the mound, showing off a pair of folded wing membranes and a spined back. Riker only noticed the lengthy tail when it uncoiled itself from the floor around him and came up with a tri-edged stinger at the tip.

"You bring me dinner, wizard?" came a voice to Riker's left. It was coming from a blinking orb held in an iron tesseract sitting in a pile of gold.

"No, my lord," said Kruzco. "We have come to make a plea for your mercy."

"You dare possess the foolish courage to confront me?" The wyvernous dragon's serpentine tongue flicked as the words came from the orb. "You, whose scent is strange to my nose but familiar... Ah, yes! Elf flesh. A taste I have not known for two hundred years or more."

"I only wish to leave these mountains with my friends," Riker replied, staring at the wyvern's blood-red scales and flicking tongue.

"Master, I —"

"Silence, wizard!" A puff of smoke and intense heat came from the nostrils. The dragon returned his attention to Riker. "Go on. You were about to start begging for your life."

For one reason or another, that snapped Riker out of his fear. "More like a warning for you not to attack me."

The dragon's neck wrenched closer to him. "That was a bold bluff."

"It's true," he continued. "I bested your wizard and showed him mercy. I will grant you the same if you bid me and my companions safe passage."

The voice from the orb started laughing. "Your attempt was most entertaining, but I will have to refuse your plea disguised in a threat. If the wizard won't kill you, then I will have to kill you both myself!" Riker dodged forward as a stream of fire came from the mouth. He was under the neck when he decided to jump up and hug the beast. "You dare? Get off me!"

Holding on for dear life and embracing burns to his skin, Riker noticed Kruzco rushing over. "Cover your eyes!" He took from his satchel a piece of long cloth and burned it in the light from his staff while forcing his eyes closed. "*Alafonslux Grandios!*" Through his eyelids, Riker noticed a tremendous light flash. The wyvern hissed and writhed causing Riker to fall to the floor.

"Traitor! Your death will be the slowest!" Now blinded, the dragon backed into the wall of gold it had crawled from, and the pieces came raining down on him. Riker and Kruzco fled behind the treasures as the beast clawed its way free. "Very clever, but you cannot hide for long. I still smell you two." Kruzco had one hand on his staff and the other on the hilt of his rapier, ready to draw as they sat and listened from behind a pile of gold. "I thought I had seen the last of your kind two hundred years ago when so much elves' blood was spilled war after war." The orb said while in the distance Riker heard claws scratching and scales slithering against stone.

The dragon breathed another burst of flame not far away from their hiding spot, which made Riker jump, but Kruzco held him in place with his staff arm. "Not yet," he whispered.

"Did he tell you how he came into my service, elf ?"

Kruzco took Riker by the wrist and led him away from the hiding spot behind their hunter's back.

"The wizard came to me wanting power after being

exiled from his coven. Lucky for him I took pity and needed a guard dog." The dragon thumped his tail. "I should have known how frail his loyalty would be." Kruzco and Riker made a hasty dash between the mounds of gold, which caught the dragon's attention. A stream of fire lashed after them, intensely warming Riker's back followed by a boom of flapping wings behind them. The dragon's tail came down and whipped at their legs, tripping them.

Back against the floor, Riker dodged the stinger while Kruzco dealt with the fire-belching head and sharp teeth. The stinger cut pieces of Riker's hair as his head narrowly escaped its tip.

The wizard cried, *"Abra tempesta-gustusa!"* and the dragon was blown back by a magick force of wind, having to flap his wings so as not to spiral away. Riker quickly stood, as the floor was scorching to the touch. Any exposed skin was numb from the heat. Riker shielded his eyes from the glow of fire that was about to descend upon him before Kruzco came before him and planted his staff in the ground. *"Boul alatempesta!"* he chanted, arms out and palms forward. An invisible barrier shielded them from the oncoming flames.

It was incredibly hot underneath the fire. Riker heard a pulsing sound, and f lames started coming through, licking at their skin. "Hold, Kruzco! Hold!"

The wizard screamed and leaned against the force of fire. "Begone, wretched dragon! *Grandios!*" The protective shield expanded, and the staff eventually fractured followed by an explosion. The two were knocked back, and Riker was thrown into a pile of dead animals. The wizard lay beside him in the gold. The wyvern flew back into a mound of gold that reached near the ceiling and started an avalanche. Realizing his fate, the dragon covered his head with his wings as thousands of gold coins rained down on him.

"Do you think he's dead?" Riker asked.

"No," Kruzco replied with a cough. The surface of the pile started to ripple, and Kruzco went over to a statue of a great hammer-wielding dwarf and used what was left of his staff to move it. "*Abra tempesta monradi!*" The statue was blown over the ripples just as the dragon's head emerged, and it collapsed on top of him, breaking into pieces.

"Now is he dead?"

"No! Let's get out of here!"

"Wait!" spoke the magick orb. "A truce."

"Kruzco, get another statue!"

"No, wait, I will grant you and yours leave," said the orb as the dragon started crawling out of the gold. "Never in two hundred years have I done battle like that. Most men would cower in fear before I charred them to the bone. Even the wizard dared not use his magick against me in the beginning. But you, you were not afraid."

"Of course I was afraid," argued Riker.

"But such bravery I've only seen in non-humans."

"You mean the dwarves."

"Dwarves, elves, other. You've reminded me of the days when man and elf fought over this realm. Of course, the elves' bravery did not see them to victory."

"Wait, you were there?"

"I was. On the side of the elves, of course. The enemy of my enemy and so on…"

"But if you were there helping the elves, then why didn't they conquer the humans?"

"Because they started fighting themselves. While they had their little war, I was left to defend myself from the Slayers."

"The Dragon Slayers."

The Dragon abruptly turned his head toward Riker. "Have you heard of them?"

"I've had the displeasure of being on the wrong end of one of their swords."

"One would think they would have disbanded given how many dragons they've slain."

"It will never be enough until anything and everything sharing blood with you is gone, or so I've been told. But wait… if you were there to witness the wars going on back then, can you tell me what happened to all the male elves? Why are what's left of the elves hiding away from the rest of the world?"

"Your questions I cannot answer, for I did not see the reason, but I can say that there were male elves. They were on the battlefield while their women used their enchantments to their advantage. All I know for sure is that when I retreated to the mountains, the scent of the males had suddenly diminished. It was like they disappeared overnight. I had not known the smell of their flesh until half-breeds like yourself came along."

What a mystery, Riker thought. Then he furrowed his brow. "So now I'm free to go? Like that?" Kruzco came up and shook him by the shoulders. "Do you want it in writing? Let's go!"

"I do want something in return," the dragon said. "I demand a favor of you when the time comes, and you will not refuse me."

"You shall receive it," Riker said, not sure how he could find him later anyway.

"Say my name and it shall bond us," came the voice as the dragon lurched forward, forcing Riker and Kruzco to step back. "Say the name given to me by the Cabal of Fire."

"Who is the Cabal of Fire?"

"An ancient organization of sorcerers,"repliedKruzco."They worshiped him like a god and believed dragons were the first sorcerers of primeval fire."

"Tell him my name, wizard. Tell him what they called me."

"Diaboli. The Red Devil."

"Say it!" came the voice from the orb.

"Diaboli," Riker echoed.

"Again!"

"Diaboli!"

The dragon's massive head took in a breath, and the hot air around them was sucked away and into the living furnace. Diaboli blew a ring of golden fire on the ground around them, which had an uncanny pull at its center. The flames from the burning ring reached higher and higher until Riker could not see in front of him. He closed his eyes and waited for what came next. When he opened them, they were standing on scorched earth in a meadow hill. Behind them was the coal mine exit blocked off by the avalanche.

"The other side," Kruzco said in a hushed tone. "I have never been allowed on the other side." They looked at each other. Covered in ash and stinking of brimstone. Riker was amused by the thought of how they should be dead, and he smiled.

"We did it," he said in disbelief. "You mad man, Kruzco! We did it! We're alive!" He grabbed the wizard by the shoulders. "I met a dragon and survived!" Kruzco began to chuckle through his teeth, and they both started howling in laughter. "Does this mean you're free of your duty?"

"I do not presume to know. Diaboli does not explain himself, and I've learned during my time in those caves not to question that serpent's motives. Come, we must find your friends before nightfall." They trekked down the hill, where they crossed an abandoned mining camp.

"Kruzco. What happened to the dwarves?"

"I don't know. When they were here, the skies smoked and the mountains thundered from their makings. One day it all stopped." He paused and leaned on his staff. "The Prydens didn't find a soul when they came up here. What remained is what you saw and see here. Soon after, the dragon moved in."

Riker stubbed his toe on something in the grass. It was a rusted pickaxe buried in the skull of a creature that resembled one of the cave dwellers. "What about the creatures that chased me and my friends?"

"Ah, yes. The kobolds. Like the elves, they are not from this world." He took a moment to stroke his beard. "Lovers of darkness and trickery. You won't find them anywhere else other than mountains like these. Once full of busy tunnels and life, but now a phantom of its former self. I will not miss it."

"Good. All the more reason to leave this place."

Chapter Fourteen

Azariah

HER EYES FLUTTERED AWAKE. She was still lying on the cot, but her aches and fever were finally gone. Sabba's bitter tea had worked, and after a week of rest, she finally started feeling like herself again. Shanani was sitting in a chair next to her and offered her a bowl of vegetable soup. She was the eldest of the sisters, but one wouldn't know it by looking at the two of them. In fact, Sabba looked more like she could be her sister's grandmother.

"Good morning," she said. "How are you feeling?"

"Like normal, thank you." She slowly sat up and noticed the watchful eyes of Mlezi, the snake coiled on his perch. She was unsure if he was a real snake. Sabba called him her familiar and repeated that he was not a pet. At times she would say a few magick words with a flick of her wrist and the snake would transform into some slender object: a spear, a broom, or a walking stick. She took the soup and started drinking the broth. "How long was I asleep this time?"

"The whole day," said Sabba from across the room. She was preparing something over the cauldron as usual. "I wanted to wake you up, but Shanani insisted you sleep."

"She finally started having pleasant dreams."

"What did you see this time?" she asked Shanani.

"It's hard to say. My sorcery allows me to feel your emotions while you sleep. It's called oneiromancy but rarely have I understood what they mean to people. You were racing toward something this time — a lot more color and fire were before you. My, I don't know what it will all be about, but you have quite a bit of excitement ahead of you, Azariah."

That was her true name. She had since accepted it when Shanani revealed she'd learned of her deceptions while she slept in her illness. Shanani didn't know what to call her power of perception when she was younger. She said as a child she started experiencing people's dreams whenever she was around them while they slept. She even predicted the future when this happened. Her mother took her to see the witch doctor one day, and she discovered she was a sorceress by way of a supposed connection to a primeval consciousness.

"Was I alone in this dream?" she asked Shanani.

"No, you felt... supported. I believe you and your friends will be united again someday." Azariah squirmed at the feeling of relief. She missed Riker and Vylasgarden and had grown to regret leaving them behind, but maybe Shanani was wrong about finding them again. It had been a week and she was still on her mission north to find the huldar.

Shanani couldn't tell her when, but she knew one day she wouldn't feel alone anymore.

"The night approaches. It's time we tell her," Sabba said. Her tone was rushed, and there was an eagerness about her.

"Let's give her time to properly wake up, sister," Shanani refuted.

"Time isn't on our side, Shanani."

Azariah stood and walked over to see what Sabba was doing. "What are you talking about?" she asked. She saw on the table an open tome and an assortment of metal tools she'd never seen before, and a chill went down her spine. "Sabba, what is this?"

"It is time I tell you what I need you to do, Azariah," she said. "Witchcraft takes a toll on the body. Unlike my sister's gifts, the magick I use cannot prolong my life. There is a trade-off every time I cast a spell, which is why finding you was like fate."

"I don't understand. You're starting to scare me." Sabba tried reaching out to her, but Azariah recoiled.

"Azariah," Shanani said from across the room. Azariah saw that they both had desperate looks. "Pryden is at war with itself," Shanani claimed. "Aside from the people rising against the king, those with magick like me and my sister have overstepped our bounds with the rule of this land, and the king has made it very hard for wizards and witches to get the supplies they need to extend their lives. Sabba is a hundred and thirty-one years old." Only eleven years older than Azariah herself. "Magick is what's keeping her together."

"Blood sheds all around us," Sabba continued. "My sister and I try to keep to ourselves and move whenever the war draws near, but my supplies run dry, and I feel my bones wither by the day. Please. I need your blood."

"My blood?"

"Blood from a true elf," Shanani followed. "Long ago when the elves came from their world to ours, humans discovered kind's affinity to longevity and believed your blood could in turn cure death itself."

"But my people live and die just as you."

"What is a century to a being that can survive a millennium?" Sabba interrupted. "I once feared the day I would no longer be with my sister, but primeval fate has sent you here to us so that I may live a new life with her."

"I don't know what to say."

"Please say yes. We will never get another chance at meeting another full-blooded elf."

Azariah sat down in a chair and waited a long while. The sisters waited with her, doing nothing but patiently watching her think. "How does this work?" she finally asked.

"All the ingredients for the potions are present," Sabba said, referring to the tome on the table. "All that I require is a thousand to fifteen hundred milliliters of your blood."

Azariah's body went cold. "How much is that?"

"It's a lot," Shanani admitted, "but not a drop will be wasted and you will be fine. We will not let any harm come to you." Seeing the uncertainty on Azariah's face, Shanani's expression softened. "Forgive us, we're desperate, and with this war all around us, we're also all we have."

"I'll do it." The women were speechless. "On one condition."

"Anything, child," replied Sabba.

"You will give me supplies that will help me reach the North Province on my own."

Without hesitation Sabba replied, "It is yours."

Chapter Fifteen

RIKER

FAR DOWN THE HILL WAS A CLIFF'S EDGE. Riker saw that they were on the north side of the same mountain. The sun was high and casting its shine on a ghost town that was carved out of the stone of the valley. "There!" someone called out below. Coming from one of the buildings were people. "It's Riker! He's alive!" It was Perry running up and waving his arms at him. Riker waved back.

"You made it!" Riker yelled.

He saw Jared, Gideon, and, to his relief, Vylasgarden too.

"This is my friend Kruzco. He helped me get out of there." Riker leaned over to Perry and whispered in his ear. "He's a wizard."

Perry began stammering. He grabbed Kruzco's massive hand and shook with both of his. "What an honor!" Perry exclaimed and practically dragged the poor old man to the rest of the group.

Vylasgarden met Riker with a clawed hand on his shoulder. "I had no doubt you would make it out of there."

"Really," he replied with an exhausted smirk. "That

makes one of us."

She sniffed him. "You smell like a chimney," she then turned her attention to Kruzco. "Thank you for bringing my friend to us."

He nodded curiously. "Forgive me. I have never met one of your kind before." Vylasgarden tilted her head in response. "I mean no offense. I'm simply incapable of knowing when my thoughts are best kept to myself."

"No, I understand how I may seem," she replied.

"It is a true pleassure, really, to meet you. Your friend was worried about all of you."

Riker left the two to converse while he met with Jared, who was counting gear with his remaining brother.

"I was sure you'd be dead," Jared said to Riker without looking at him. Riker said nothing. "We shouldn't have followed you. We should have turned back as I said."

"Jared, I —"

"My brother is dead because I listened to you!" Jared screamed. The echo silenced Kruzco and Vylasgarden's conversation.

"I know what you are going through —"

"You know nothing," Jared said, facing Riker.

"Stand back," Vylasgarden said, and Jared took a step backward.

"Look, Gideon, he hides behind his beast."

Gideon kept his attention on the items they were

counting. "Let it go, brother."

"None of us knew what was going to happen," Riker continued. "It could have been any of us. We can't turn against each other. We still have a ways to go to get out of here. The full moon is coming and —"

"You may not have known, Riker, but I knew better, and I should have listened to myslef," Jared interrupted. "I will get us out of here and you will lead no one."

"Lead the way then," Riker relented, annoyed. He was too exhausted to reason with them any further. Maybe Jared needed that time to grieve in his own way.

Perry, Vylasgarden, Kruzco, and Riker set up a day camp while Jared and Gideon conversed amongst themselves and looked at Jared's map. While Perry was entertaining Kruzco with his books, Vylasgarden sat and spoke near a sleepy Riker. "We need to be careful, Riker," she said in a hushed tone. "They're not just dangerous, now they're angry. I need you to know I will not hesitate to kill them."

"I know. There isn't going back," he replied. "I won't hesitate either.

But what about the boy?"

"Perry is a good boy," she replied to him. "A good human. Whatever happens, I think we should take him with us." She saw the reluctance on his face. "I will take him and find him a new home."

"We don't owe them anything, Vylasgarden. They saved

our lives and we returned the favor. Asghar is gone but that wasn't on us. I say we leave with the wizard as soon as possible."

Riker woke up hours later to the group packing up their belongings. The twilight sky was upon them. "Kruzco is going to lead us out the mountains," Perry said to him, helping Riker off the ground. As they all walked through new caverns and more abandoned mining sites, Riker moved as if he'd had no rest at all. It was days later when they finally saw flat land again. During which they were foraging wild vegetables, hunting, and listening to Perry asking Kruzco endless questions about wizardry. The old man was patient enough to answer each one.

By the time they made it past the last mountain, Riker knew more about magick and had eaten more strange creatures than he cared for. They were making their way down the east side of the northernmost mountain when they came across a village in a meadow valley. Beyond that was an immense desert. "This is where we part ways, friends," Kruzco announced to the group.

"No! Please come with us," Perry pleaded.

"I'm afraid I can't, young apprentice. I have to go my own way now," Kruzco said with hands on the boy's shoulders. He looked at Riker. "Follow down the path and you will reach the village I mentioned by nightfall."

"I don't think I can thank you enough," Riker said.

"You know who you should be thanking," the wizard said with a wink. "Pray he doesn't come to collect." Riker nodded. "Oh! I almost forgot. Here." He handed Riker his rapier.

"Kruzco, I couldn't take this from you."

"I don't need it! I'm a damn wizard! Take it!" Riker took the weapon by the hilt. It was old and tarnished but noticeably well sharpened.

"You'll need it until you find some new instruments."

"I can't argue with that. Thank you, my friend."

The wizard bowed and started to make his way back up the mountains. He held a hand with Vylasgarden as he passed her, and they exchanged a smile. When he disappeared behind the rocks, Vylasgarden came up to Riker and asked, "Who was he talking about?"

"What?"

"Who should you be thanking?"

Part of Riker wanted to tell Vylasgarden about the dragon, but he felt it best not to distract from the task at hand. "Oh! He's mistaken. You know wizards are kind of weird." The group walked down the path, and they soon noticed a village near a lake in the valley. On the other side was a vast desert with the sun setting in the west behind massive dunes of sand before them. "We're running out of daylight," Riker said and led them all across the meadow and into the surprisingly quiet village with a noticeably large graveyard. The surrounding grasses whispered to them as the gentle breeze swept through. No one was outside, but many homes were illuminated from the inside. Thankfully for the group, they found a boarding house at the village center next to a stable.

The building's lobby was cozy-looking with rancher's paraphernalia as the decor, and the fireplace had a caldron burning in it. Riker could smell the lamb stew brewing from within. He couldn't resist licking his lips. "Good evening, travelers. Will you be staying with us this evening?" said a homely man, coming up to greet them nervously. He was middle-aged, dark-skinned, dressed in sheep's wool, and had a bald, shiny head. Riker noticed the young girl sitting behind the counter drawing with parchment and a piece of charcoal. Her thick hair was pulled back and held together by a golden cuff.

"Yes, my friends and I are quite tired," Riker responded taking off his knapsack. "It was almost like you were expecting us."

"It isn't often we have folk come through this way, but you will find we are always prepared so long as you leave tomorrow morning, of course," he said with a smile.

"I'm sorry, did you say tomorrow?" replied Jared. "The following night is the full moon."

"Yes, an unfortunate series of events, but our village does not permit outsiders on the nights of a full moon."

Riker grew suspicious.

"Look, Daddy, a dragon!" the little girl said, hopping down the counter and running over to Vylasgarden.

"Semira, let the creature be," the man called to the girl. His smile melting away.

"It is alright," Vylasgarden assured him. "Can I see your tail?" Semira asked.

"Semira, don't be rude to our guests," the man called a second time. He was much more stern.

"No, she is fine," Vylasgarden insisted. She demonstrated that she, in fact, did not have a tail.

"What happened to it?" Semira asked.

"I was hatched without one," Vylasgarden explained.

"Hatched?" Semira responded. At this point, the child appeared more confused than before. Vylasgarden exchanged a look with the man, and it was apparent that this was a talk he was not ready to have with his daughter.

"Perhaps your father will tell you about it one day," Vylasgarden answered. The child looked on with astonishment. As the two conversed, Riker and the rest of the group approached the counter. On their left was an entrance into a separate room; it looked to be a lounge that had a long table covered in a bounty of food and drink. Numerous villagers were quietly eating and drinking.

"Curious," Riker said to himself.

"What do you think?" Jared whispered to him.

"I think something is going on here," he whispered back. "We should play along. Let's get some rest tonight and worry about tomorrow in the morning." Jared nodded and stepped aside for Riker to speak. "Good sir, my friends and I have been endlessly traveling and have gone through a couple of miserable days. We do not have much for payment, though we are prepared to offer dried meats from our travels and a few assorted items," Riker said to the building's manager.

"Alright, young man," the man replied. "Let us make a bargain. Show me what you have." As he and the group sorted through the materials, Vylasgarden continued entertaining Semira, who seemed to have endless questions and observations.

"You are beautiful," Semira said to Vylasgarden.

Vylasgarden smiled and said, "Thank you, Semira. Most people look at me and see a monster."

"Why do they see a monster?" the girl asked with fingers in her mouth. Vylasgarden paused and considered what to say next.

She took a breath and said, "Your elders fear what they do not understand." Her voice was soft and kind to the child.

Semira stared into the distance and said, "Daddy says that the dragons are all gone now." She looked back at Vylasgarden. "But you're a dragon."

"I'm like the dragon's baby cousin," Vylasgarden said,

kneeling closer to Semira's level. "My people come from an old dragon and mountain fairies."

"They were your mommies and daddies. Daddy says the fairies in these mountains are dangerous."

"Yes, we know," interrupted Gideon at the counter. As Vylasgarden's conversation with the little girl continued, Riker and the rest managed a deal with the man using gold from the cockatrice's lair and things of no importance to them.

"Vylasgarden, it's time we go," Riker said to her.

Vylasgarden looked down at Semira. "Farewell, little one."

"Goodnight, Miss Dragon Lady!" Semira called as the group went upstairs. The room reserved for Riker and Vylasgarden was small and a bit cramped, but they managed to fit inside along with what was left of their belongings.

"The man could have mentioned that the rooms were this small," Riker commented, frustrated beyond belief.

"That would have been nice to know," Vylasgarden said exhausted herself, and going to close the door behind them, but then she stopped.

"What is it?"

"I heard something just now. Downstairs," Vylasgarden said, her eyes lingering at the door.

"Yeah, there are people drinking down there," Riker

reasoned. Vylasgarden put her ear against the door.

"No, it sounded like... nailing."

"I knew something was going on," said Riker. "It is quite late for an activity that would require nailing." Then came a knock at the door.

Vylasgarden hesitantly answered. It was Semira. "What is the matter, Semira?" Vylasgarden asked.

"Is it true that dragons lived a really long time?" the girl asked.

"Semira, perhaps you and Vylasgarden can talk about this in the morning," Riker suggested. "Do you know what is happening downstairs?"

"Father is boarding up the house," Semira said plainly.

Riker perked up. "Why would he do that?" he asked, stepping into the little girl's view.

"I dun know, he says it keeps the monsters away," Semira replied casually.

Riker and Vylasgarden exited the room and went to the stairs.

"Go get Jared and the others and meet me in the lobby," Riker told Vylasgarden, and he made for the stairs. Semira followed him.

"Do all elves look like you?" Semira asked him. "Not now, little girl," Riker hissed.

"Okay then." Semira took a second to think. "What

about the food you eat? Is it the same as what we eat?" Riker stopped at the head of the stairs and turned to her, grim with exhaustion.

"No, we usually eat little girls who ask too many questions," he growled with a twisted smile. Semira gasped. "Now go away before I develop a craving," Riker said, clawing his fingers toward her. The little girl yelped but only stepped back. Riker sighed and turned his attention downstairs. The bottom floor had every person from the lounge congregating in the lobby. They were spectating as the manager nailed boards and iron grates over the windows.

"What is going on down here?" Riker asked just after the rest of the party joined him. Everyone stopped and turned to look at them.

"What is all this?" Jared asked.

"Everything will be okay. Just go back upstairs. You are safe here," the man reassured them. Nothing in his voice seemed certain of safety.

"That is not what I asked," Jared pressed. "I will tear down those barricades, so I suggest you tell us what is going on." There was a pause. No one moved or spoke, but the people looked at each other as if waiting for someone else to speak up. Jared started pushing his way through the crowd.

"No! Please, I will tell you!" a man said from the crowd. He was old and hearty-looking. One could have assumed he was a carpenter or a smith of sorts. "Once a month during the full moon, our village is haunted by a beast that comes from the Dark Realm. While the ghosts of our dead roam without bother, the beast – a werehyena – torments us. She kills at least one person every moon." No one interrupted him, and when he paused, no one dared to speak. "We thought at first it was a coincidence. Monsters crossed into our village during the moon before, but she came back every time."

"She killed every person caught outside during the first moons of her attacks," said another person.

"You said she. You know that the beast is female?" Jared asked.

The people looked among themselves again. One of the villagers, a middle-aged woman, pointed a finger at an elderly man sitting at a small corner table and drinking from a large bottle. "He is the one to blame for this!" she yelled. "I do not know why we protect him; all he does is get drunk, and we barely have enough for us all to drink away our sorrows. We should have thrown him out many times over. Maybe then she will go away for good!"

"Why? What did he do?" Riker insisted.

Another woman spoke and held the manager's arm. "Before all this, he was our shepherd, but he kept losing our cattle to the lions, jackals, and hyenas. We lost a lot of food because of that waste of a man's drunkenness, so one day our chieftain asked him to make a sacrifice to our gods

188

so that they would bestow upon us a guardian to protect us from the predators. But instead of sacrificing a dog or our best goat, he sacrificed his virgin daughter!"

The shepherd began to sob over the table.

"His mistake became our punishment," a man said. "It angered our god, so he sent her back as that thing to torment and punish us."

"Why haven't you hired a professional to handle this?" Riker asked.

"What choice do we have?" stated an older woman. "Magicians are outlawed by the crown and no warlock will set foot in Pryden lands so long as the Order of Fire watches its borders. The only thing that can harm her without magick is a silver blade, and no one who's gone looking for silver in the mountains has come back from the journey."

Gideon spoke. "If we get rid of your beast, will you give us your horses?"

Jared's face flashed with anger. "What are you doing?"

"No one is doing anything but staying here," Vylasgarden said. "We cannot help these people."

"I believe we can," Gideon suggested, "with this." He put on a leather glove and carefully took out a bundle of feathers and a jar of blood from his travel bag. "You may not have silver, but perhaps this can kill her."

"What is it?" Riker asked.

"Cockatrice blood and feathers. I meant to sell this, but a horse is more valuable to us right now."

"We won't," argued Jared, "it's too dangerous."

Gideon held Jared by the shoulders. "What's this, huh? I know the loss of our brother still stings, but this is what we do, Jared. We're not getting anywhere without a horse."

"We've always hunted together. The three of us. I'd rather take the horses by force," Jared replied under his breath.

"That's never been our way," Gideon assured him.

"Her mortal form is possessed by a demon called a bouda which transforms her into that beast," informed the elderly woman. "If these are true cockatrice remains, then it may be enough to destroy the body and set the bouda free."

"Then it looks like it is settled. We kill your monster in exchange for your horses," Riker concluded.

"You really want to do this?" Vylasgarden asked, astounded.

"If you succeed in ending this nightmare, our horses will be yours," the woman assured them all.

"Fine, we'll need a good plan," Jared conceded. "No mistakes and full cooperation from the entire village." The villagers' faces lit up throughout the room. The former shepherd took a long drink from his bottle and covered his face with his hands. He began sobbing again.

"While you plan for the next night tomorrow, bring the

cockatrice remains to me," the elderly woman instructed. "You will find me at the cemetery."

With little else to talk about, everyone dispersed, and Riker noticed Jared watching him as he and Vylasgarden went back upstairs.

The next morning, the day before the full moon, the group met with volunteers from the village. They huddled around the counter on the first floor with a map of the village and a meaty breakfast given to them by the boarding house's manager. When Riker met eyes with Jared, the two nodded to each other as one of the villagers explained the bouda's behavior. "She spends the beginning of the night with the herd of sheep before running through the neighborhood cackling like a true hyena," he said.

"I think we should set up an ambush and use the sheep as bait," Jared offered.

"We will need to fashion a net or some kind of trap to slow her down," Riker added.

A villager came up and said, "We can weave a net with some loose rope over by the forge."

"Great! Once she's caught, the rest of us will distract her while Gideon somehow uses the cockatrice's blood to kill the mortal body."

Vylasgarden shook her head. "That seems too simple of

a plan. A lot can go wrong with this."

Riker shrugged. "We can't have anything set in stone until Gideon gets back with whatever the woman from last night made with the blood."

Vylasgarden stayed inside with Perry while Jared and Riker went out to look for Gideon. The tension between them was ever present, but Riker felt he had done his part in trying to mend things. Whatever Jared was feeling inside, Riker hoped that he had the capacity to put their differences aside for the night to come. They found Gideon coming back on the path.

"What happened with the woman?"

"She took the jar and sent me away," he pouted.

Jared threw up his arms. "You left it with her?"

"She said she can't work 'under watchful eyes' and that she'll bring what she's crafted before sunset." Gideon turned to Riker. "She asked for you."

"Me? Why?"

"You think she'd tell me?" He stormed off, Jared following behind.

With nothing else to do, Riker went to the graveyard and found the woman performing a ritual in front of its gates. "You wanted to see me?"

"Thank you for coming," she said, not turning to face him. Something was smoking in her hands. "Look at the fence around the burials and tell me what you see."

"I see an iron fence that's meant to keep the dead from leaving their resting place."

She finally turned around. She was holding a smudge stick. "The truth is, without magick, the fence does nothing to prevent the dead from roaming. My rituals have been keeping them at peace for decades like my mother did before me."

"Why are you telling me this?"

She was smiling at him. "I had a feeling that you should know that the dead don't like to be manipulated."

"You had a feeling?"

"They especially don't like the presence of black magick. If one were to be wielding that kind of power without knowing how to control it…"

"Are — are you a sorceress?" "Officially, no," she replied, turning back around to continue her ritual in front of the gate. "That would be an affront to the king. I'm just a healer to my people."

"I've been hearing a lot about this king. Who is he?"

"Theod-Rah is an immortal man. There are those who worship the ground he claims his family paved. The rest of us are just living in his world."

"Why doesn't anyone move out of his reach?"

"Because Pryden is our home and the sun eventually sets on all dynasties. Some of us, like you and me, have the time to wait it out." Riker pondered what she'd said and thanked her for the information.

"Wait," she demanded. "I have something else for you. Come with me."

Riker followed her to her home, where numerous wooden windchimes decorated the front. "Doesn't the noise bother you after a while?" he asked.

"It's better for private conversation, and the wind often tells me things your ears cannot perceive." She invited him in. It was a single room overwhelmed with scents and herbs. She led him to the cauldron over a fire in the back.

"A cauldron," he observed. "That's more in line with your witchy rivals, isn't it?"

With a flick of her wrist, the woman produced a gust of wind that snuffed out the fire. "Take this to the counter, will you?" she asked him, and Riker obliged. "'Rival,'" she mocked and waved her hand over the counter, blowing away the leaves and powders in the way of the cauldron. "Sorcery and witchcraft, or wizardry, are all the same to an extent. It's just a matter of how you wish to get your desired result. Why should I limit myself to my primeval gift if I can gain so much more with study? I've had a long life. Learning witchcraft saved me from boredom." Riker chuckled politely. "I brought you here to give you these." She put on a leather glove, reached into the caldron, and pulled out three arrows. "Recognize the fletchings?"

"Are those the cockatrice feathers?"

"It wasn't an easy fix, but luckily I had the blood and all

the necessary ingredients to produce legend worthy petrifying arrows."

Riker reached out to them. "Incredible…"

She pulled them away. "Didn't you hear me, boy? Pe-tri-fy-ing! You'll die with a single touch!"

"Well, how do we fire an untouchable arrow?" She threw the right-hand leather glove at him with her free hand. "Of course…"

"Take this too." She put Gideon's jar on the counter. It had a lot of blood left in it.

"Thank you for all of this, but why give it to me? It wasn't my idea to use these."

"When you have a gift like mine, and the wind tells you something about the people around you, you'd best listen. I believe we all have gifts like this; it's called intuition. Be sure to listen to it when it's talking to you." Riker thanked her again and left her home with their secret weapon. On his way back to the boarding house, he felt someone's eyes on him. It was the village's former shepherd approaching Riker, and by the looks of him, he was still drunk.

"Thank you," he slurred. The scent of spirit was strong on his breath. Riker looked at the pathetic old man and put his arm over his shoulders as they walked back together.

The night was young when the last lock turned in the village. Riker was perched on the roof of the boarding house, as it had been decided that he was the best archer there. He had given the rest of the blood back to Gideon after they finished with the plans. The nearly complete moon took up the sky and dwarfed clusters of stars. He had never been outside on the night of a full moon (or as far away from a city) and noticed its brilliance. It was so large that looked to have been dragging the sky below it. There was an unnatural chill in the windless air, and at times the silence became deafening until he started hearing the baaing of sheep. As part of the plan, Jared's group released the herd on the village road.

He spotted everyone at their stations and waited. He wasn't sure what to expect, but he trusted that the plan would work. *It must work,* he thought. For a long while, nothing happened, but eventually, she appeared in the hills. A young, bare, and ghastly Pryden woman stepped through a black mirage and, upon the moonlight illuminating her, started transforming. Growing muscle enlarged her body as it became covered in spotted fur. Riker shuddered listening to her bones breaking from across the village as her agonized screams turned into animalistic cackles.

He was certain he would never forget the event if he survived the night. She was quicker than any horse running across the fields and into the village. She crept toward the herd, and none of the sheep seemed to be bothered by her presence. She greeted some of them with nuzzles and licked the lambs. Being that close, Riker saw that she was more hideous than any werewolf he'd ever seen depicted. He felt time passing, and if they didn't finish her before the moon was complete, she'd become too powerful. He gave the signal, shining a mirror in the moonlight to Jared's station. Moments later Jared stepped out into the road. The bouda noticed him and raised her muscly neck in curiosity. Jared maintained his position in wait as the sheep parted for her. Her dagger-shaped ears pointed upward as she came to him, more curious than threatening. Gideon came from the dark and tackled her to the ground right on Perry's station, where the bouda bucked Gideon off and stood on top of the net trap that Perry triggered — ensnaring her up in the air from a tree. But it failed and brought her back down.

Panicked, Vylasgarden came and attempted to pin her down. Seeing that the plan was failing, Riker prepped a bow and arrow from the rooftop. As Vylasgarden wrestled with the monster, Jared approached slowly but with determination, drawing his sword. Vylasgarden was on the ground with the bouda on top of her attempting to bite at her face, and Riker wanted to take the shot, but Jared stood in his way. "What are you waiting for? Stab it," Riker whispered to himself. He glanced at the moon. It was looking as full as it was going to be. Gideon and Perry came up to them and said something to Jared, to which he replied and glanced up at Riker coldly.

Riker shook his head and swore. He released the arrow. Jared dodged it in time for it to pass him and meet the bouda in the neck. Vylasgarden threw the beast off and charged after Jared. "Die beast!" Perry shouted, throwing stones at her. Gideon came from behind and bludgeoned her at the knee with the sheath of his sword before drawing his blade from it. "Perry, what are you doing?" she said with hurt in her voice. Riker took a shot at Gideon but missed narrowly. He was never a good archer and suspected this was their plan all along. Gideon advanced on Vylasgarden while Perry kept throwing things at her. They backed her to the boarding house, which made it impossible for Riker to shoot. He stood up to move positions but was met by Jared, who climbed up on the roof and tackled him. They rolled all the way off and fell two stories. Jared came on top, landing on Riker when they met the ground.

There was a wave of pain from Riker's chest. Jared stood and started pacing around Riker. "The bouda..." Riker managed to say between gasps of air.

"Yes, I think you killed it," Jared replied, drawing his sword. Behind him, Vylasgarden was roaring defending herself from Gideon. "Get up! I won't kill you lying down."

Riker slowly stood and felt the second wave of pain in his chest. He winced, freeing the rapier from its sheath. "This won't bring him back, Jared. It was no one's fault."

"I don't care. I never liked you, anyway." He whirled the hilt of his sword and advanced. Riker stepped back and blocked himself from the attacks. Riker noticed the moon's position in the sky and looked at the dead witch's pendant on Jared's necklace. Suddenly he recognized what the woman was trying to tell him and started running away in the direction of the graveyard. "Coward!" Jared said behind him. The resting place for the village's dead was immense, and after seeing the bouda up close, Riker understood she needed to be stopped to end the death. He went in past the gate and waited for Jared, who soon lumbered in after him. "The dead won't save you, Riker!"

Riker revealed himself from behind the tombstone. "You said you wanted magick…" There was a pulsing sound, and the world and its dark reflection became one; what color was in the night seeped away, leaving behind saturated grays and darkness blending Riker in with the shadows. "…be carful of what you wish for."

Jared noticed that the pendant was vibrating and glowing as the wraiths started to claw themselves free from their graves. Their ethereal forms came at Jared making gutteral, disgusting noises and Riker ran for the entrance. He did not look back when he heard Jared screaming behind him. "Get away from me! Get back!" Riker managed to close the iron gates behind him right before the undead could pull him back inside. One reached its gaunt, wispy arm through the bars, and it burned into glowing ash. The orange from the rotten embers was the only color in the night. The rest were dragging Jared into the depths of a hollow graze as Riker backed away.

The victory was cut short by distant cackles. "The bouda!" Riker ran back into the village, passing weird and grotesque limbs lunging for him in the dark. The full moon's white light was all that he had to guide him back to the village proper. He found a frightened Perry being shielded by Vylasgarden as the recovered bouda was mauling Gideon across their way.

Riker ran over to Vylasgarden. "We need the arrows!" she said to him. She had a few abrasions on her face, shoulder, and arms.

"Jared is gone. We're on our own." He looked down at Perry, disapprovingly.

"He's just a child."

Riker said nothing. He looked back and witnessed Gideon forcing his fist into the bouda's mouth; it began shredding his arm with her sharp teeth and started working her way to his shoulder. The jar of cockatrice blood came from Gideon's bag on his back and rolled away from the assault. "Cover the boy's eyes." Riker ran up, catching the jar in his hands, and stood over the beast as she took Gideon's throat in her mouth — his eyes pleading. Riker removed the lid and poured the blood over the bouda and Gideon. There was a whimper from the bouda, and she suddenly stiffened and shriveled with Gideon's dying scream beneath her. Riker picked up Gideon's sword and brought the edge down on them, creating a cloud of dusty and rubbled flesh. Riker fell to his knees, screaming in the black night.

"This is all my fault," the former shepherd said mourning over what remained of his daughter's monstrous corpse. The wind shifted in the cold morning air as the color returned to the world. And so, the moon's cycle was anew and with it the Dark Realm took away its creatures and oddities from the dark.

"With a proper burial, she will never return," claimed the village's shawoman. "Thank you." The village gave them food, water, and the horses as promised. "Be wary of the desert ahead. It is full of the bones of those before you who tried to cross it in search of the Shining City," she told Riker.

"I have no interest in the Shining City," he replied impatiently. "The nearest road to Southaven will do me just fine."

"Back around the mountain with you then. There is a pass called the Peddlersroad that will take you south."

"But what about Perry?" Vylasgarden asked.

"His life is his own now," Riker replied, "and that is that."

"He was doing what he was told, Riker," Vylasgarden said, raising her voice.

"He helped in trying to kill you, Vylasgarden! Where is that rage I once saw in you?"

"My rage is only for the Dragon Slayers."

Riker sighed. "The most I will grant is to not lay a hand on him." He walked away and said, "Let's get out of here." They each had a horse leaving the third for Perry. At the edge of the village, Perry was waiting for them. Riker dismounted the horse and stepped toward him. The boy was nearly taller than him. Riker met Perry's eyes and said, "This is goodbye." His voice was soft and calm, but Perry stared at him blankly like he had just said something frightening. "How long did they plan to betray us?"

Perry averted his eyes. "Since Jared thought you died in the moun tains. He said that your group would have turned on us eventually."

"Look at me." Riker lifted his right hand and slapped the boy across the face. Perry held his cheek and fought back tears. "Good luck," he said to him, returning to his horse. He and Vylasgarden rode off, leaving Perry behind as the sun rose in the east.

Chapter Sixteen

AZARIAH

THEY WAITED FOR WHAT SABBA CALLED the witching hour. She said it was the second most opportune time when raw magick was its most powerful during the day and she could perform the ritual with the least risk. They had her drink a watery elixir and lie on the cot for Mlezi to wrap himself around her arm above the elbow. "Thank you for doing this," Shanani whispered after kissing Azariah on the forehead. She wanted to say something like It's the least I can do, but the words wouldn't come out. Sabba began to chant in the background as thunder slowly rumbled outside. Mlezi slowly tightened around her arm, and Azariah fought against the urge to flee. Sabba came to her wearing white paint on her face and holding a needle with some kind of flexible tube attached to it.

Azariah held her breath, waiting for the pain, but only felt a sharp prick against her forearm. "It will be over soon," Sabba assured her before returning to her chants. There was a sensation in Azariah, but she trusted Sabba and Shanani that this was expected. Moments passed and she was starting to feel tired and lightheaded. A clap of thunder erupted, and it made her jump, which did something, because she started feeling her warm blood drain down her arm to her fingers. "Wait, stop!" cried Sabba, but she was already sitting up, which sent her mind into a daze. The next thing she knew, she was lying on the ground being hoisted up by the women. They laid her on the cot, and Azariah made out a few words they exchanged.

"She needs to rest."

"We don't have time to wait!"

"We'll kill her if we push her more."

"We may never get this chance again!"

When Mlezi released her, Azariah got up from the cot and ran out of the white canvas tent. Outside, the cool air brought Azariah back to her senses. She held pressure against her wound to try to stop the bleeding as she ran into the savanna. "Azariah, stop! Come back!" Shanani called after her, but she kept running towards the mountains, where the nightly clouds lit up with the rolling thunder. She thought her mind was playing tricks on her, because she noticed a cluster of stars floating about in the blue night. She wiped her eyes with her forearm and saw that the stars came towards her. They were people carrying bronze torches on the backs of flying cats with great bird-like wings.

The cats roared as they flew down and surrounded her.

"I told you we'd find something," said a dark-skinned human male. He had an accent similar to Sabba and

Shanani's.

"What is she?" said a similar looking woman. Her cat was white, unlike the rest, which were all a variety of yellow-gold to reddish-brown.

"She's a witch in a different form," accused a third. "Eh! Do you speak?"

Azariah began to stutter.

"Look! She's hurt," noticed a fourth. His skin wasn't as dark as the others, and he looked much older than them. He was surprisingly skinny and wore a golden cape over his white robe. "What happened to you, girl?"

"She is with me," said Shanani. She came into the light, and the snarling cats parted ways for her. "We strayed too far from camp. Come along, Azariah."

"Where is your camp?" asked the old man. "There isn't a campfire around here for miles. I can sense these things, you know." His eyes gleamed with a fiery haze.

Shanani's eyes widened with realization. "I recognize the Order of Fire, my lord." She gave a quick bow to the old man, who seemed unamused. "We're in a cave not far from around the hill," Shanani insisted. Azariah noticed one of the cats sniffing at the ground before them.

"Something isn't right, yeah?"

The woman on her cat curled her lip. "She's a witch, Lord Zitane."

"No! I'm not a witch!"

"The king doesn't like witches. No witch, no sorcery that isn't the Order of Fire. Which are you? Tell us now and we will spare the white one," said one of the followers.

"She isn't a witch,"Azariah managed to say. "I was attacked by an animal in the grass," she showed them the wound on her arm. "She was helping me." The cat jockeys circled them for a moment.

"Okay, you're good this time, but be careful," said the old man. "There be witches in these hills, and they're most powerful during the —" The man and his cat combusted into flames after a bolt of lightning struck them from the clouds above.

"Ambush! Ambush!" called the woman, and she held up her hands, which ignited with fire. She reached out, and the flames engulfed Shanani, who used herself to shield Azariah from the fire. Shanani fell over, burning to the ground next to Azariah, who cowered as more lightning rained down from all around her. It was Sabba in the distance, chanting and using Mlezi in the form of a rod to channel her witchcraft power. The old man from before — she'd thought him to be dead after the lightning strike — came over and seized Azariah away. He was naked from all his clothing disintegrating and was surprisingly strong for his frame. He carried her off to one of the remaining winged cats as lightning and thunder struck his compatriots. Each bolt of lightning briefly illuminated the darkness of the night as the rest of the cat jockeys swiftly and narrowly avoided the strikes descending upon them. Azariah watched, fighting against her captor's grip as the cats surrounded Sabba and mauled the old witch to death.

Chapter Seventeen

KING THEOD-RAH

THE KING WAS ALONE AT A MIRROR, angrily pulling gray hairs from his chin and head. When his advisors came to him, he startled before regaining his composure. "Forgive me, Your Majesty," one of them said.

"What is the meaning of this?" he said, turning to face them.

"It's Zitane," said one of the others. "He's returned with one of the champions."

The king smiled. "Where is Zitane? Bring him here."

"At once, my king." The advisors left the room, leaving the king with his thoughts. After all that time, fate was finally catching up with him.

Zitane came into the room, bringing his aurora of powerful incense with him. "Your Majesty."

The king greeted him with a hug, which felt inappropriate after the act. "Pardon the expression, Zitane. I fealt the occasion called for it."

"No, you are within your right, my king. The moment does call for high spirits."

"So you found him alone? Did he say anything about the

other two?"

"My acolytes and I found *her* during the last witching hour near the border with the Hara Province. She was accompanied by illegal practitioners: a witch and a sorceress we've been tracking for years."

"Strange, we often don't see those types working together," the king stated.

"My spies tell me that the insurectionists are growing more desperate."

"Wait, did you say, her? Which one is it?"

"The woman of light, Your Majesty. She's the elfess. She hasn't said much, but I did find this on the remains of one of the magicians she was with." Zitane showed the king a vial of blood.

"What's this?"

"The alchemists confirmed that it's blood, and we believe it's hers. What a witch was wanting with elf 's blood is what we're trying to unravel. So far, she's refused to answer any questions. If you permit it, I can force answers out of her."

"No, we need her on our side for now," the king declared. "I will try my hand at getting answers from our guest. Take me to her." The door to the room she was kept in was guarded by four of the Throne's Guard, and a party of handmaids left the room when he entered. Seeing the elf brought the king memories from years past. "You're more beautiful than the descriptions I've heard from the soothsayers." He sat in a chair near the door. "You must be wondering why you were brought here."

"Who the hell are you?" she said to him.

"My name is Theod-Rah. I am the king of these lands." He showed her the vial of blood. "My assistants found this on your friend when they killed her. Care to tell me what you were doing with a pair of dangerous magicians?"

"The only dangerous magicians I saw were your 'assistants' when they used their beasts to tear Sabba apart. It was barbaric."

"You think your Sabba was innocent? Those beasts attack anything that poses a threat to the normal people under my care. That witch and her sister sorceress burned my crops that were meant to feed people, and healed the traitors wanting to put my head on a pike."

"They were good people!"

"They're rebels looking to overthrow me," he said, remaining in his seat. "Without me, this whole continent would fall apart, and you can trust that."

"This realm isn't yours to conquer. You can't just kill anyone who opposes you."

"No, but I will kill anyone who threatens to change the way things are." He smiled. "The status quo keeps the world in line. I'll ask again in a different way. Why did they want your blood?" She didn't answer him. She only stared scornfully with crossed arms. There was something familiar about the way she looked at him with those pale green eyes. "Hav — have we met before?"

She considered him in a way that could only come from royalty. "No."

"Holy fires, you're her."

"You know me? That's impossible. I'm older than your bloodline's eldest grand-sire."

"Do not presume," he said seriously. "You're the elves' prophetic First Born. I saw you on your name day when you were suckling from your mother's breast. She signed a peace treaty with man's armies."

She dropped her arms to her side. "Peace treaty? It was said the sisterhood fought mankind and sealed the new home away so that war could be avoided."

The king snickered. "My dear, you've been misled. If I wanted to, I could rally my allies and march to the Land of Elves and break down the weak magick that is the door of your society. The only reason I won't is because she gave me something very important, something I need your help getting back."

"My help? There is nothing I can do to help you. You're mistaken."

"Haven't you learned by now that you are in no position to be right about anything going on here?" His king's fury was coming out. "I am not mistaken. I've seen several sorcerers who all tell me that you and your companions are fated to reclaim your mother's gift to me."

"My companions? You don't mean —"

"The bard and the blue beast. I've spent months exhausting resources and manpower, but in turning to magick I only found that you three will be the ones to find it. So, where are the other two?"

"I don't know. I left them weeks ago."

The king sat back in his chair, twisting the rings on his fingers and contemplating what to do next. He couldn't go to his usual torture methods if he was to get what he wanted from her. The power was in her hands, and perhaps she knew it. "Well, enjoy the view," he said, standing and gesturing to the barred window. He placed a gold bell on the vanity mirror beside the chair. "Ring this for when you need something. I'll return after you've had some time to process all this." He started to leave.

"Wait." The king smiled, stopped short of turning the door knob. "What was it my mother gave you to end the war?"

"The exchange was for her to grant my father's wish for a long life, and him to grant her all of mankind's armies to put down her other enemy. I'm sure you can surmise who that was."

Chapter Eighteen
VYLASGARDEN

THE HARDER HE PUSHED THEM to find Peddlersroad, the more lost they seemed to be. "I wish we had a map," Riker swore.

Vylasgarden rode up and put a clawed hand on his shoulder. "Take it easy, friend. If we keep going like this, we'll have no water left for us and the horses. It may be best if we go back through the mountains."

"Trust me, Vylasgarden. You wouldn't be saying that if you saw what I did up there. The Thundering Mountains should be our last option. Forgive me. I'm both tired and running out of patience. I should have been home by now, perhaps with Raven, tuning a new lute." Vylasgarden acknowledged him with a nod. "What of you? Will you continue your crusade against the Slayers?"

"I will, eventually," she admitted. "These last few days haven't given me much time to think about it. I worry about Llorva and what's come of her. I worry about what might be swimming in your mind." They were in the sand now, losing track of the savanna grasses while keeping the mountain range to their right.

"What do you mean?"

"Have you fully taken a life before?"

"I would hardly call what happened to Jared and Gideon murder," he stated irritably, "but I would be lying if I said it didn't bother me. These last few hours, Jared's screams have been echoing in my mind. I know the moon and its wraiths took him."

"It would haunt anyone, Riker. Give it time."

With no sleep from the previous night, Vylasgarden could barely keep her eyes open. The setting sun was meeting the horizon in the orange sky, and the day was still hot. "Riding by day was a mistake," Riker huffed. "We may have to keep riding through the night so we can rest tomorrow." He was sweating faster than he was drinking water. He started to say something else, but Vylasgarden became distracted by a mirage in the sky. It was the silhouette of a box carried by some great flying things.

"Riker, do you see it?"

"What is that?"

"I don't know." Vylasgarden dug her heels in her horse and took off ahead of Riker.

"Vylasgarden, wait!" She ignored him, chasing after the silhouette in the sky, but it started to disappear behind the ever-present mirage. There was no chance of catching up with it. Surely it was headed toward the famous Shining City she'd heard of many times before. Without wings, they would surly die if they continued after it.

"No, no, no. Come back," she pleaded. Riker's horse was fast approaching when the silhouette finally vanished. All at once, Vylasgarden grew frustrated and she roared loudly. Louder than she ever had before, to her surprise, as if she were twice her own size. A bolt of lightning struck the sand, closely followed by ground-shaking thunder. The horses brayed fearfully, and Vylasgarden struggled to console hers.

"Did you do that?" They went over to where the lightning had struck the ground. In its place was a seven-foot semi-arch of fused sand. "Wow, Vylasgarden! I didn't know you had that in you."

"Neither did I," she said, staring at the structure. "If they'd lived to see it, my clan wouldn't have believed it either."

"Looks like it did the trick," he said, pointing up at the sky. The silhouette was now coming towards them. "Let's hope they're friendly."

"We've had worse odds," she replied, dismounting her horse. The sun was setting, casting the sky orange like molten steel as the flying creatures and their box came swooping down on them. The creatures in chains were great white bulls. They were no smaller than sixteen feet from head to ground and possessed beautiful copper wings and horns. Their riders were Pryden men dressed in robes as white as the bulls. They had golden capes upon their shoulders and amber eyes. They started talking to each other in an unfamiliar language while observing Riker and Vylasgarden.

"Do you speak Common?" one eventually asked them.

"Yes," Vylasgarden and Riker said together. One dismounted his bull and looked at them for a long while before saying something to his companion. The other man dismounted and started opening the box from his side. Vylasgarden's heart started to pound in her chest. Perhaps it was a mistake trying to get their attention. The box creaked open, and the man pulled at a chain. From the box came another human man that looked a lot like Kruzco, only his beard and hair were singed and he was beaten and gagged. "That's Kruzco!" exclaimed Riker. He dismounted his horse and ran to him while Vylasgarden maintained eye contact with Kruzco's captors. She was tired, but she had enough fight in her to take on a few more men.

Riker removed the gag from Kruzco's mouth. "What did they do to you?"

"Thank fate, they found you," the wizard said. "I was sure to be dead soon."

"Kruzco, what happened?"

"These fire sorcerers are looking for you. Something about a king needing your help."

"I don't understand. You're not making sense."

"They bested me and started asking me questions about other magicians. Forgive me, Riker, they would have killed me. When I mentioned that I knew a bard that could bring a mountain down with a flute, they became curious and started speaking their damned sorcery speak."

"Kruzco, how could they have defeated you? I've seen what you can do."

"Wizards and sorcerers are rivals, boy. We know each other's secrets. They got the jump on me and gaged me before I could utter a spell. Without my mouth, I'm as useless as any other old man."

Riker felt Kruzco's singed hair and offered him water before walking up to one of the men. "What is all this about a king?"

"You and your monster are coming with us," the sorcerer said in his funny accent.

"The hell we are!" Vylasgarden growled.

"You come with us or your wizard friend dies. It is the law of the land. The king may spare the deviant if you accompany him," said the other one.

Riker looked over at Vylasgarden. She gave him a shrug. They stood no chance fighting sorcerers in the state they were in, especially since Riker had no instrument to conjure his own magick and she doubted she could summon lightning again effectively. "Why does the king want us?" Riker asked next.

"That is not for us to know. We only follow orders. All your questions will be answered when you meet His

Majesty, Theod-Rah."

"Theod-Rah?"

"This cannot be a coincidence," Vylasgarden replied.

"And we don't have a choice." Riker went to retrieve his steed. "If he wants to see us then he'll pay our price."

Vylasgarden shook her head. "I don't follow."

"A man this powerful has connections I'm sure can get you back on the Dragon Slayer's trail, and depending on what he wants, I can leverage some gold for my travels."

"Always the schemer, I see."

He smiled mischievously. "We'll go with you," he said to the sorcerers, "on the condition that the wizard remains unharmed."

"Not another hair will burn by our hands," swore one of them. The other laughed to himself. It took another two days for them to arrive at their destination. Riker suspected the box they were carried in was meant for livestock because the inside smelled of manure. It provided protection from the sun, but they drank the rest of their water the day after the bulls carried them away. Through the air holes, all Vylasgarden could see was miles and miles of sand dunes until they arrived at an island in the sea on sand. It was a kingdom made of sandstone and gold inside a lush green oasis.

When the box opened, Riker and Kruzco were pushed out, but some strong men with catchpoles tried noosing

Vylasgarden's neck and arms. Something snapped inside her. Perhaps it was the thirst or tiredness, but she raged when they pulled her out in the sun.

"How dare you!" she roared, and they pulled her down to the ground, where she struggled to stand up.

"Stop!" Riker called. One of them got close with his noose to beat her with a club in his other hand. Vylasgarden scratched his face with her claws, and the man screamed, dropping the tools.

"Someone get in there and control that beast!" said a man standing off to the side. He wore a similar robe to the sorcerers but looked much older than them. As more came up to restrain her, Vylasgarden reared her head and roared once more, and a clap of thunder followed and the sky turning gray. A heavy rain started coming down. They all stopped dropping their ropes and poles to hold their hands out to the water.

"Rain," they all echoed. "It's been so long…"

The older sorcerer came up to Vylasgarden. His eyes were fiery orange with a hint of a glow. "Behave yourself, monster. Otherwise, you will regret it." Vylasgarden groaned and ripped the ropes off herself as the sorcerer walked to the steps of a palace before them. Riker and Kruzco ran up to her while their keepers were distracted with the rest awed by the rain. "This way, if you please. The king is not a patient man."

Chapter Nineteen

AZARIAH

AS THE KING HAD SAID, the bathhouse was vacant. He mentioned that there was a surprise for her inside, which made Azariah's skin crawl. She'd learned in her time imprisoned in his palace that to refuse him was futile. Fortunately, he never wanted anything more than for her to go places. She found a changing room and saw that a pile of soaps and a basket of roses were waiting for her. *How did they…? Those mind-prodding sorcerers…*

She realized then that her secrets (what few were left) were no longer hers. She undressed and caught a glimpse of herself in a mirror as she wrapped herself in a towel. The alfr in the reflection had scars and bruises across her body. She was amused that she was not fazed by how she looked. As she walked down the hallway with a fistful of plum-scented soaps and the basket of rose petals, she heard singing. She found a new door where the singing was coming from and opened it. Steam swept through the threshold, and the voice became familiar:

…I see no rescuer in the sea's storm
I was finding my own way but I was torn

The sirens were calling, but I heard the sheep at home,
bawling

My mind was going like before I was born.

It was Riker who was singing. He was alone on the far side of the room full of baths, his naked back facing her as he sang:

The rapids were churning and I had no place to look,

But I maintained slow and still like a forest brook.

"Ahem!"

"Llorva, is that you?"

"Don't turn around. I'm behind you," she said, approaching. He said nothing as she spread the petals in her own bath behind him. She submerged herself, and the water gradually warmed her aches away as she sank down to her neck. She undid her braid, allowing her silky silver hair in the water, and gave a pleasant sigh. "So, how are you?"

"Alive," he answered. She was disappointed by the lack of enthusiasm in his voice. "We have had a few close calls since you left. I don't think either of us thought we would have met again like this."

Azariah brought her fingers to her lips. He sounded melancholy. "You're not wrong about that. Listen, about me leaving —"

"You don't need to say anything. You were probably right to have left; Jared's group are all dead except for Perry. We left the boy in a village in the mountains."

"What happened to them?"

It took him a while to answer. "Wraiths from the full moon took them. They died saving our lives. I was told you arrived a few days before the full moon."

Azariah frowned. "Yes, I don't know what you know, but the three of us reuniting here was no accident."

"Mm-hmm. I suspected as much."

"Is Vylasgarden okay?"

"She is," he said, somber. "They treated her like a wild animal when we came here. They won't even let her go any farther than the palace courtyard."

"They don't know her as we do," she said to him, "and hopefully we won't have to stay here for long. The king thinks we're connected to some kind of magick object that was stolen from him." An awkward silence took hold of them. Her thoughts swam in her mind as she tried to figure out what to say next and water dripped somewhere in the distance. She debated with herself whether she should tell him about Sabba and Shanani but settled on something more important to share. "Hey, look at me." They both turned and faced each other. He looked skinnier than before, and his hair was longer too. "There's something else I need to tell you. My name isn't Llorva; it's Azariah. I'm the princess of Foss Sergens." He stared at her for a moment.

"It all makes sense now." He turned back around and sank into his bath.

"Say something, Riker."

"What needs to be said? I understand why you lied."

"The veil of my mother's lies became too thin. I realized what my mother was teaching me about our relationship with the outside world was all a lie. I hoped that finding the huldar in the north would lead to some kind of truth."

"Azariah."

"Yes?"

"No, I was just trying it out." He chuckled, which made her feel better.

"That's right. Get used to it."

"You know Vylasgarden will not take this news well."

"Let's not keep her and our host waiting. I have a feeling we're not going to like what he has to say."

The four of them met at a long table overlooking the oasis. Azariah reunited with Vylasgarden and met the wizard named Kruzco, who greeted her with a kiss on the hand. "I've heard good things," he said to her.

"I wish I could say the same," she replied with a forced smile. Azariah didn't like the idea of a new member to their trio. They ate and drank for hours into the night, and when the king finally made his presence known, the merriment ceased.

"I'm pleased to see you've made yourself at home," he said. "I think it's time I show you all why you are here." Theod-Rah personally escorted the party through his halls with the royal guard on either side. "For me to explain and for you to understand what happened, we must go som where to avoid prying ears," he said, stopping in front of an unassuming wall. A servant handed him an oil lamp, and two of the guards pushed against the wall, revealing a secret passage. The king led them all down spiraling stairs that took them underneath the palace. At the base of the stairs was a wide hall illuminated by a line of braziers at the center. On either end was a row of additional guards standing in wait. Azariah assumed they all were ready to defend what was at the opposite end of the hall: a chamber of riches with a decadent fountain at its center.

The guards bowed as the king and the party passed by. Each said "Your Majesty," as their ruler strolled past them with the party and the royal guard following behind. Right above them, to Azariah's shock, was a mounted dragon's head on the archway opposite the chamber entrance. Vylasgarden made a concerning noise, and Azariah went over to console her friend. Staring at the head, Azariah realized that it was the first time she had seen a dragon in real life (or what was left of one). Its sharp rows of teeth were as large as daggers.

"What is this place?" Kruzco asked. "I sense magick like

no other."

"Right you are, wizard. This is my personal vault," Theod-Rah replied as if impressed with himself. "A long time ago, Pryden and much of the world was underwater," the king started as he welcomed the party to gather around the fountain. There was a pedestal in the fountain with a triangular decanter positioned on top of it from which a steady stream of water flowed. "Some million years later, the oceans receded and the age of dragons and men started. Before the Dragon Wars, my nomadic ancestors traversed this desert, believing their old gods were leading them to new fertile lands, and legend says a lot of them died of thirst, but they never gave up on what they believed was the fate of the gods. They all would have perished if not for what my forefather found digging in the sand." He gestured to the decanter, which was still pouring an endless stream of water from its finite space. "The decanter was found in the dead skull of a ginormous sea beast. When he found it, the rest praised their gods, but my forefather in all his wisdom made them praise him for water."

"Who's to say the gods didn't lead your forefather to the Decanter of Endless Water?" Riker interrupted.

"I say it ultimately doesn't matter. To the people of this province, my family are gods incarnate," the king answered, visibly annoyed. "The water brought the oasis, and while the rest of mankind was fighting dragons, my forefathers were conquering the rest of Pryden." He walked over to another, more elaborate pedestal made of bronze, though it had nothing featured. "The reason you are here is because you three are prophesied to find the missing second wonder discovered by my father, a relic from the elves called the Phoenix Flame."

Azariah's heart stopped. *"Phoenix Flame?"*

The king twisted a smile as if expecting Azariah's reaction. "I'm not surprised that you know of it. Where the decanter gave life to my kingdom, the Phoenix Flame gave me everlasting life, but something or someone stole it from me not long ago. I want it back, and somehow you three are the only ones capable of finding it."

"Us?" uttered Vylasgarden. Her booming voice bounced off the walls. "We can't possibly be who you're looking for. We hardly know each other, let alone anything about your stolen magick."

"Azariah seems familiar," Riker pointed out.

"I'm familiar with the birds," she said innocently. "We have one in Foss Sergens. Apparently, my mother gave one of the feathers to the king's father before the end of the civil war."

"King's father?" questioned the wizard. "But that was over two hundred years ago."

"Quite the thinker, aren't you, wizard?" the king interjected. "I'm sure you can figure out why getting the feather back is important to me, which is why, since the three of you are destined to find it, I'm prepared to offer you a deal in exchange for its return."

"What did you have in mind?" Riker asked.

"A hundred gold coins to each of you."

Vylasgarden stepped forward and said, "We also want your knowledge on the Dragon Slayers' organization."

"What? What would you want with the Dragon Slayers?"

"They massacred my people," Vylasgarden answered. "Keep my share of the gold. I just want a name and location."

The king grinned. "I can certainly do that. When you've done your job, it does not matter to me what becomes of you afterward. If it's the Slayers you want, then you'll have them. Now I'd like to have everyone but the princess leave this room," he commanded. The guards left, but Riker, Vylasgarden, and Kruzco lingered. "Don't have me ask again," he said threateningly to them. Azariah gave them a slow nod, and they all reluctantly went out into the hall. The king approached her closely. "You're probably wondering a lot of things right now, so as a show of good faith, I'll tell you. My people killed your people and yours killed a lot of humans, that's history, and both our worlds are better off separated if time tells us anything. What matters right now is that you help get my father's souvenir from the war back to me." Azariah's face flushed. "In truth, that feather was the only thing that saved the rest of your people. Bring me the feather and I won't need to revisit your former home."

"I'll have it."

"Good. I'm patient enough," he replied, "but I'm also running out of time. The longer you make me wait, the more desperate I will become. Do keep that in mind." He started to walk away and join the rest of the party in the hall. Azariah was left there with panic building in her chest, but she composed herself, relying on the behavior she'd learned to exude growing up and followed the king out of the chamber.

Later that night, Azariah grew restless and paced back and forth in her assigned room. Earlier she'd insisted that Vylasgarden stays with her, which Theod-Rah reluctantly obliged. She didn't care for his anger and she didn't want to care for the demands he made of her, but her mind was racing with all the implied reasons she should care. Vylasgarden observed her from the window. "You have to calm down," she urged her. Vylasgarden sat on the floor with crossed legs. "Come meditate with me?"

"Meditate? What good would that do?"

"I learned it at the monastery after escaping the Dragon Slayers in Froisia. The humans there said it helps calm and focus the mind. Try it with me." Realizing she was biting her lip, Azariah begrudgingly joined Vylasgarden on the floor. She instructed her to breathe deeply and try thinking of nothing.

"Vylasgarden, that is impossible."

"Shh! No talking! Only breathing!" she growled at her lightly. Azariah remained quiet, but the intrusive thoughts kept emerging. "How do you feel?" she asked after a minute or two.

"Better," Azariah admitted. "Thank you."

"You're welcome. Now, what's got you this worked up?"

She considered what to say and found what was bothering her the most. "He threatened to attack my home if we don't succeed in finding the Phoenix Flame."

"Princess —"

"Do not call me that," Azariah interrupted and got up from the floor.

"Azariah," Vylasgarden started again. "Humans like him only make threats like that because he doesn't feel he is in control. This is ultimately a good thing because he has something to lose."

"His loss could mean the end of what's left of the alfar, and it's up to me to get between it all."

"First of all, you have me, Riker, and now Kruzco to do this with you.

We're all in this together."

Azariah felt tears swelling in her eyes. "I don't deserve you," she whispered in a quaking voice. "I left you. Lied to you about my name. Why aren't you angry with me?"

"Because I understand, Azariah."

She waited for Vylasgarden to continue, but that was all she said. "I wish I could give you your people back. I don't know anyone who suffered more than you."

Vylasgarden stood and came to her. She seemed more giant than ever before. "Just promise me one thing."

"Yes?"

"For as long as we will know each other, our relationship will be an honest one."

"Yes, of course. I just —"

"I understand why you lied, and I do not blame you for distrusting us at first, but now more than ever, we need to rely on one another to survive what comes next. Can you do that?" Azariah jumped up and threw her arms over Vylasgarden's broad shoulders and, after a moment, felt Vylasgarden's powerful arms gently surround her. She patted Azariah on the back. During the quiet moment, Azariah noticed talking outside their door.

"Do you hear that?"

"I do." It was their guards addressing someone in the hall. Paranoia began to settle in her again as Azariah perked her hearing and put her head quietly against the door. She could hear someone informing the two guards that Riker and the wizard had gone missing.

"What is it?" Vylasgarden whispered.

"It's Riker," Azariah whispered back. "He left us."

"No, no. It's something else. Why would the king keep

us separated?"

"Do you think he's doing something to them?"

"Only one way to find out." Vylasgarden picked up a chair and blocked the doorknob with it. From across the room, she charged at the barred window — breaking the glass and pushing the bars free from the sandstone. "Do you want to go after them?"

Azariah took her clawed hand and replied with haste, "Yes."

Chapter Twenty

RIKER

RIKER AND KRUZCO SNUCK through the palace halls. They had just escaped their room after Riker convinced the guards to fetch him an instrument native to Pryden, claiming that he'd impress them with his skills or bore them both to sleep. When they brought him a stringed instrument, Riker played them a quick magick lullaby, and the guards fell into a slumber. "I guess I was wrong," he said mischievously.

"I've never seen such a spell in action," Kruzco remarked, impressed. It made Riker proud of his ability.

"I can't say you'd be able to do it," he replied, keeping an eye out for more guards. "It's more or less all in my fingers."

"What exactly is the plan here, Riker?"

"We're going to see this golden city for ourselves and hopefully find you a conduit for your magick. I don't know, I do these things before the plan is fully realized." They found a window on the first floor and used it to make their escape.

"Maybe we can make it back in time before they notice we left." They found themselves in a garden with great big hedges in the shapes of animals towering over them. Across the way was a fifteen-foot wall that had guards patrolling the top. They quietly followed a guard up some stairs and slid down the slope that made up the wall's other side.

"Easier getting out than getting back in, I'm sure."

"Best to leave that problem to the future, my friend. We are out of that prison for the time being!" Riker spread his arms and did a twirl. The streets were full of life. Performers belched fire tricks and a man played his drums while a pair of scantily-clad women dressed in reds danced provocatively for onlookers. The great bonfire in front of them stretched the dancers' shadows up against the palace wall.

"What are we looking for, Riker?"

"I'm not sure," he replied. "I'll know it when I see it." He noticed people staring and pointing at him and realized how he was going to stick out of the crowd. "First thing first, I need a disguise." He found a woman with a scarf over her hair and thought it would do nicely. "Get ready to run."

Kruzco jolted. "Wait, huh?" Riker positioned himself on the side of the woman and tapped her on the opposite shoulder. Once she was distracted, he freed her long, lustrous hair from its covering and started running away with it.

"Stop! Thief!" screamed the woman.

Kruzco swore. "Oh, now you did it!"

"Come on!" They found an alley and ran through it but saw some city guards coming in the opposite direction. "Uh oh!" He looked around and found an open window just out of reach. "Quick, give me a boost!" Kruzco knelt against the wall, held out his hands for Riker's foot, and lifted him. He overshot the window, and Riker caught the ledge by his feet. Arms swinging for balance, he quickly slipped inside and poked his head and arm out for Kruzco. "Give me your hand!" Kruzco jumped up and nearly pulled Riker back out. The wizard was heavier than he looked.

"How is it that you weigh this much?"

Kruzco huffed. "You watch your mouth!" The guards caught up to them, and Kruzco swung on Riker's arm and used the momentum to kick them back. "Pull me up!" Riker reached down with his other arm and caught the wizard by the collar. "Heave-ho!" With his feet against the wall, Riker slowly lifted the wizard into the window as the guards were recovering from Kruzco's kick. Riker slammed the window closed on one of their fingers as he tried climbing in after them. "You don't think they saw our faces, do you?"

"Uh." Riker wrapped his prize across his nose and mouth. "Let's not worry about it." They found an exit somewhere on the other side and watched for guards before stepping out. "Quick, there's something going on over here." He led them to another crowded area on an open square, where more of those winged bulls stood around, chained to decorative living wagons and boxes similar to the one they came in. Grand braziers and bonfires lit up the event with pillars of colorful tribal masks and banners that enlightened the amusement of the people. It wasn't until Riker heard music that he slowed to a stop.

"What's the matter?" Kruzco asked.

"I know that music…" He searched around and followed the music until the smell of food grabbed him. "Do you smell that?" It reminded him of the food back in Bloowood. They were smells he hadn't known since he'd left home. Riker smiled. "I can't believe it." He pushed through the crowd passing the puppet show about the founding of the elves, and he followed the music past the archers demonstrating their skills to an audience enjoying meals and drinks straight from his hometown. The music was coming from a tent, and inside elves and half-elves danced to the music of the orchestra performing in the back. That was where he saw her playing on the harp: Raven Ralohana, the woman he loved. His hands were shaking as he watched her. Seeing her, it was like time hadn't passed between them. Her hair was still as black as her namesake, and she still had the aura of friendliness that had drawn him in so many years ago.

Kruzco shook his shoulder. "Are you all right? You look like you've seen a ghost."

"Yeah, I, uh, just saw someone."

Kruzco followed his gaze. "Oh! I see." They waited

there, watching the entire show, and Kruzco didn't complain. He got comfortable and somehow got his hands on some food and a mug of mead. "What's the plan?" he said with a mouthful of pheasant.

"I'm going to go talk to her." Once the final dance was over and the orchestra concluded the finale, the tent erupted in applause. "Best we get out of the way of the crowd," he said, and Kruzco agreed. They went off to the side so that Raven stayed within view as the musicians started packing their instruments. "Kruzco, I think it would be best if —"

"Say no more, lad. I'll be close by."

"We need a signal."

"How about I crow like a rooster?"

"Umm, what else you got?"

"Hmm, I can do a really good vampire bat hiss."

"Wouldn't that just sound like a snake?"

"No, no. It's all in the back of the throat. Here, listen —" Riker placed a hand on Kruzco's shoulder.

"I'll take your word for it. Wish me luck."

"Good luck, lad." Riker followed the last musician behind the tent where they all were turning in for the night at their parked living spaces. He saw Raven speaking with a group of other half-elves. Were they her friends? Hopefully, none of them was a romantic rival. He waited for their conversation to end and followed her all the way to a wagon, where she struggled to carry her harp up the steps.

He rushed up and said, "Allow me."

"Thank you," she said, not looking at him. She seemed distracted by her exhaustion. They got it up to the doorframe, but the top kept knocking against the harp. "The damned thing won't go in this way. We have to turn —" She suddenly dropped the harp, and the thing fell over with a loud crash.

"Raven, are you all right?" someone said, running up to the scene. Her eyes were locked on Riker.

"Yes, everything is alright," she said before shaking her head, and the three of them stood the harp up. "Come in. Please," she said to Riker and held the door for him. Inside, the wagon looked like the room she'd kept back in Bloowood all those years ago. "How did you find me?"

"I'm still asking that question myself," he replied cautiously. She wasn't as enthusiastic as he had been expecting. "I know this is a lot to take in."

She didn't reply, only stared at him for a moment before sitting down on the window seat. "Sit with me." She reached out her hand and took his. Her fingers were just as calloused as his from playing strings in years past. "You've gotten darker."

"I've spent this time in the Southern Seas." He didn't know what to say next. Before, he had it all rehearsed, but seeing her there unexpectedly made his mind go blank. "I missed you, Raven."

She smiled at him. A good sign. "Oh, Barron." She was the only one who called him by his first name. "So much has changed since you last saw me."

"Is there someone else?" He regretted speaking the words as he said them.

She grinned. "No. I've not loved again since…"

"I should have never left."

"No, you were discovering yourself, remember? We agreed not to hold each other back from our dreams."

"I never found mine," he admitted. "I thought of you constantly. It's why I'm here. You wouldn't believe what I've been through to be right here." She patted him on the hand, and he sensed something wasn't right. "What's wrong?"

She leaned in and kissed him. Riker's eyes rolled to the back of his head as their lips locked. *Intoxicating,* he thought. It was better than he'd dreamt. "I didn't think I would ever see you again," Raven told him, still holding his body.

"I'm here now, Raven." An intrusive thought reminded him of his agreement with Theod-Rah. "But unfortunately, our reunion must be short."

The words seemed to wound her. "Why?"

"It's hard to explain but —" He was interrupted by awkward hissing noises outside. He looked out the window and saw a firelight approaching. He turned back to her.

"I'm in business with the king."

"What?"

A hard knock came at the door, and Riker went to open it. Outside were over a dozen guards on horseback surrounding the wagon. Leading them upon a black steed with golden shoes and bridle was King Theod-Rah. He was smiling, wearing a crown and a dark cape. "If you wanted the pleasures of a woman, all you had to do was ask." His smile turned to an angry frown, and some guards brought out Azariah, Kruzco, and Vylasgarden in chains. "You didn't have to assault my guards and then rampage through my city unsupervised."

"This doesn't involve them, Your Majesty. It isn't what it seems," Riker told him.

"Isn't it?" the king refuted. "I sure hope it is. Otherwise, it would have been a waste as far as I'm concerned." He snapped his fingers, and the guards parted ways for a pair of bulls pulling a box forward.

Something inside roared and shook the box. "What is that?" Riker asked, trying to stay calm.

"Who's in there with you?"

Riker hesitated.

"Open it!" Some guards moved the bulls out of the way, and another pair pushed in the sliding lock. "Last chance."

Riker threw up his hand. "Okay!" Raven came out timidly.

"Oh, how charming," the king said, mewing. "What's your name, girl?"

Riker stepped in front of her. "You don't need to know her name."

"You don't give the orders here!" Theod-Rah shouted.

Raven shrilled her own name.

"What are you to him, Raven, dear?" She hesitated. "Speak while I'm still in a good mood!"

"We're lovers," she said. Riker felt a bit of relief at that admission.

The king nodded slowly and then snapped his fingers again, and the guards pulled the box door open, unleashing a monstrosity that jumped out at them. It was a ferocious lion with a pair of leathery wings and a long tail barbed with spines on the end. Its jaw overextended, revealing additional rows of teeth that chomped at Raven and Riker. It was inches away from them, but the chain around its neck prevented it from getting closer. "Let me make myself very clear, Barron Von Riker," started the king. "You and your friends may think you are in control, but I am here to remind you that you are gravely mistaken. Do you hear me?"

"Yes! I hear you!"

The monster kept chomping and swiping its claws at them. "The next time you undermine me, I will force you to watch my maneater tear your love apart, and I will make sure he is fed so that he eats slowly like a predator playing with its meal." Spit flew as he spoke. "Do you understand me, you mutt?"

"I understand." The king snapped his fingers again, and his guards used wheels on either side of the box to pull the monster back inside by the chain. Its oddly human eyes stayed on Riker as it was pulled back into the dark box. "I will work for you, but you have to let her go."

The king laughed. "I don't need to keep her to make my threats real, boy. There is no place out of my reach. Now say your goodbyes before I change my mind."

Riker turned to Raven and held her face in his hands. She was trembling. "I will find you again. Do you hear me? When I'm done, I will find you and buy you that home in the Bloowood we talked about years ago." Raven started to cry. "Say you'll marry me," he said desperately.

"What?"

"Marry me," he said again, more softly. "I want to be your everything and you mine. May our love be ever tangled in each other's lives."

"I — I can't."

A pair of guards came for him. "It's okay," he said. "You'll see.

Everything will be fine." They dragged him away from her and put him in chains with the others. "Everything will be fine." They were escorted back to the palace and given their own individual rooms without a window. Despite everything that had happened the night before, Riker managed to sleep well in his assigned bed. The next day, he woke to the sound of a knock at the door.

He answered it, and a team of people flooded into the room. "Today is the day!" They all cheered, and a pair of women dressed him in a shirt and a fine black leather jerkin and bracers. The look was completed with a pair of fingerless gloves.

"Black isn't really my color," he started to say, but a third woman came up and force-fed him food and wine as the other two put on his fine black boots. He was getting a shave when a table with musical instruments was laid before him. A man waited patiently for him to choose as the barber finished his hair. "He's letting me have these?" Riker asked.

"Choose two," the man said in a deep voice. Riker looked at his options and noticed many instruments were from Southaven. He would have chosen a lute, but there wasn't one present. He went with a cow horn with five finger holes and a dark wood square lyre. "Excellent choice," said the man though Riker felt he'd say that to anything Riker would have chosen. "Your weapons will be waiting for you outside after His Majesty's debriefing." Riker was taken to the back of the palace, where the gardens seemed to stretch all the way around. There was always a guard within five feet of him, and he didn't see any of his friends until he reached the stables, where men rode horses on a dirt track behind it in the morning sun. Vylasgarden hugged him when she saw him. He noticed she was bruised all over when he got a good look at her.

"What did they do to you?" Azariah said when she came around the corner with her own guards. She was dressed in a brown leather studded corset, green leggings to match her eyes, and knee-high boots with holsters on the side to hold a pair of concealed daggers. She seemingly ignored Riker, not acknowledging his presence and looking Vylasgarden over. Vylasgarden didn't seem to have gotten anything more than a beating. Courtesy of the king's men. A man who referred to himself as the royal treasurer came to them and handed Azariah a purse of coins. "What's this for?" she asked skeptically.

"His Majesty wishes for the expedition to go well and has entrusted you, Your Highness, with the funds. He also wanted me to remind each of you of your gold rewards as good faith, in light of last night's unpleasantry."

"Is that what he's calling it?" Riker asked angrily.

"Let it go, Riker," Vylasgarden insisted.

"No," Azariah said. "He had my friends afraid and brutalized. I shall have a word with the king before we depart."

"I'm afraid that won't be possible," the treasurer said with a pained smile. "He is away handling affairs regarding the rebellion elsewhere in Pryden, but he did want me to inform you all that he is watching and trusts you will fulfill your destinies."

"Where is the wizard?" Riker asked seriously.

"He awaits along with your weapons, magick bard." The treasurer pointed, and across the field was a pair of winged bulls chained to a carrier box with Kruzco riding horseback in front of it. He wore a tight hair bun and a well-fitted cloak with one of his goat pelts shawled over the shoulders. His face looked as well-groomed as Riker, though his beard was still intact.

"They tried cutting my beard," he roared to them as they approached.

Happy to see him, Riker shook Kruzco's hand. "What? Don't they know your power comes from your beard?" he half-heartedly jested.

"I'd gladly trade my beard if it meant keeping this." Kruzco showed them a beautiful chromatic crystal wand he was hiding in his sleeve. "Amazing, isn't it? A wand of this quality is a catch-all for spells. I won't need a talisman, ingredients, or time crystals. It's all here in this wand."

"Truly outstanding," Riker said, failing to seem amazed.

"How are you doing?" Kruzco asked him.

"I'm ready to get this over with," he replied somberly. Some servants brought over additional horses for Riker, Azariah, and Vylasgarden to match Kruzco's.

"These are the swiftest steeds you'll ever ride," said the treasurer.

Riker petted his horse, which was complete with a saddle and bridle. The horses were taller than average by the legs and had long, arching necks, small heads, and high tail carriages. "They're beautiful," Azariah remarked. More servants brought over the rest of their belongings. Everything was present and presumably cleaned; Riker even noticed that the rapier Kruzco gifted him had been reforged. Gone were the rusty stains that had given it age and personality.

With the horses put in the carrier and their supplies double-checked, Riker went to talk to the treasurer for the final time. "We keep being told that we're meant to find this phoenix feather, but none of us has seen it, let alone knows where to look for it."

"The lamassu riders will drop you off where His Majesty's private trackers last made contact with a carrier," informed the treasurer. "Lucky for you elves, it was addressed near the border with Southaven." He handed Azariah a small scroll. "It was received a week ago. Details inside should point you in the direction of your destiny."

Kruzco scoffed. "Destiny and fate are the products a sorcerer peddles to cheat poor folks out of what little they have."

"Spoken like a true wizard," the treasurer mocked. "You have your orders. Best be on your way. His Majesty is not a patient man."

PART THREE

The Land of the Elves

Chapter Twenty-one
VYLASGARDEN

IT TOOK A WEEK OF MISERABLE TRAVEL for the bulls to reach the province border. They had to land twice after coming far from the desert, and the entire time it was relatively quiet among the party. Each seemingly in their own thoughts. They were dropped off at the location in the message the trackers had sent the king. "Do you think we'll run into them?" Vylasgarden asked.

"We wouldn't know if we did," Kruzco answered. The two of them were waiting outside while Azariah and Riker went inside the hold of the noble whose bird had sent the trackers' message to the Shining City.

"He says they left a day later and headed south to cross the border in the nearby woods," said Azariah. She had assumed leadership ever since they'd landed. "He said they were checking on a lead about a fisherman seeing a ghost figure with a burning feather hanging around a ruin on the river in the woods."

"That was more than a week ago," Kruzco complained. "They could be far gone by now."

"I'm sorry, I don't recall why you're still here," Azariah argued. "Theod-Rah and his followers never mentioned you in their prophecy."

Kruzco chuckled a bit. "Don't get all upset, princess. Wizards and witches are cloaked from a sorcerer's divination. I hate to disappoint you, but you're stuck with me because you need me." Azariah scoffed dismissively.

"He's right," argued Riker. "His power is unmatched by any of us. We don't know what we're up against and need all the help we can get." Riker sounded so broken ever since he was humiliated by the human king. Vylasgarden wanted to ask about Raven but felt it might be too painful for him.

"Fine," Azariah said fustratingly. "We'll follow the lead and hopefully find something along the way." When they came off the main road and into the forest marked on the map, storm clouds were forming above. Vylasgarden was leading on the path and took note of the sudden stale scent in the air. There were a lot of fallen trees and dead wood in the area. It was nearly dusk, and they came across plenty of desolate homes overtaken by the brush.

"We should pick one of these for camp soon," Vylasgarden announced.

"We can't be too far from the river. Has anyone else noticed there aren't any animals here?" Azariah mentioned.

"Yeah, the quiet is making me uneasy. I'm not sure what to make of it," concluded Riker. "Kruzco?"

"I sense no magick at work. None that I can detect anyway."

The group persisted, and eventually, they came across the sound of rushing water. "The river!" Azariah cried. "We're close!" She galloped ahead of them, and when they caught up to her, she was looking over a slope to a river and found that there were isles in the middle with a stone building on one of them.

"Can it be?"

"This has to be it," Azariah affirmed. The structure cast a large shadow over the water and was marked on the outside with elf-like effigies that guarded an entrance.

"You think someone is home?" said Kruzco.

"I hope not..." Riker said.

Azariah seemed to shake her caution and started moving toward the river. "Only one way to find out," she said, being the first to dismount and tie her horse to a tree.

Vylasgarden considered the situation. "Perhaps we should go in fresh, Azariah."

"We shouldn't wait. Whoever has the Phoenix Flame can't be far.

They may be ahead, and I'd rather close the gap as soon as possible." She went to the water in a hurry and was the first to wade into the chill. Layers of ice on the surface broke apart as they all got closer to the isle. They immediately noticed that something or someone had smashed the pair of iron doors off the hinges. Together they quietly flanked the entrance as light rain started;

Vylasgarden and Azariah were on the left and Riker and Kruzco were on the right. They slowly stepped inside. An eroded hole in the ceiling brought light in, but it was the burning torch on the floor that brought attention to the two corpses lying in front of the entry to an underground. The corpses were humans dressed in leather and animal skins. They were males, perhaps from the oasis.

"These could be Theod-Rah's trackers," said Kruzco, kneeling over them. He examined the wound in one of the necks and then turned the other over, revealing a slash in his upper inner thigh. "They bled out recently."

"Which means the killer may still be here," Riker said.

"Probably with the Phoenix Flame." Vylasgarden looked down into the dark hole that gave a chilling, howling wind from underneath. "Who should go first?"

"I'll go," said Azariah.

"No, let me," insisted Riker.

"It should be me," argued Vylasgarden, and they all looked at Kruzco.

It took him a moment to notice their eyes on him, and he shook his beard. "I don't want to go first," he answered.

Vylasgarden took up the burning torch on the ground. "I will go." She dropped the torch in the hole, and it fell several feet to a stone floor. She followed in after it and surveyed the surrounding dark, feeling the gentle gust blow harder and noticing the smell of mildew in its wake. She caught each of them as they hopped down to join her, and with torches in hand, they followed her deeper into the catacomb. It became a maze with recesses in the walls where they found innumerable urns sitting in the pockets. Vylasgarden noticed that Azariah was falling behind looking at the urns. "Azariah," Vylasgarden called in a whisper. Azariah didn't seem to hear her, but Riker and Kruzco were now looking back at her.

They came up behind Azariah, who was holding an urn in her hand and reading the elf language inscribed on it. "What is it?" asked Riker.

Azariah was transfixed, not taking her eyes off the urn. "I — I think these are all the male alfar. This is what happened to them after the wars."

"If that were true, then that means the elves came this far from Foss Sergens," Kruzco claimed.

"It would have to have been a large group of them to have built this tomb," Vylasgarden argued. She looked across the walls and expected the line of urns to continue down the maze. Azariah was still enthralled with the urns as they spoke, walking down the rows of her dead male ancestors.

"No one has seen an elf outside Southaven since the war except maybe your huldar in the north," said Riker close behind her.

"This isn't making sense to me..." Azariah said.

"What does the sisterhood know about this place?"

Riker asked.

"Nothing," she replied, astounded. "None of it makes sense. Unless there are more of my mother's lies to be unraveled." She started speaking in Elfish as if quoting something.

"What are you saying?"

"The words to an alfar rite: *We burn our dead for their bodies are now hollow.* A ritual of cremation makes sense but…" She picked up another urn off the shelf. She recited once more and translated her words. *"Fire is the beginning and so it must be the end so that life can renew. We give the ashes back to nature so that the alfar become one with our forests."*

"With no forest to call home, it looks like whoever burned the dead here skipped the final step," Kruzco said, observing more urns. "There's something else." They all looked at him. "Ever since we entered this place, I've sensed an aura of magick. Our Phoenix Flame may be here."

Azariah scowled. "Why didn't you say anything?"

"Because I was putting pieces together." Kruzco stroked his beard. "Something tells me we're about to learn what all this means."

"We better move then," Vylasgarden urged, and they followed the maze with greater haste. Ahead of them was candlelight, and they all extinguished their own in a puddle of water. Slowly and quietly they came upon the scene.

They were at the end of the catacomb where a stone sar-cophagus sat in the center of the room with lit candles around it in a circle. In front of it was a figure in a dark cloak, kneeling with a great bow and arrows before it. The figure then manifested something in his left hand. It was radiant and gave off a sound like a raging hearth. Vylasgarden knew this was the Phoenix Flame. When the figure in the cloak started chanting, she became agitated with dread. She looked at the others for what to do, and Riker had an all-too-familiar expression of a poorly thought out plan. Once he was sure they understood what to do, he signaled for them all to split up. The cloaked figure, meanwhile, continued his ritual and chants by placing the Phoenix Flame inside the sarcophagus. He raised his hands and chanted louder. It had the effect of setting the stone sarcophagus ablaze in a gold fire; which startled everyone out of hiding.

They surrounded the figure, who slowly stood and took down the cloak over his head. He was bald, from his head to the eyebrows, and was as pale as a ghost. He seemed ancient and sinister, with large bulging black eyes but had other features that resembled the grace of an elf, like Azariah. He pointed a bony finger at Azariah and said something in what Vylasgarden assumed was Elfish. Kruzco lifted his wand and said, *"Abrafulgur Monradi!"* A bolt of crackling energy shot from the wand at the figure, who wrapped himself in his cloak as the bolt connected and vanished before their eyes.

Riker rushed over to the burning stone coffin. "Did you kill him?"

"Unlikely," replied Kruzco, blowing on the smoking wand. "He's disappeared using that cloak of his. We best get that feather out of there and go." As he and Riker used the great bow to wrench the sarcophagus open, Vylasgarden noticed Azariah standing still.

"What did he say to you?" she asked her gently.

Azariah blinked hard, shaking her head. "It's not important right now. Let's help them open the damn thing." She helped pry with the bow, and Vylasgarden shoved the top with her bare claws. The gold fire didn't hurt much; instead, it felt more like it was crawling like leeches on her scaly flesh. It burned yet felt good in a way she couldn't explain. Just when they were getting the lid to move, the gold fire died and the lid popped open. "Get back!" The foursome retreated to the catacombs and hid with their backs against a wall; they listened to stone grinding against stone and the grunts of something that was emerging from the box.

"Hmmrrr…" came from the other side along with fleshy footsteps on the stone floor. Riker slowly unsheathed his rapier, and Azariah reached into her boot for daggers. Vylasgarden was tall enough to see over the wall, and she peeked to see what was on the other side. It had an elf's height but was hunched over as if its back was failing to support it. It had no nose or lips, and in the place of its eyes

were golden flames; in its right hand, it held the Phoenix Flame as if it were a part of it. It noticed the bow and arrows on the floor and picked them up as if it recognized them and then looked back and forth between the weapon and the flaming feather, deciding to throw the flame down in exchange for the weapon. It aimlessly marched towards them.

"It's coming," Vylasgarden warned.

Kruzco readied his wand for another spell, but Riker put out a hand. "I got this one." Riker freed his cow's horn from the leather straps and stepped into the creature's path. It tilted its head unexpectedly at him. Riker used the horn to cast a spell of his own, blowing into it hunched over and then rearing up at the ceiling. Vylasgarden could see the sound waves coming from the horn that rang out and vibrated the bones in her body but also shook the walls and ceiling. The creature notched an arrow in its oversized bow, and Azariah reacted with a knife thrown into its shoulder just before the ceiling came down on top of it.

Vylasgarden's heart raced, waiting for the dust to settle. "Let's find that flame before the rest of the tomb comes down on us." Vylasgarden went straight to the spot where the creature had thrown the flame down, and, underneath a foot of heavy stone, she could see its light. "It's here!" she started to say before the ceiling cracked again.

"Get out of there!" cried Azariah. Vylasgarden dug her hands into the stone, but with all her strength she struggled to make the rubble budge. The second collapse came down on her, and the next thing she knew, she came to some time later under loose soil. Her head was pounding when she surfaced and saw that she was alone. The rain washed away the dirt on her face, and the flashes of lightning in the sky showed that there were mounds of dirt where the catacombs were.

"Riker!" She found where the rest of the tomb hadn't collapsed. "Azariah!" She slid in the mud into the darkness, where it was still submerged and somewhat dry. "Kruzco?" She wandered a bit, backtracking in the maze with only the moonlight in the cracks permitting her to see. She found Riker struggling to light a torch with his tinderbox. Azariah approached him first. Her cloak appeared odd on her shoulders; it was blackened and singed as if it had been raked through coals. Riker put down his tools and met with her.

"Oh good, you're alright. Have you seen the others?" He was answered by Azariah delivering a dagger into his stomach.

"Abomination," she said with her other hand holding his head.

Vylasgarden cried, "No!"

Azariah pulled the dagger free and bolted when she saw Vylasgarden charging at her. Vylasgarden caught Riker as he fell. She roared mournfully as he bled through his jerkin and blood pooled in his mouth. He reached up for her face, and she noticed the color had gone from his hand. He was shaking dreadfully and tried saying something but choked on the words. Vylasgarden could only cry tearlessly and continue to whimper in sorrowful growls. His arm finally dangled when Kruzco found them. "What happened?" he said.

"She stabbed him." Vylasgarden barely believed her own words.

"No, she didn't."

"She did!"

"No! Vylasgarden. She didn't." Kruzco nodded over her shoulder, where Azariah stood in shock. Her cloak was like it had been before. She came to his side to hold his limp hand.

"It wasn't me, Riker," she sobbed. "It wasn't me." He didn't hear her, though. He had died moments before, trying to speak his last words.

"He's gone," Kruzco declared with his head down.

Azariah wiped her tears. "No," she said defiantly. "Where is the feather? The Phoenix Flame will revive him if we don't wait long. You two go. I will stay with him." Vylasgarden exchanged a look with Kruzco. "It will work! Go before it's too late!"

Without a second thought, Vylasgarden ran with Kruzco to the spot where she had dug herself free, and they started digging deeper into the rubble as it rained. They came to the stone covering the flame and the two of them struggled to move it. The ground shook, and the creature from the sarcophagus came from underneath the rocks, three times the size it had been before. It disturbed enough rubble to unearth the flame that continued to rage its golden light in the rain. Vylasgarden and Kruzco froze in place as the creature towered over them. It was gray and malevolent looking. Vylasgarden had never felt so small before that moment staring back into its fiery eyes. It lumbered over the crater and walked into the river before disappearing in the darkness between the trees.

They returned to Azariah with the Phoenix Flame in Kruzco's hands. "Lay him on the floor," Kruzco commanded. Azariah had been crying, but she perked up when she saw the flame. "I hope you know what you're doing. I've never practiced necromancy."

"This isn't magick you would know," she said. "Have you done this before?" Vylasgarden asked.

"I've seen it done... on animals." She took the feather in her hand and used her other to separate a wisp of gold fire from it. The intensity of the feather dimmed, and the flame it held shrank a bit. She spoke Elfish again and laid the wisp of gold fire to the wound in Riker's stomach. She gave the flame to Kruzco and used both hands to spread the fire across Riker's abdomen. With one hand on his wound and the other's thumb on his forehead, she chanted Elfish intently over and over. She removed her hands and sat back, waiting. It was a long while before the gold fire dimmed like a dying candle.

"Maybe we need to do it again," Kruzco suggested.

"No, be patient," Azariah insisted, but Riker remained motionless.

"Agh!" cried Kruzco. Something slashed at his wrist and caused him to drop the Phoenix Flame. Its light revealed a shape in the dark.

"It's the imposter!" exclaimed Vylasgarden. She went to tackle him but missed as the Phoenix Flame whipped about and she felt a blow to the head. The flame shot off in the dark. Vylasgarden started to chase after it, but Kruzco stopped her.

"Not now," he said before pulling her back. There in the dark, Riker suddenly gasped awake.

Chapter Twenty-two

THE NEKODARZ

AS THE DAWNING SUN ROSE, the warm feeling that was inside had dwindled to cold. Like before when there was nothing. The Nekodarz was marching all night with no destination in mind. He was trying to put the pieces of what was left of his mind together. Everywhere he went the cold followed him, leaving frost wherever he touched. He went east for a while until a memory told him to go south. The Nekodarz ground his rotted teeth, fighting to remember why that direction meant something to him. A gentle breeze blew through the nearby woodland that linked the southeast border of Pryden and the northeast border of Southaven. A howl pierced the air between the two lands as a pack of wolves emerged from the forest's edge. The Nekodarz followed them into a clearing in Southaven where, like a muscle, he shrank down to normal size. He watched them with familiar curiousity as they preyed upon a herd of grazing deer.

In the far distance, a short mountain range was erected across the fields like a great wall. He knew those mountains somehow. Near them were a forest with the tallest trees, wild orchards, clearest waters, and a place he may have once called home. The Nekodarz watched the wolves eat; seeing the blood brought about an emotion that had perhaps been dormant before. He looked upon his decrepit form and decided he favored the wolf, so he changed into the wolf. He was bigger to compensate for his mass, and he found this form to be superior. This wolf was old; he had various scars and matted fur, and his white eyes were full of gold fire. When he ambled to the pack, he was greeted with snarls. One bark was all it took to send them running. Eating the deer needlessly, the Nekodarz tried remembering more from his past life, but the harder he tried, the more the memories ran from him.

"I knew I'd find you here," a feminine voice said in the wind. At the tree line, he saw the familiar shape of the one who had thrown the knife at him. He bounded to her with bared teeth but stopped when she commanded him in words that brought a flood of memories to him. "I see you remember some things about us." She dropped her tattered cloak and changed into a male that would have resembled him if he had not decayed.

He changed too, back into his decrepit form, and the Other revealed to him the bow and arrows from the night before and a crown made of stage antlers. The Nekodarz took them in his withered hands. "Vilhjalmur Sergens, First King of the New Realm, All-father to the Changelings and the Alfar Race and Master rider of the Wild Hunt. I am yours to command." The Other knelt before him. "Much has changed since the civil war, my king, but with this…" He produced the gold burning feather from before. The fire that had brought him life again, the very thing he disregarded before escaping his tomb. "We can pick up where we left off."

"Left off…"

He remembered then. The migration. The war with humans. The betrayal from the sisters and his queen. He remembered what was taken from him and the enchantment he put on himself to preserve his soul so that he might rise again like the phoenix bird. He placed his crown on his head. "I was all that was left," the Other mentioned. "This world is especially cruel to our kind, but when we take back Foss Sergens, there will be no more hiding for us, right? We will conquer this world as you promised." The Nekodarz took the phoenix feather in his free hand and, remembering what he was meant to do with it, took an arrow and amended the fletching with the burning feather. He notched the flaming arrow beneath the bow's notching point and faced the clearing. The Other joined him at his side. "Hundreds of brothers died here. There were too few left alive to cremate all the dead." The Nekodarz aimed high and released. The arrow came down in a murder of crows who took wing as the golden fire caught in the field. Like an infection, the fire scorched the clearing in a wave. The blackened ground began to roll as its smooth surface fractured and cracked, revealing the remains of hundreds of hundred-year-old buried corpses of their brethren and their horses.

The eyes of the dead kindled with magickal fire that breathed new life into them. They were no longer youthful, and their numbers weren't where they had been before, but the Wild Hunt had never looked more ready for war. The Other looked on, horrified, but remained at his master's side. The Nekodarz put an affirming hand on his shoulder and nodded, then stepped out to his army and cried a ghastly sound. From the field, six wolves dug themselves free from the dirt and ran up to the Nekodarz at the top of the hill. Each of the six was uniquely scarred and decayed. They transformed as he had into their former naked changeling forms – wearing nothing but tattered wolf pelts. "Your berserkers, All-father," announced the Other. Each of the six's eyes burned with gold fire, and they knelt before him.

Chapter Twenty-three

AZARIAH

AZARIAH WATCHED RIKER SLEEP while Vylasgarden and Kruzco discussed plans by the hearth. She listened to the pitter-patter on the window of one of the abandoned homes they accommodated, which kept her calm enough not to scream. Vylasgarden and the wizard were arguing about what happened. "That thing will use the Phoenix Flame to raise an undead army," she said to quell their argument. "It's called the Wild Hunt. They were male warriors that defended Foss Sergens during times of war," she said calmly, not taking her eyes off Riker.

"What about the other one?" Vylasgarden said. "Why did it take your form?"

"He was a full-blooded male elf, a changeling," she replied. "I have never seen one before but I know they have a unique ability to take the form of others. They were all supposed to be dead before I was born."

"Riker doesn't look like that ugly oaf," said Kruzco.

"Riker shares blood with the sisterhood. He wouldn't have inherited the changelings' power. What we should be focusing on is what happens next. The changeling used the Phoenix Flame to resurrect someone, and I'm certain they're going to use the flame again to raise the Wild Hunt and resume the civil war. We need to get to Foss Sergens and warn the sisters as soon as possible."

"Forget the elves," interrupted Kruzco. "What about the towns and villages between here and Foss Sergens? If what you say is true, they'll tear those homes apart. Folks will think it's the end of the world seeing the undead marching through their streets."

"Then they will buy us some time."

Kruzco scowled at her.

"Look, this isn't easy for me," she shouted at the wizard. "This dying and living and living for a chance to die again. I'm not made for it. Right now the home that I ran away from has another war coming for it and there is no way I can get there in time to convince them to listen to me... Riker actually died and may never be the same after I did something unnatural and brought him back to life. I have to live with that, and you're sitting there pouting because humans you don't know may die." She realized she was standing and sat back down. They all became silent with only the pitter-patter of rain and the crackling of the fire to disturb the silence.

"I know what to do," Kruzco finally said. "I will go to the nearest town and have them send a messenger bird to the elves."

"It won't work," Azariah replied. "They will shoot it down before it gets too far past the border. I will go. I have the best chance at getting a word in before they kill me."

"No! We stay together," declared Vylasgarden.

"We aren't going anywhere so long he stays like this," Azariah replied, packing her things. "Someone will have to stay with Riker."

Kruzco raised his hand. "I'll stay with him."

Azariah shook her head. "As much as I'd prefer it, you will have to come with me. Your magick will be needed, and frankly, I trust Vylasgarden's bedside manner more than yours."

Kruzco grumbled. "Fine!"

Azariah hugged Vylasgarden at the door. "Make sure he knows —"

"I will," she assured her. "Be smart out there and don't do anything rash without the rest of us." With that in mind, Azariah and Kruzco saddled up and galloped into the night, heading toward Southaven.

They did a day of hard riding. Azariah was sore and blistered by the time she and Kruzco came across the crossroads. He insisted taking the road would get them there sooner than going through the wilderness. By then, the horses' legs were shaking with fatigue. "We best give them a break," she told him, and they dismounted in front of the signs. The scenery was awe-inspiring. Off in the far west was a white castle standing picturesque alongside the blue sky and green meadow that stretched for miles. Azariah drew herself away and read the two signs: one pointed east, labeled Aquarin, and the other pointed west, labeled Bloowood. "Bloowood is Riker's town. He once mentioned Foss Sergens is a day's travel south from there."

"Then that is where we go. Pray we aren't too late."

A cobblestone path led into Bloowood, where they were stopped at a golden gate with a sigil on it of a blue sparrow in flight carrying a white begonia. "Go no farther and state your business," a guard said to them.

"Look! Bailey, have you seen an elfess like that one? Look at the silver hair on her!" commented another.

"We've come to warn the town. Trouble is on the way."

"Oh yeah?" questioned the first, named Bailey. "What trouble would that be?"

Azariah exchanged a pained look with Kruzco. "It would be best if I spoke directly with who is in charge here."

"Well, Your Ma-je-sty! As far as you're concerned, I am in charge here."

"Bailey!" came a man's voice. "This is no way to treat guests." He was dressed in a fine doublet and held a book in his hands. He was tall but a bit fleshy and had even-cut dandelion-yellow hair with a sharp trimmed mustache. "Vartan Miraven at your service. Come, you may discuss your matter with me and leave Ser Bailey to his morning."

"As you wish," Azariah hesitantly abided.

Vartan Miraven showed them to his manor, a two-story home surrounded by a rose garden. The property was enclosed by a stone wall that had short iron pines atop it to discourage vaulting. A servant opened the door for them. "I lead the town's league of historians. I was just visiting the library before joining my family for breakfast," said Miraven, entering his home. "Care to join us?"

Azariah took down her hood and nodded graciously. "That would be kind, thank you."

He led them to the dining room, which had a long table and a view of the yard in the back. An older woman and two children sat at the table. They seemed to have been waiting for him. "Dear, who are these people?" said the woman.

"Family, we are honored today to welcome royalty to our home."

"I never said —"

"I knew from the moment I saw your silver hair, princess. Few elves' hair shine as brightly and there were books written about your historic birth." He walked over to the lady of the house who remained in her chair. "Named after the human woman who save the All-mother's life in the first Human-Elf War; Princess Azariah was the first full-blooded elf born to this world. Come join us, please." Before she could fully accept, Kruzco was already sitting at the table. They were served a whole turkey, a suckling pig, and a banquet of fruits and wine.

"I wish I could say that we're here under more favorable circumstances," Azariah started to say. She was distracted by Kruzco's noisy eating. "My wizard compatriot and I came to warn the town that a war with an army of undead is coming this way."

"Did she say undead?" asked the lady of the house.

"I know how this sounds, but you have to believe what I say. We've seen it. Kruzco?"

Kruzco looked up from the meal with a turkey bone in his mouth. "Ahem! Yes, the princess speaks true, my lord. Two nights ago, we witnessed the start of it. Plainly put, we believe that the elves from the losing side of that old civil war will have risen by now, and will come through your town to get to the Land of Elves. We came to send word for evacuation with your fastest birds to every settlement between here and there."

Miraven and his family sat with mouths agape. Miraven himself expressed amusement. "Well, I'm certainly floored, princess. Say I believe this. What series of events would bring upon an undead elfish army?" he asked skeptically. "It would be the first of its kind. The world has been at near peace for nearly a century."

"Then don't you think it is overdue?" Kruzco suggested a bit too sternly.

Miraven grew more serious. "Beth, dear. I'm afraid I will have to make up for our plans today. It would seem I should entertain our guests." He stood from his chair at the head of the table and walked over to Azariah. "Come, let us discuss this further in privacy," he said to her. He led them to a separate room on the same floor that was blocked off by a cluster of objects. He welcomed them into the space and went over to unveil the curtain, throwing up dust from the windowsill. On either side of the room was a simple bookshelf, and at its center in front of Miraven was a table with several sheets of parchment lying on it. He unrolled a large piece, revealing a detailed map of Southaven. Miraven looked at Azariah and Kruzco with intrigue. "I drew this up almost ten years ago. Bid me everything you know." He wrote as quickly as he could on a script as they spoke over each other. They told him about Theod-Rah and the Phoenix Feather at the end of the Human-Elf War and how it had been stolen two hundred years later. "Are you sure about this?" he asked her for the fourth time.

"Yes! Every bit of it," Azariah replied, worked up and in a sweat. "I imagine this army draws nearer by the minute."

Miraven called for a servant and handed him what he had written. "Take this to the roof and send a carrier to the barracks immediately," he ordered, "and prepare a carriage for my family at once. Tell them that we're going to the winter home for a while." The servant bowed and went off with the message.

"What did you write?" Azariah asked.

"I wrote the necessity of the matter. For guards to be on

alert for an invading force."

"Wait, that isn't enough," objected Kruzco, "There has to be a full-body evacuation."

"Do you have any idea what it would take to evacuate a third of Southaven? You're lucky you gained this much success. The city guard will spread the word of a potential attack and for the time being the country will keep both eyes open."

"My lord, we're talking about an undead army of warrior elves. Don't you think we should proceed with greater concern?"

"My dear princess. With no offense to your crown, mankind defeated your warriors when they were alive. Reason stands to suggest we can handle them again, half dead, and in our sleep."

Azariah held her breath, and a touch from Kruzco made her let it go. "Come on," the wizard said, "we did our part here." On their way out, they were intercepted in the dining room by guards rushing into the house. Azariah noticed a sudden chill in the air.

"Everyone stay calm. Close the doors and draw the curtains," said the guard named Bailey. He came in and laid his weapon on the long table.

"What is the meaning of this, Bailey?" demanded the lady of the house.

"Don't you worry, Lady Miraven, everything is under

control. We just have a situation at Townsquare."

"What sort of situation?" asked Vartan, entering the dining room. There was a level of concern in his voice that may have not been there if not for the previous conversations. "A parade of wildlings came from nowhere on horseback and started siccing their dogs on the winos. It was a hell of a scene. Saw it with my own two eyes. Say, you wouldn't be connected to this, would you?" Bailey asked Azariah and Kruzco.

"Come on Bailey, look at them," Vartan said but looked at Kruzco suspiciously. "Well, I'm certain of her. No offense to you," he said to the wizard. Kruzco shrugged. "They've been here with me the whole time," he answered for them. "Why aren't you out there handling the situation?"

"I came to check on you and yours, my lord. I see something strange happen and I remember an hour before some riffraff came into town and you welcomed them into your home like they own the place."

"Mind your tongue, Bailey. Go ring the bell. Southaven is under attack." He turned his attention to another guard. "And get a carrier raven to every settlement from here to the Land of Elves telling people to evacuate their homes."

Suddenly, a long, haunting howl filled the space. Azariah went to the window and saw shadows casting down from the sky. It started with a few, but the sun was soon blocked by sheer numbers. "They're here," she announced. There came a crash on the roof, and Miraven's children screamed.

"Vartan, what is happening?" asked his wife. She was clutching her necklace.

"We'll be fine," he answered, and urged his family away from the windows. "Go gather your things." A loud, deep horn sounded not far away. Miraven reconvened with Azariah after the family had left the dining room.

"We must get ahead of this," Azariah told him.

"Right. Once I've sent my family away, I will do what I can here." He took her by the hand. "Thank you, princess. I shouldn't have doubted you." She nodded with a despondent smile and went outside with Kruzco, where it looked like a nightmare had become real. Dead changelings on horseback galloped overhead accompanied by large wolves on the ground charging through the streets.

"Come! Your horses are this way!" said a swordsman shouting through his helmet. They followed him to the stable while Kruzco provided cover using magick words to keep the attack off them. "Continue south. You'll find the other end of the town where the road continues into the Blue Woods. It will be a long ride but eventually you will find a new clearing."

"Thank you."

She and Kruzco mounted and burst out of the stable, galloping down the streets of Bloowood where a violent snow fell and Azariah could hear flying hooves trampling the rooftops. The riders had gray skin and the all-too-familiar gold fire burning in their eyes. They were gaunt yet powerful as she noticed them tearing apart doors and throwing the town's defenders from their horses. The air smelled of rotten flesh, and when she looked back, she saw that more were coming as the stormy sky was blackened by the Wild Hunt's swarming. Azariah snapped her head forward, and, after a mile riding through the chaos, she and Kruzco finally saw the end of Bloowood. Tall timbers encroaching the town's wall were the gate to freedom.

They were flanked by a pair of guards on horseback. "Lord Miraven sent us to accompany you!" one shouted to her.

"We've got your back, Your Highness!" shouted the other. Together they entered the Blue Woods on their way to Foss Sergens, her home. Her last sight of Riker's home was of the dead descending upon the town like locusts to a field of crops. The settlement started to blaze in the snow as messenger birds took flight in all directions.

Chapter Twenty-four

THE NEKODARZ

THE NEKODARZ FELT A STRENGTH growing within him. Every death at the hand of his hunt fueled the magick flame within him and in turn, brought memories to him. When he saw her, the female that had thrown the knife into him, he changed from his wolf form along with his six berserkers. "There isn't much here of use except the armory in the barracks," said the Other, approaching him. He had been acting as lieutenant to the Hunt. The Nekodarz didn't respond. Not that he could with many words. Still, he kept his gaze at the south gate, staring into the dark timber forest.

"I saw her too. They must have gotten ahead of us. No matter, my king. No amount of preparation will stop us from claiming victory over Foss Sergens."

The Nekodarz went over to one of the six and put a hand on changeling's. *"Go,"* he managed to say.

"There isn't a need to send a hound after her, my king," interrupted the Other, which angered the Nekodarz. He stood over The Other, burning his golden fire eyes and saying nothing. "Of course, if you think it necessary…"

Without taking his eye off the Other, the Nekodarz

repeated, *"Go,"* and one of the six transformed into a wolf and chased after the female. The Other slunk away and the remaining five of his hounds went rampaging through the town. Standing there alone, the Nekodarz felt something sting his back. He turned around to see the annoyance and found his first challengers. A man and woman in heavy armor started to surround him.

"En garde!" cried the male, and he lunged forward with his blade and sliced the end off the Nekodarz's bow. The Nekodarz sensed the first female attacking from behind, and he turned gaseous, an ability he remembered he had. She went right through him, and her blade fell into her companion's body, between the armor plates.

The Nekodarz in his gaseous form came to the other side and manifested his burning eyes to look at her horrified face. "What are you?" she said, quivering. Before she knew it, he had weeds growing from underneath her, entangling her feet and wrapping around her and the fallen male's body. The Nekodarz slowly took his normal form as she became intertwined with vines and stems. She managed a scream before the plants completely wrapped around her head.

Pleased with his work, the Nekodarz looked around at the burning buildings and fresh corpses in the street becoming burried in the snow he summoned. The Hunt had successfully taken this unsuspecting settlement, and he knew they were stronger for it. He would take the next one and the next one with greater confidence that Foss Sergens would be his again. He raised his rotting head and howled, summoning the wind. The Hunt howled with him like a chorus of hounds on the scent of their prey.

He took the wolf's form again and caught up to the front lines, where he led the Hunt off-road and into the winds of the sky to spot the next unfortunate farm or village on which to rain down and take whatever would make him stronger for war.

Chapter Twenty-five

AZARIAH

AS NIGHT TOOK HOLD and the moon rose high, they rode through the Blue Woods and Azariah heard a howl behind them. It made the hair on her neck stand on end. "We're being followed," said Kruzco.

"We can't afford to stop," she replied.

"Go ahead," said one of Bloowood's guards. "I'll check it out and warn of any danger."

"Luke, are you sure?" asked the other guard.

"No reason to slow the party," Luke replied, stopping his horse and brandishing his sword. Azariah and the rest continued. Part of her believed it was nothing but an actual wolf in these woods, but the other part reminded her of the howling in the wind that had come before Bloowood was attacked. They stopped when Luke's screams pierced the quiet of the night.

The other guard dismounted his horse. "Luke, no!" He unsheathed his sword; its blade shone in the moonlight. "Go on ahead," he commanded.

"We're not leaving you," argued Kruzco. He swung his wand out from his sleeve. Azariah took out her knives, and they waited in the arch of the trees, listening to the leaves rustling in the wind.

There was a low growl, and Kruzco shot his magick blindly into the trees, saying, *"Abrafulgur monradi!"*

"Careful with that!" warned the guard.

From the shadows of the trees, Azariah made out a milky white body coming their way. "There!" Kruzco cast the spell again, but it met a tree, leaving a burn on the wood. The assailant leaped out and scrimmaged with the guard, who sliced across his bare, undead chest with his sword. He staggered back, and the guard advanced, slicing through his belly. The changeling huntsman fell to the ground against a tree. He started mumbling in Alfletani. "Keep your distance!" Kruzco warned.

"Best I behead it," said the guard, and he raised his blade over his shoulder. "Any last words, monster?"

The changeling said, *"Ridi gibfa meir styrk!"* He caught the blade mid-swing and grew an additional two feet over the guard. His white skin turned blood red, and Azariah watched his wounds heal. He snapped the blade in half with his fist and used his other fist to punch the guard through the chest armor. She heard the ribs crunch. Azariah threw one of her knives at the changeling's face, but it ricocheted and stuck in an adjacent tree.

"Kruzco, do something!"

Kruzco pointed his wand at it. *"Magas Abjure!"* The huntsman suddenly started changing back, staggered and confused. "That actually worked..." Azariah jumped down off her horse and threw another pair of knives at the changeling: one in its neck and the other in its head. Then she picked up the shattered sword by the hilt and swung, cleaving his head. She let go, and it slumped lifelessly. The gold fire in its eyes extinguished. "That one was different from the rest," the wizard pointed out.

Azariah stared into the night. "Come on, let's go before another one comes." They rode hard until the horses refused to move any faster than a trot.

Azariah swore.

"We'll get there," Kruzco assured her.

"But not fast enough," she replied, vexed. They were surrounded by green fields in every direction, and Azariah was growing more desperate by the minute. They came up a hill, and she jumped off her mare when she saw the mountains again and, more importantly, the forests before it. "There! We made it!"

"How can you be sure?"

"I'd never forget those trees." They came to a ravine and traveled east until they found a bridge. There was a boulder off to the side with Alfletani etched into it. Azariah noticed Kruzco's interest in it and spoke the runes aloud. "It welcomes us to the Land of the Elves." It was there they saw the smoke on the other side and the camp that produced it.

"What is that?"

"Retribution," she said, drawing her hood over her head. The closer they got to the camp, the more effigies they saw in the field, made of animal remains and dressed in wildflowers and alfr spider silks. The camp proper was right up against Foss Sergens' trees and was made of temporary living. Its people were made of human women and a variety of sister alfarwho once chose to leave Foss Sergens but yearned to return. The halfar were diverse in human heritage with hair textures of all kinds and skin tones reaching as light as her to as dark as humans from Pryden Province. Some of them were shorter and was uniquely dark as true black. These peculiar halfar had their dull hair in their faces and had an aura about them that made Azariah uneasy looking at them. When they all saw Azariah and Kruzco coming, they met them, forming a wall with their bodies. At the front was a stoic elderly woman with flowers in her long gray hair. She had a taller-than-average alfr sister standing beside her, wearing body paint and a deer antler headdress.

"Come no farther!" warned the elder. "You are not welcomed here!"

"Neither are you," replied Azariah. "I did not know there were alfar and humans living this close to the new kingdom," she said with her hands up. "I came to see you before wanting to go inside."

"You must come from a faraway place if you believe you can go in there freely," the elder mocked. "All who goes in pays with their life."

"Do you aim to stop us?" Kruzco questioned. Azariah wanted to scold him for speaking.

"That is not our purpose. She may pass and do as she likes, but the only thing waiting for her on the other side is death."

"It is forbidden by the All-mother," declared the deer-alfr. "None can go without paying for it with their lives. Though our efforts are futile, we pray to the sisters and hope that someday the All-mother may let us in."

Azariah asked, "Who are you women?"

"We are the Sisters of Mourning; we are made of regretful elves forever shunned from returning to their former paradise and widowers and ladies wanting to escape this imperfect world," replied their leader. "I invite you, sister, to join us, but the man must go. He reeks of human's magick."

Kruzco laughed.

"Control yourself !" Azariah hissed at him. "Stay here and keep watch."

"What? You need me, remember? How do I know they won't kill you?"

"You already know the answer to that. Try to convince them of what is coming," she answered, and before he could argue, Azariah noticed something coming in the distance. "Kruzco, look!" She pointed up at a black horse galloping in the sky towards them. Kruzco took out his wand and pointed at it.

The wizard spoke, *"Magas Conjure-ignis!"* His wand flashed, ablaze with fire, and he brought up his second hand. *"Boul alaignis!"* He pushed his free hand forward, and a ball of fire flew from the wand and toward the rider in the sky. It caught the rider, bringing the horse down and raining fire to the ground. They along with the alfr in the headdress came up to the crash and saw that it was one of the Wild Hunt's horses. With her hood still over her head, Azariah cautiously approached and saw that it was the changeling that had killed Riker that was riding; his leg was caught under the horse's body. Azariah swore.

The changeling put his hands up. "Wait! Stop! I beg you!" His pale skin started crawling and changing colors from blue to red and green.

"By the All-mother," said the alfr, "that's a changeling!" She tried to move the dead horse.

Azariah got in her way. "What are you doing?"

"He can help us find more. We can save our race from dying off!"

"He killed my friend!" she yelled, and the alfr relented. "He killed my

friend and resurrected the Wild Hunt."

"I made a mistake," he said.

"What did you say?"

"I made a mistake bringing them back. I thought the phoenix's feather would bring my brothers back as they were, but I waited too long. The brothers I knew before are gone. They're nothing more than rotten flesh on bone. The magick wasn't strong enough to bring them fully back. I'm sorry."

"You're sorry? How many lives did you take before making your mistakes?"

The changeling refused to answer. "Wizard, stand on the horse."

"Wait, no!"

Kruzco stepped on the dead again animal, applying pressure to the changeling's leg.

"Agh! Please, stop! I came to help you stop him! I know how to stop him!"

Azariah signaled for Kruzco to stop, and she kneeled over the changeling. "Speak!"

"Most of the feather's power is within the king of the Hunt. Without the flame powering him, the rest of the hunt's flames burn out."

Azariah looked at him pitifully. "Sister, tell the others what you saw here." She took off her hood and revealed her face. The alfr waited and stared at Azariah behind her deer skull mask before taking it off her face. "All-dottir, First Born..." The alfr stood and walked back to the camp. Azariah returned her attention to the changeling.

"You know I have to kill you."

"But I came to help you fight against the Wild Hunt. I've changed!"

"Even if you hadn't killed my friend, I still would kill you for the lives that will soon be lost." She took out one of her daggers, and Kruzco held the changeling's arm. His skin was violently changing shape and color.

He settled on changing to Riker's shape. "Please don't do this."

With gritted teeth, Azariah pushed the blade through his neck all the way to the hilt and watched the life fade from his eyes. When it was done, Kruzco came over and put an arm around her. "Are you okay?" he asked. She shrugged him off, pulled the dagger free, and started walking back to the camp.

When she returned, all the alfar and human women of the camp knelt before her. "Welcome home, First Born," said their leader.

Azariah strode into camp. "My sisters, prepare for war. I'm going in to warn the All-mother." She was back on her mare when Kruzco came up to her. "Be sure to signal when the Wild Hunt is near," she said to him.

"How am I supposed to do that?" he whined.

"You will think of something!" Azariah rode through the part that the Sisters of Mourning had made for her. As expected, there was no path at the tree line. The foliage was as thick as the day she'd torn and scratched her legs to escape the place. Now she was going back in. *I want them to know I'm coming,* she thought, going right up to a spruce tree. She heard singing and saw that the alfar and halfar of the camp had followed her. The song was one that the sisterhood would sing at times of a pyre burning. In all her years, Azariah had only heard it twice. She closed her eyes, placed a hand on the trunk, and began to hum. She waited for a feeling between her and the tree before whispering an enchantment.

"Opna hlidas."

There was a loud crack, and the trees began to sway and bend. A path was made into the woods as the trees moved aside on their own. One of the alfar cried, "Go, sister! Go!"

Suddenly, her mare reared and took off in a full gallop. Azariah lowered her head as branches swept past and whipped her arms and hands as she held on tight. Afraid she would run into something, she looked up and saw that the woods were parting mere feet before the mare's hooves. One passing branch snatched and tore away her cloak, which disappeared behind her as the portal of trees closed behind. There came a white light, and in an instant, her mare halted in a grove full of birch trees with golden leaves. Azariah dismounted her mare and rid her of her reins and saddle. The mare, which she never named, trotted away as if by command. Azariah weaved through the birch, following another light that felt like emerging into a new world, but it was a world she knew all too well. She knew she was home when the air from her mouth condensed from the cold. Before her was a lake, a network of green hills and waterfalls over it all.

A soaring arrow grazed her ear — cutting away strands of her hair. It was meant as a distraction because when she looked up, she was met by a sentry wielding a bow. She was as naked as her first name day, and her eyes, lips, and hair were as red as an apple. "You should not have returned, All-dottir," she said to her.

Other sentries emerged from the trunks of their trees and surrounded her. Before Azariah could get a word in, she was bound and gagged by the sisters. "Death cannot be given to the First Born without remarks from the All-mother. She will know what to do with you." Knowing there was no use fighting, Azariah willingly went all the way to Bjortheim, the brightest building she had ever known and had once considered her home and prison. It was at the top of Foss Sergen's tallest hill that oversaw the kingdom's orchards and garden of relics from the Old World. She was taken directly to the court where her mother's throne was. All in attendance wore their finest white silks, which enriched their ethereal radiance. Her mother, the queen of the alfar, sat straight in her high seat with a shawl wrapped around her forearms and her hands clasped in her lap. The gold phoenix bird (the root of her troubles) was perched beside her and screeched when the sentries brought Azariah before her. "All-mother. The All-dottir has returned to us."

"Daughter, welcome home," her mother said after a dramatic wait. Azariah would have tried speaking, but her mouth remained gagged. "Temptation of the outside world was always a bane of the sisterhood, but learning that you betrayed us broke me," she said without emotion. "It broke all our hearts, daughter."

"All our hearts," the rest echoed.

"Look at you," her mother continued. Her voice was ever patronizing. "Your shine has faded and you've disgraced us by returning in man's clothing." There was another dramatic pause before her mother stung her with, "At least you didn't let any of them touch you," she said disgustedly. She stood from her seat with her hands still clasped. "Still, part of me wishes you had stayed away because by returning you've forced my hand. You've known the law of our new home ever since you were born in it, and now I must decide if my own blood deserves mercy where others did not." Azariah tried speaking through the silk in her mouth. "Allow her to speak," the queen commanded, and the sentry removed the silk.

"I only came back to warn you of what's coming. The Wild Hunt are back, and they're coming to take Foss Sergens."

Murmuring started in the court.

"That is impossible!" exclaimed one of her mother's advisors, a member of the ever-wise Pheonix Flock. "The Wild Hunt and all the changeling males are dead."

Azariah grew impatient."I saw them myself. The feather the All-mother gave the humans was used to resurrect the entire army. They're coming for revenge." The murmurs grew louder.

"Are we to go to war again?" someone asked, and one of the sisters screamed, creating an outcry in the court.

"Enough!"cried the All-mother. Her circlet of light was shining intensely. She adjusted it ever so slightly so as to not imbalance the piece. "She speaks the truth," she said plainly. "What's left of the changelings have been walking among men since the end of the war, sisters."

This surprised the entire court, including Azariah. "You've known?"

"So long as they did not move against us, I thought it was unnecessary to mention."

"My queen," started a member of the court, "you've led us to believe that there was no hope for our race to continue. That the males had all gone." Her piercing blue eyes shot at the court.

"And they have all gone. Gone the way of humans and raised their hounds against us. Or have you forgotten how many sisters we lost in those days?"

"Your grace, none of us has forgotten, but this changes

everything. We no longer need the phoenix to preserve our people. We can make peace with the —"

"No!" the All-mother yelled before returning to her controlled voice. "None shall pass these borders. We are safe here, and whatever comes from the other side is corrupt. We don't need it." She turned her attention to Azariah. "And we don't need you. Betrayer." The court fell silent.

Azariah grimaced. "All my life you've been lying to me. You've been lying to all of us, and for what? Because you're afraid of something?"

"Silence, girl!" her mother said with a hand up.

"I'm not afraid!" Azariah yelled back. "I'm not afraid of the world, of man, and I'm not afraid of you anymore! You want to know why we keep leaving, why we all keep leaving? It's because you are a terrible queen and a terrible mother!"

The All-mother came down from her throne and slapped Azariah across the face. "Take her to the Underground," she said, "and leave her there until this is all resolved." As she returned to her seat, the sentries took Azariah away. She felt conflicted, both relief and regret. Anger and satisfaction.

The Underground was a network of dungeons below the kingdom. She was under a mound near the waterfalls where the only light one would see was from her own body. It was the only place Azariah thought was worse than her tower in Bjortheim. There in the dark, she came to terms with things. At least she got to warn them, but what good did it do if her mother knew about it all along? "First Born?" she heard after some time in the dark.

"Who's there?" She saw another body of light come into the dark.

The red sentry that had found her and cut her ear. "It's you."

"My name is Iona, and I'm going to set you free."

"You'll disobey the All-mother for me?"

"I was going to leave Foss Sergens tomorrow with my love, Savania. A lot of sisters agree with your words, First Born. The queen in all her wisdom is wrong. If it is true that the Wild Hunt is coming, Foss Sergens doesn't stand a chance at stopping them." Iona freed Azariah from her prison, and they stepped out of the Underground. Waiting for them outside was Iona's lover, Savania, a sister from the hills with gold hair and dressed in white silk. She was mounted on a white horse and had Azariah's mare with her.

She greeted Azariah. "All-dottir, First Born."

"Thank you, but I can't leave. Not yet."

Iona took her by the shoulders. "Listen to me, child. There is no hope for this kingdom."

"I'm sorry, but I didn't come all this way just to abandon my people again." She mounted her mare. "You're going to need a name," she said, petting her mane. "I understand more than anyone why you'd want to leave this place, but I'm going to do everything I can to change that." Right then, the clear sky unnaturally formed gray clouds. Snow started to fall right before a flash of lightning grounded outside Foss Sergens, followed by a crack of thunder that was so loud that it convinced Azariah that it had to have come from the wizard.

Chapter Twenty-six

RIKER

HE WAS DROWNING when he came to. He gripped the sheets on the bed he was lying on and wrenched over to spew the liquid from his mouth, which was his own blood. Then something blue and terrifying came up to him. He screamed as it tried grabbing at him and pulling him closer. "Riker, stop!" it said to him, and all he wanted was to get away from it and start making sense of what was going on around him. He fell over as he was trying to run away, and he started crawling on the floor. "Calm down, Riker! You have to calm down!"

"Why are you calling me that?" he screamed. "What are you?"

"You're safe with me. I'm your friend, Vylasgarden." He became dizzy and threw up more blood near the hearth. The monster stepped away from him. "I knew I was going to be the worst one to stay with him," it said to itself. "Don't you remember your friends? Azariah, Vylasgarden and Kruzco?"

Those names were familiar. They were coming to him slowly at least. "You called me Riker..."

"That is your name. Barron Von Riker. You're a

musician who uses your instruments to cast magick spells."

"Magick?" The concept was also coming to him along with his sense of self. He put his hand to his head. "Oh, Vylasgarden. What happened to me?"

"What do you remember?"

"I remember… drowning in ice water. It was so cold. Then it was dark. I couldn't see anything as I held my breath down there, and no matter how hard I swam I couldn't see the surface." He threw up more blood and shivered. "I'm so cold!" He crawled over to the fire and threw more logs in. "So cold…"

Vylasgarden came over with a blanket. "Riker, you died."

"What?" He was breathing into his hands.

"You died saving our lives from a male elf that Azariah called a changeling. He was disguised as her and stabbed you in the stomach."

He felt his stomach, where dry blood stained his shirt. He felt for the hole in it and touched his bare skin, where he felt a thick scar on his belly. "I… don't remember." He looked around. "Where are the others?"

"They went to warn people about the army."

"Army? What army?"

"The army of undead the changeling hopes to awaken with the Phoenix Flame." Riker remembered something then. In the dark when he was drowning, he remembered seeing stars like he was somewhere in the aether. There was this land before him with burning hills and mountains with lakes of fire. As he floated above it all, he saw a great firebird meeting him in the aether where it dwarfed him among the stars. He didn't remember what happened after that. "... Riker, are you listening to me?"

"I'm sorry, I need some air." He stood, shaking, and slowly walked to the door and stepped outside. The air was frigid, but it felt good filling his lungs. He surprised a doe and fawn that stared at him from across the way.

"You should come back inside," Vylasgarden said behind him.

Riker wanted to cry but didn't have the tears. "Okay," he said with a shudder. He ate all the food they had. Vylasgarden watched him nervously from across the table. "What?"

"I don't know what to make of this."

"How do you think I feel?" he asked her before eating the last spoonful of venison soup she'd made for him. "You just told me I died and came back to life. We're talking necromancy, the forbidden black magick. How do I know that this isn't temporary or that I'm even fully alive?"

"Azariah said that it isn't necromancy. She used the Phoenix Flame to bring you back."

"Like how my murderer intends to use it to raise an army that's been dead for a century. Vylasgarden, I think I should be dead."

"Don't say that."

"No, this is wrong. I shouldn't be here."

"If it were true, you wouldn't have gotten this second chance, now would you?"

He didn't have an answer for that.

"We leave for Foss Sergens in the morning. I'd say get some rest, but you've been dead for a whole day." He said nothing. "That was a joke."

The next day, they gathered their things, and Riker took one last look at the blood all around the abandoned home before putting on his jerkin and closing the door behind him. "Do you remember the way?" Vylasgarden asked.

"I do," he replied regretfully. They rode together on the path Vylasgarden said Azariah and Kruzco had taken. The whole time, he was holding his hand over the scar on his belly. It wasn't long until they came across the great valley known as Death's Vale.

"What happened here?" Vylasgarden asked.

"He succeeded." The entire field was uprooted where countless elfish bodies had been laid to rest during the last fight of their lives. "They call this place Death's Vale because it's where the male elves took their last stand against the human race."

"This is where he used the Phoenix Flame. Come! We may not be too late." Vylasgarden rode off, but Riker remained where he was. She came back to him. "What are you doing?"

"We lost."

"We don't know that."

"The feather is gone, Vylasgarden! The whole reason we came this far is gone!"

"What about our friends, Riker? They need us. They need us now more than ever, and we're not going to stop until we know they're safe. Now, am I going to have to drag you all the way to Foss Sergens or will you ride with me?"

Riker hesitated.

"Will you ride with me?" she repeated, growling, and held out her arm. He grabbed her by the forearm and nodded, and they continued, eventually coming across what was left of Bloowood. The snow had covered the carnage that ensued before. Riker could smell the fires from the buildings.

"This is my home..." They rode past the college, Townsquare, and even his father's home, where Riker had hoped to raise a family with Raven. He remembered her then and what she meant to him. By then he could cry tears. "Dammit all! They will pay for this."

"Then we best be moving. Another day's travel, is it?"

"Yeah, let's go." They were leading their horses on foot when they saw the smoke over a hill. They ran to the top and saw Foss Sergens burning in the distance. "Oh no! We are too late." They galloped to the bridge over the ravine, where they found hundreds of men in armor gathering. They rode up while a leader was giving a speech to the crowd of soldiers. There were explosions of fire in the distance closer to the conflict. Riker started recognizing bannermen colors from all over Southaven, like Wingston and Taglignton further south and the Aquarin men from the eastern seafront wielding their tridents on horseback. He even found soldiers from Bloowood in their golden armor.

"What in all the realm is that?" someone said, and all eyes fell on them as they came through. "It's a dragon on a horse!"

"Have you come to fight?" the leader asked them. He was a balding gray-haired man dressed in plate mail armor and wore a black cap that flapped in the wind.

"We have," Vylasgarden spoke for them.

"Bloody hell! It speaks!" someone said in the crowd.

"My name is Vylasgarden of Froisia, and I came to defend Southaven from the evils of the dead."

A large portion of the crowd cheered in hurrah.

The leader grinned and nodded approvingly. "Brothers and sisters of the Southaven. It looks as though the gods smile upon us this day. For we have a dragon on our side to fight this war with us." The crowd hurrahed once more.

"Riker! Is that you?" someone called from the crowd.

"Vartan? Vartan Miraven?"

A yellow-haired man stepped out of the crowd and approached Riker's horse. He looked like one of his professors, Vartan Miraven, from Lone Oak College back in Bloowood, but this man was dressed in knight's armor and carried a greatsword on his back. "What are you doing here, son?"

"I... It's a long story. What are you doing?"

"You won't believe it, but the princess of the Land of Elves came and warned us of the return of the evil elves."

"You saw Azariah?" Vylasgarden asked him. "Where did she go? Is she in there?"

"I believe so. She came moments before their army tore through Bloowood."

"Wait!" called the leader. "You know the elfish princess?"

"She's our friend," answered Vylasgarden. "We're here to assist her in battle."

"You won't be alone," said Professor Miraven.

"The houses of Southaven have gathered to assist the elves and defend the realm from these undead bastards!"

The crowd cheered again. "Huraah! Hooff! Hooff! Hooff!"

Riker was tuning his lyre while Vylasgarden was invited to discuss the plan of attack on the bridge with the leader of the cavalry: a man named Lord Jason Lynch of Croftboulder Keep in Wingston. "Why are you bringing that into battle? I don't think my lessons on music theory will do you much good in there." Professor Miraven said, walking up to him.

Riker looked at the instrument as if he knew no better than the professor. "It's my weapon of choice," he said, a bit bewildered with himself. Miraven arched an eyebrow as he sat across from him. "Forgive me, professor, I haven't been feeling like myself since I've been back in Southaven."

"Who could blame you, son. Did you see Bloowood before you got here?"

"I did."

"I'm sorry you had to see it like that. We got as many as we could out of there. Fortunately, my family is far from this."

"Why are you here? The last I remember, you weren't a soldier."

"I'm not a soldier, but I served as a squire in my youth. This was long, long ago, before Bloowood was built."

"Were you knighted?"

"I was supposed to, but my day never came."

"Why?"

"Why else, son? I have elf blood in me. In those days,

men like you and me didn't have titles. Today the world sings a different tune, which is why I have to fight and make sure this is all still here for my son to inherit."

Riker smiled at that. "As noble a reason as any." It was the first smile since he'd awakened from death.

Vylasgarden came up to them. "It's time." He and Miraven joined her on the bridge with Lord Lynch.

"There is a good chance we don't survive this," Lynch said earnestly. "We're up against a magick force we do not understand, and we have only swords and spears."

"Not entirely true," Riker pointed out. "I can't speak about the elves inside, but we have a wizard on the inside who I'm sure is doing a great deal of hurt to the enemy."

"Not to mention we have him with us," Vylasgarden said, gesturing to Riker.

"You're magick, son?" Miraven asked.

"I can use music to give us an edge," he admitted.

"Good!" declared Lord Lynch not asking how. "We'll want you on the front lines with the horn players then." He brought his attention to Vylasgarden. "Are you sure you can't grow fifty feet, sprout wings, and breathe fire?"

"No, I cannot."

Lord Lynch scoffed a bit amused with himself. "It was worth a shot. This is already strange as it is." He went to a soldier wearing his colors and said, "Ready the men for battle."

They were across the bridge with Riker, Vylasgarden, and Lord Lynch at the front line. The woods before them were in a fiery rage. Riker lifted his horn and blew into it, followed by the other horn player, who echoed his call. The cavalry charged, and Riker blew into the horn again, this time producing a spell that created a force of sound in front of his steed. The other horn players joined in, which allowed the spell to expand across the front line of the charge and shield them from the impact with the trees and burning brush. They came out to the other side, where they drove their horses over the undead.

The cavalry broke off, taking the fight where it was needed. Swords clashed and bones were broken as men joined the elves against the undead. Riker saw Foss Sergens for the first time, but it was not as he had imagined it. The trees were on fire, the waterfalls were frozen, and the ground was covered with slain elf women. He looked up into the gray sky and saw the end of the world staring back at him. Dead men on horseback flew with flocks of crows wielding bows and shooting flaming arrows upon the ground as what remained of the elves fought back using the cover of trees to shield themselves and shoot back up at their enemy with radiant magick.

A group of decayed wolves came up to his horse and started biting at him, making the horse buck and kick. Riker brought the steed to a gallop, but the wolves persisted, following him into the battlefield. "Riker! This way!" It was Kruzco. He was standing over the frozen pond at the top of the frozen waterfall. Riker drove his horse over the ice, and the wolves followed. "Brace yourself!" Kruzco yelled as he raised his crystal wand. *"Abrafulgur monradi!"* A bolt of lightning came from the sky and struck the waterfall, creating an avalanche of ice over the pond. Riker's horse missed it in time for the ice to crash over the wolves and sink them in the water. Riker met the wizard on the side of the hill. "Ha! Ha! I saved your life again," Kruzco said, grabbing Riker by the forearm and shaking it.

"Believe me," Riker said with a smile. "I am keeping count."

Chapter Twenty-seven
KRUZCO

"WHERE IS AZARIAH?" Riker asked, still on his horse.

"How should I know? She took off without me. She could be anywhere." "Then we best meet up with Vylasgarden first. She can't be too far away." Kruzco grunted, agreeing. An arrow flew past his head and shot through the eye socket of an undead huntsman sneaking up on them. It was the elf wearing the deer skull over her face from the Sisters of Mourning. She walked up to them.

"Wizard."

"Deerwoman."

"You two know each other?" Riker asked.

"Just making friends, lad. Come on, let's go find the dragon lady." Kruzco climbed up on Riker's saddle, and the three of them went into the fray between the Wild Hunt and the defense of man and elves. They eventually came upon a stone structure in the orchards. It had walls and plenty of archways for the elves to make a stand in. There Kruzco saw Sisters of Mourning, some soldiers of Southaven, and Vylasgarden fighting off hordes of huntsmen. As Riker circled the horse around the structure, Kruzco used his spells to thin the attack. The next he knew, the horse was tripped up and crashing to the ground. Kruzco and Riker tumbled. "Get up, lad!" Kruzco said, stumbling to his feet. "The fight's not done." He saw that Riker was lying on the ground, unresponsive.

He went to him but was kicked over by a huntsman wielding a mace. Kruzco pointed with his wand and cast, *"Abra tempesta!"* He dodged a swing of the mace. *"Gustusa!"* A whirl of wind spat from the wand which was unfortunately not aimed well. The huntsman swung again and narrowly missed Kruzco's face. Someone from behind brought a heavy mallet down on the huntsman's undead head, splintering it to pieces under the weight.

It was Vylasgarden who'd saved Kruzco. She nodded to him and pulled him out of the corner he'd backed himself into. "Riker." They went to him, but he was still unconscious from the fall.

"Here, give him this." It was Deerwoman. She handed Kruzco some dried herbs that smelled of mint and citrus. "Break it apart under his nose." The scent brought Riker back.

"Are you alright?" asked one of the soldiers. He was half-elf like Riker with ocher-colored hair.

"Is it over?" Riker groaned.

"Afraid not," Vylasgarden answered. "We can't keep fighting like this," said Kruzco. "We need to find Azariah and take the fight to the king of the Hunt. Wherever he is."

Riker stood and pointed up the hill. "She may be in the

castle with her mother."

"We can't all go," insisted Vylasgarden. "The fight is mostly down here, and it would take too long getting through the horde to reach the top."

Riker snapped his fingers. "Only if we all go. Kruzco! You can travel between spaces!" Kruzco nodded, not sure where he was going with the thought. "If I go alone to the top, do you think you can travel through the Time Dimension to my location?"

"It's not a bad plan, but it's a costly spell. I'd need to know exactly where you are up there in order for it to work."

"I can help with that," said Deerwoman. She pulled out a cylinder from her quiver. "The Sisters of Mourning would use these to signal to each other when we circled around Foss Sergens. You can use it to signal for the wizard. Take the string and use this flint to spark it. When it starts going, keep your distance." Riker took the flint and cylinder and thanked her.

"We'll make you a path," said Vylasgarden, slapping her mallet in her clawed hand. Riker made for the steps up the Foss Sergens hills. The party used brute force, magick, and arrows to form a path through the Wild Hunt. There were so many that the plan seemed futile until they noticed from the hills a legion of six white horses leaping down from great heights in formation. Their riders were armored elves wearing winged helmets. They wielded silver scythes and used then to cut down the undead in their way. This gave enough space for Riker to reach the steps.

"Who are they?" Kruzco asked.

"The All-mother's warmaidens," answered Deerwoman before notching another arrow and running to join the fight. Kruzco put his hands to his hips and briefly watched the new elves turn the tide in the area before joining in. "I think I'm in love," he said to himself. He too leapt into battle, casting spells and following directions as to where to aim his magick. Though he grew tired, Kruzco had never felt more purpose in those moments. He knew that if he survived the day, his elderly body would be bedridden for weeks, if not months. He cast his bolts of lightning and fireballs less intensely, trying to conserve his energy for when Riker eventually signaled for him.

Chapter Twenty-eight
VYLASGARDEN

WITH THE HELP OF THE SIX elfish warmaidens, the party had a moment to breathe. The elfess dressed in paint and deer remains followed the ones with curved blades into a grove to finish off stragglers from the undead while Vylasgarden, Kruzco, and Vartan Miraven caught their bearings. "I was worried this wasn't going too well," said Miraven, leaning over.

"The fight isn't done yet," said Vylasgarden, watching for a sneak attack. Kruzco limped over to a fallen tree, which had been burned in the fight.

"My feet hurt like I've been running through coals!" He sat down and pulled one of his feet up to rub. "I wish I still had my walking staff," he mumbled. Vylasgarden was prepared to relax too but heard a cry in the distance. One of the warmaidens flew through the air and crashed through the trees behind them. "What in hell…"

The other five backed toward them while being pursued by five hulking undead tearing through foliage to get at them. They were tall for changelings, and their bare skin was a deep red. They screamed while wielding axes that they used to cut through anything that was in their way. The elfess in the deer skull mask shot at one of them, but the arrow bounced off him like his skin was steel. "I'm running out of arrows!" she cried. "I've got to make the rest of these count!" One of the scythe-wielders said something to her in their elf language, and she nodded, replying the same. While Kruzco and Miraven assisted in the fight, Vylasgarden watched two of the five remaining scythe-wielders rush up and grapple one of the Reds by the arms, and the elfess shot two arrows behind herself. Vylasgarden saw that arrow pass through a tree and emerge from another in front of the restrained attacker, which pierced through both his eyes.

Seeing an opportunity, Vylasgarden ran up and smote the Red in head with the mallet Lord Lynch gave her — only stunning him.

Kruzco came up and pointed his wand at him and said, *"Magas Abjure!"* The Red shrank down, and his skin turned white as death again. "Now, Vylasgarden!" She followed the cue and swung the mallet again — crushing the head. The elfesses looked at Vylasgarden, impressed, remarking in their unique language. "We must get them out of their enraged forms," Kruzco informed.

Vylasgarden nodded, understanding. "Then we will set them up, and you take away their magick." She ran with the elves to join the rest, fighting the remaining four. Their blades sparked off the Red's skin as they countered the swings of their axes. The elfess in the deer mask used the trees to their advantage a few more times but often missed and soon ran out of arrows.

"I'm out," she said before a Red free from his ax came over and took her by her wrists. She kicked at him but stopped and screamed when he crushed her arms in his hands. Kruzco stunned him with his spell, and Miraven fished him off with his sword. Kruzco knelt beside the elfess as she continued screaming and Vylasgarden and the other elves continued fighting. One by one the scythe-wielders were being picked off without Kruzco's spell to help them.

Vylasgarden even sustained a few blows from fist and ax — whose sharp edges scaled her skin. "Kruzco, we need you!" she yelled back at him, but he did not respond. She noticed then that she had been cut badly in the abdomen. Her warm red blood glazed over her clawed blue hand. *This is it...* she thought. This was how she was going to die. For a kingdom of elves and not for the people she vowed to avenge.

In those passing moments, she thought of the family she'd started before the Slayers came for them. Her hatchling pair, a rare occurrence, weren't even a week old before they were taken from her. Their faces flashed in her mind, and it brought her peace right before she took another blow to the face, sending her flying back against a tree. She was ready to die then and see her family in whatever afterlife awaited her. In her dreariness, she suddenly thought it strange that she would want to die. She couldn't, because she had more work to do. The Dragon Slayers were still out there, and she was their reckoning.

She dug deep to find the fight still inside herself and felt something growing from within. There against a tree she saw the last three Reds approach. Vartan Miraven was the last to stand against them, and they cut him down easily, tearing him apart. Anguished, Vylasgarden roared and the sky crackled with thunder and lightning which, to her surprise, also stopped the three Reds in their tracks. Surprised, they looked at each other before charging after her. She gave another thunderous roar, this time discharging a bit of lightning from her gaping mouth. Like a second wind, it rejuvenated her, and she stood on her feet. *It was in me the whole time,* she thought. The Reds closed in on her, and she dug in her heels, crouching, ready to unleash the dragon.

Chapter Twenty-nine

RIKER

RIKER HEARD THE THUNDER while fighting his way up the stairs of Foss Sergens. He helped the allies on the hill the best he could, cutting down any undead in his way with his rapier. Fortunately, the magick of the phoenix feather was spread thin enough to make the undead functionally sluggard on their own. He kept his eye on the elves' keep the whole way up. A weak arrow bounced off his leather jerkin, and it sent Riker into a panic. He took cover behind a statue and collected himself, breathing heavily and trying his best to swallow fear. Looking back up at his path on the right where the stairs continued, he realized how congested the fight was getting. Collectively the undead overwhelmed the elves with their relentless stamina and ignorance to pain. They were slowly but effectively making their way to Azariah, and Riker had to beat them to the keep.

He noticed a lone deadman wielding a sword. He came past the statue but paid no mind to Riker, instead passing him to go into the garden on his left. Riker heard, *"Ljosberi ah!"* and the undead was met by a blast of white light, which left nothing of the undead behind but the sword it had been wielding. It was a battalion of elfesses dressed in white gowns defending the garden from invasion on both sides. Upon a closer look, Riker saw that they were defending the roots of a great tree above the garden on the cliff of the hill. If one were to climb it, they would reach the elf 's keep in half the time. Riker sheathed his rapier and picked up the sword on the ground. He cautiously approached the elves.

One of them yelled at him in Alfletani. "I come in peace!" he yelled back with his hand and sword up. He noticed their attention drawn behind him, and he swung around, meeting another undead with the sword in its chest. He kicked the body free of the blade, then swung again at the head — crushing the skull and killing it. He turned and saw that the elves were distracted from the undead shooting arrows at them from the other side. "Look out!" He tackled one of them to the ground, narrowly missing an arrow to their heads. On the ground behind cover, she shoved him off her, yelling in Alfletani. "I don't understand what you're saying! Azariah! Do you know Princess Azariah?"

"Azariah?" the elfess echoed.

"Yes! Yes!" He pointed to himself. "I need to get to her. Can you help me get to the tree?" He pointed at the roots sticking out of the cliff and pulled his hand back when an arrow whizzed past it. "Help me!"

The elfess slowly nodded and called out to her sisters in Alfletani. The rest of them responded something in unison, and the elfess pushed Riker out from cover. He ran toward the roots. Heart racing, he blindly dodged arrows and magick light missiles as he traversed the garden wielding the sword with both hands. When he reached the cliff face, he dropped the sword and had to jump off a rock a few times before catching a root by the hand, but he couldn't lift himself up to catch his second hand. He felt his fingers slipping but received a boost underneath. It was the battalion. Riker climbed the network of roots as arrows shot through the spaces. He relied on the excitement to carry him all the way until he reached the cliff's edge and nearly slipped off.

When he climbed up, he took a moment to look over the hills. There was an uncanny power lighting up the gray sky and the thunder shook the earth as black birds took flight. Bodies rained down off their horses with the snow over the men and women of Southaven who continued the fight on the ground. Riker took out Kruzco's signal and flint and stuck the cylinder object to the ground. He pulled the string from it and started sparking the flint against a stone. "Come on, come on." Eventually a spark caught on the string, and it started to spark like crazy, quickly burning up until it reached the cylinder, which started crackling. Riker ran, and soon after the cylinder exploded, firing a colorful missile into the sky.

Riker pumped his first. "Yes!" In an instant he heard Kruzco's voice in the void and both he and Vylasgarden appeared out of thin air, bloody and crazed with fight.

Kruzco came over and clapped Riker on the back. "I knew you could do it! Come! We have a kingdom to save!" Vylasgarden's roar coincided with rumbling crashes thunder and sparks of lightning all around her, and together the three charged into the fray in front of the elves' keep. There were elves on the wall blasting swarms of crows with their light magick while spear-bearers and archers fought off sword-wielding undead on the steps leading up to the front gate. Vylasgarden cleared a path using her lightning breath; she charred the enemy's flesh and the rest that was out of the path turned their attention on them.

"Go, Riker! Get in there! We've got this!" shouted Kruzco. Riker whipped out his horn and blew into it, creating another blast of sound to knock back the enemy and coincidentally a few of the elves as well. "While they're down! Go!" Riker charged past the elves and to the gate of the keep's courtyard.

Behind him came a cloud of black smoke that materialized on the other side of the gate as a familiar dead face wearing stag horns as a crown. Riker nearly fell over from the shock. He looked at Riker on the other side, then looked up at the keep. A blast of light magick threw Riker back, and its power passed through the Stag King as he turned back to smoke. Riker collided with an archway pillar and fell to the ground. The pain was so great that he hoped that it would kill him. Ready to give up, he heard his name.

"Riker... Riker..." He looked up from the ground, and through blurry vision he saw Azariah coming to him from the keep's wall.

Chapter Thirty

AZARIAH

SHE SAW HIM STAND, holding his shoulder. "Riker!" she called again. She rode a thick vine down the thirty-foot wall and ran to him. "You're alive! You're alive!" He limped to her, and they came into each other's arms.

"I had to come and repay the favor," he groaned. "You saved my life, after all."

She kissed him then. It was the first time she'd kissed anyone, and there were tears in her eyes. "Damn you!" She embraced him again. "Did you see him?"

"Yeah, he made it past the gate."

"We have to go. I think he's going to try to kill my mother."

"We can't go without Kruzco and Vylasgarden."

"There isn't time! Let's go!" She pulled him up to the gate, where she spoke Alfletani words, *"Opna hlidas!"* The gate swung open, and they rushed in. "Once we kill him again and for the final time, this will all be over."

"How can you be so sure?" he asked as they entered the keep.

"Your murderer told me so," she said, wielding both of

her daggers. The keep seemed abandoned on the inside. When she led Riker to the Court of the Phoenix Flock, they found that none of the members were present. "Where is my mother?" she said under her breath. The silence was broken by the sound of a struggle upstairs. "This way!" Together they went out to the keep's courtyard, where the World Tree that had brought the alfar to the realm all those years ago was grown. They found the All-mother up on the loggia defending herself from the leader of the Hunt. "Mother!" Azariah said.

"Azariah! What are you doing here?" She was swift, missing attacks narrowly. She would counter with blasts magick radiance. "Leave, daughter. You shouldn't be here." The All-mother said before shielding herself from a wall of ice the leader of the Hunt produced from the water coming from a waterskin at his side. The floor they were fighting on crumbled, and the loggia crashed down to the courtyard. Riker pulled out his horn, and before the huntsman was standing, he materialized an ice spike and threw it at Riker's hand-piercing it and shattering the instrument. The huntsman growled at Azariah and stood between her and her mother. His golden-fiery eyes burned intensely.

Her mother stood, holding her side. Blood was coming through her silk gown. "Please, don't do this. Not in front of her." With what little water he had left in his waterskin, he manifested another ice spike in his hand and stepped toward the All-mother. It was then that Azariah ran up and impaled the huntsman with both of her daggers and managed to topple him. The huntsman roared ghastly as Azariah jumped off him and kicked him until he fell to his side. She stood between him and her mother. With the spike still in his hand, the huntsman slowly rose.

"Today, you die for good," Azariah threatened, and a clap of thunder struck the still air right before it started sleeting in the courtyard. Azariah's heart pounded. She heard her mother saying something, but she was too focused on the undead king changeling in front of her to hear it. Riker came to her side, armed with his rapier in his none dominant hand, and the three of them stood their ground. The huntsman advanced, his attack lumbering. The All-mother distracted him with a flash of her magick while Riker and Azariah slashed and stabbed him with their blades, but he didn't stop coming for them.

Just when Azariah was feeling the excitement wear off, she heard Vylasgarden's voice from across the courtyard. "Move!" Vylasgarden ran up, and tackled the huntsman to the raging sound of thunder. She stood over him and beat on him with her fists. To Azariah's surprise, a chain of lightning came from Vylasgarden's mouth like a dragon would breathe fire. The lightning struck the huntsman while he was down and when she was done, he lay motionless. Kruzco was there, wrapping Riker's hand with a bandage.

Vylasgarden started to sway tiredly, and Azariah

approached cautiously. "Are you all right, Vylasgarden?" She looked at Azariah with weary eyes and took a step toward her, but the huntsman grabbed her suddenly and used his other hand to stab Vylasgarden in the side with his ice spike. There was a flash of lightning as Vylasgarden roared in pain. "No!" Azariah screamed and threw her daggers into the huntsman as he tried rising off the ground. "Why won't you die already?"

"Azariah, wait!" Riker called. He was holding his bag and an arrow by the cloth of his bandage. "Move out of the way!" The huntsman was pulling Azariah's daggers free just as Riker was aiming the arrow like a javelin. "Kruzco! An assist please!" He threw the arrow, and as it arced, the wizard pointed his wand, saying, *"Magas a la manas!"*

From the wand came a pulse of energy and a phantom hand that grasped the arrow, delivering it into the huntsman's chest just before he could grab Azariah with his decayed hands. The huntsman suddenly froze, fingers were inches away from Azariah's face. He fought against whatever was happening to him but his fingers near her face snapped apart from his hand. The rest of his body started disintegrating into a pile of dust and bone with only the horned crown remaining in his remains. The fire from the eyes of his skull snuffed to embers. The sleet suddenly stopped as they gathered around Vylasgarden. "Is it over?" she said, holding her side. Azariah knelt beside her friend and assisted with slowing Vylasgarden's bleeding.

Azariah looked up and saw that the clouds had parted and the sun was shining through. "It's finally done," she said, exhausted.

"The flames from that cursed phoenix feather have died out," said her mother. "And so too will anything else it brought to life." Azariah's relief faded when she realized what that meant and she turned her attention to Riker. He was lying motionless on the ground in Kruzco's arms. Kruzco brought him over to them while Azariah fought back the tears.

"This is how it's meant to be," she told herself. She noticed her mother looking at her, trying to understand. Azariah felt like running away all over again. "Don't look at me like that," she said.

"Who is this halfr?" her mother asked.

"He saved our lives," Vylasgarden answered. She crawled over to Riker, still holding her blood inside herself, and lay beside him.

"He saved my life countless times in the beginning and I failed to save his…" Azariah said next, holding his hand.

Her mother took Azariah's other hand. "You used the feather to resurrect him?" Azariah nodded, whipping tears away. "He must have meant a lot to you, daughter. What was his name?"

"Barron Von Riker."

The All-mother raised an arm and whistled loudly. From

the sky, her phoenix flew gracefully into the courtyard and landed on her forearm. "I should have never given that feather away," she said softly. "If he is so worthy, daughter, then I owe him a debt for guarding your life."

Azariah stood to meet her gaze. "Thank you."

The All-mother gave her a warm and assuring smile then plucked a feather from the bird's plumage, and the feather started to burn a golden fire between her fingers. "I fear the consequences of this act. They were only meant to extend the lives of the alfar people." She laid the feather on Riker's body, and the fire started to consume him. "Join hands," she commanded. The All-mother and Azariah knelt to take Vylasgarden and Kruzco's hands around Riker's body. The All-mother began the ritual enchantment, retrieving Riker's fleeting soul. She removed the feather from his body and the fire covering him died slowly, leaving Riker naked. Kruzco covered him with his cloak.

Riker then gasped awake screaming.

"It's okay," Azariah said to him soothingly, but she saw fear in his eyes.

He started to weep. "I can't do this anymore," he said. "You should have let me die."

The All-mother stood over him. "Whether it be a blessing or curse, you have my daughter to thank." She then addressed everyone. "We will never speak of what happened here. This secret of the phoenix feathers is ours to bear alone."

"What did you see?" Kruzco asked him.

Riker shook his head. "There's nothing but darkness and fire," he started to say. "There is nothing but fire at the end."

It was a day later when Azariah saw Riker again. Vylasgarden convinced her and Kruzco that Riker would need time to put his mind back together. To distract herself, Azariah joined the efforts in counting the casualties. Like the changeling had said, the flames inside the rest of the Wild Hunt had died when their leader fell. Many sisters and human allies died as well, and Azariah couldn't help but think of the phoenix bird and the guilt she felt for keeping an important secret. Her mother told her in private that the lie would become easier to bare with time.

With the barrier of trees burned down, the survivors came and went as the sisters started to rebuild. On her way to meet with her mother, Azariah looked over the hills and saw that groups of humans from the neighboring settlements had come to help rebuild Foss Sergens. "It seems a new dawn is upon us," the All-mother said, surprising Azariah from behind.

"What does it mean?" she asked.

The All-mother waited to answer. "Perhaps greater changes are necessary for us to mend what was broken before." She reached for Azariah's hand and she accepted it. They stood there watching in silence for a while before her mother said, "I know this was all my fault. If I hadn't turned on the changelings the way I did and given away that feather, none of this would have happened."

"Perhaps those were the changes that were necessary for us to come to this point, mother. We have to be better. I need you to be better," Azariah replied, not looking at her. "What will we do next?"

"The council and I have agreed with some of the human leaders. In exchange for supplies to rebuild and further ensure a greater alliance, Foss Sergens will integrate with the rest of Southaven." Azariah almost couldn't believe what she was hearing. "It's been time. I see that now. It took you leaving and then returning with a war for me to see the error in my ways." Azariah had no words, but she smiled politely. "Azariah, I'm sorry for hurting you. I thought I was protecting you and preserving something worth keeping."

"I forgive you, mother," Azariah said looking at her. "Not All of it is worth loosing either. I believe there is room for the old ways and this new world. I have to believe it. I think I can accept the responsibility of the All-dottir and bridge the gaps."

The All-mother was holding the staghorn crown that belonged to the leader of the Wild Hunt. "Thank you, but I know I have more work to do in earning your full trust. I will start someday soon with the truth about why we broke away from the changelings and the Wild Hunt, but first, I want you to introduce me to your companions." They went inside Bjortheim and met with Kruzco, who finished speaking with the council.

"Now that Foss Sergens is welcoming humans in its borders, we'll need a human wizard to advise us about foreign magicks. I couldn't possibly offer the role to anyone else," Azariah said to him.

"As great as an offer that is, princess, there is another war I must go to. It seems a mutual enemy of ours is occupied fighting his people in Pryden. Soon he will notice we haven't returned his precious feather and I intend to help keep his attention divided."

"The powers of Foss Sergens are in your debt, wizard," stated the All-mother. "The threat of Theod-Rah looms over us all. When the time comes, you can count on the alfar for aid."

Kruzco nodded politely and started walking away but Azariah intercepted him with a hug. "Thank you. For everything."

"Don't get all weepy on me," he said hugging her back. "You'll make an excellent leader someday. I'd gladly follow you to hell and back."

They parted and Azariah watched him leave the front steps. She and the All-mother went to Riker's room in the keep and found him talking with Vylasgarden on the balcony. His phoenix feather was burning inside an open glass jar on the dresser next to his lyre and rapier. The All-mother took the jar in her hands and they joined them on the balcony. Vylasgarden was well-bandaged around the waist and she walked around the keep with an improvised cane. "You two seem to be recovering well," the All-mother said to Riker, "Keep this close," she said referring to his phoenix feather. "Without it, death will seize you once again."

"Yes, Your Majesty," he replied, accepting it in his hands. "Thank you for giving me a third chance at life."

"The thanks is mine for you saving my daughter's life. You must mean a great deal to her for her to use our ancient magick in this way."

"We wouldn't have gotten far without each other," he said, looking at Azariah but she kept from meeting his gaze.

"What will you two do next?" Azariah asked to change the subject.

"I have to go back into the world and find Raven again. I have to make sure she's safe from Theod-Rah's reach."

Raven, Azariah thought. She was his reason for fighting. Azariah grinned. "Of course you do."

"I will be back," he assured them. "We'll come back to Bloowood and help rebuild there."

"I also must go," said Vylasgarden.

"You shouldn't go after the Dragon Slayers alone," Azariah warned.

Vylasgarden grinned. "The Slayers can wait a while. I think I deserve to live without vengeance consuming me every waking day. Helping others will bring some balance to my life. I'm going to help rebuild in Southaven for a while."

Azariah gave a sad smile. "I didn't think we'd go our separate ways like this."

"We still have time," Riker told her. The three of them hugged, Riker's arms intertwined with hers and Vylasgarden's around them both.

"I know we'll cross paths again someday," Vylasgarden told them.

"We'll be different then," Riker said.

"Imagine the stories we'll have to tell."